D0996441

TAKE IT TO THE LIMIT

Other books by Lucy Rees

WILD PONY
HORSE OF AIR

Take It To The Limit

a novel by

LUCY REES and ALAN HARRIS

DIADEM BOOKS LIMITED
LONDON
1981

© by Lucy Rees and Alan Harris, 1981

First published in 1981 by
Diadem Books Limited, London

All trade enquiries to Cordee,
249 Knighton Church Road, Leicester

ISBN 0 906371 80 5

Printed in Great Britain by
Butler & Tanner Ltd, Frome and London

Contents

The Old Man of Hoy

CHAPTER 1

Get Your Kicks

They had been walking fast up the railway track for half an hour before they reached the shack that marked the halfway point. Two other climbers were there, sitting listlessly outside. Bob nodded to them, dropped the sack and turned to Jonathan.

"They make the best lemonade in the world here."

"Sounds good."

Bob went in for some; Jonathan, still hot, rubbed his neck and glanced up the mountain. The top of the cliff stuck up over the ridge, a dark line. The other pair did not move. Their silence made him nervous; he wondered what they were aiming for, what they thought he was aiming for. He tried to look as if it did not concern him. Finishing their meditation they grunted, got up, swung the sacks on their shoulders and trudged on up the track. Bob re-emerged with the lemonades.

"She makes it herself with the spring water here. It's famous for it."

"Yeah, I heard." He could not talk about lemonade with the cliff hanging up there, but gazed across the bleak cwm. Presently another couple came up the track, a man and a girl. They had no sacks: walkers, not climbers.

"Hello," Bob said, surprised. "Didn't know you were coming up this way."

"Thought we'd go up this way and down the Pyg track," said the man. "Didn't expect you up here either."

"Jonathan's never been up to Clog, so we thought we'd take a look"

"Should be dry, anyway," said the man, with a sideways look at Jonathan. "What were you thinking of doing?"

"Oh, I don't know," Bob said, turning to Jonathan to

explain: "Carver's the bloke I was telling you about, the one I usually climb with; but it looks as if we've lost him now." He grinned at the girl, but she seemed not to understand. Unable to join in their desultory conversation Jonathan started to move away, forcing himself to curb his impatience. Even from so far away the cliff looked big.

When finally they went on to the top of the rise and its full height was revealed, he was more impressed than he would have cared to admit. He knew, of course, what it looked like; he had heard, too often, about its remote, forbidding atmosphere, its steepness and size; the stories of its more eventful ascents were better known to him than his own family history. People talked of it with an air of reverence that irritated him. Nevertheless, it hit him hard.

It was massive, its montrous bulk looming squat and savage, the hunched shoulders of its buttresses formidably compressed, like some petrified prizefighter's. Shunning the spring sunlight, its dark face was scarred by deep-shadowed overlaps, pockmarked with overhangs.

"I expected it to be big," he said at last, "but it's huge, isn't it?"

"It gets you every time," Bob said, sitting on a rock to roll a cigarette, but Jonathan did not want to be reminded of his ignorance: he took the tobacco from Bob and started to trace out the climbs and features from memory: "Woubits, the Pinnacle, Curving Crack, Great Wall, Black Cleft. That's Sunset Crack, isn't it, and Llithrig goes up there, right?"

"Right."

They sat and smoked, then picked their way round the rubble-flanked lake and up the scree to the central walls. The cliff towered above them, brooding, shutting all sound out of the dark hollow. They fell to wondering about each other.

Both partnerless, they had met for the first time in the Pass the previous day, knocked off a couple of good routes together and watched each other like hawks. Bob was steady and capable, a powerful, methodical mover; Jonathan climbed fast and furiously, as if used to short steep outcrops. They had done well, and when Jonathan had proposed trying Llithrig Bob had readily agreed. Yet they were both wishing they knew each other better. The cliff was big . . . I'm not going to let it get to me, Jonathan thought, you can put yourself right off if you get gripped before you start. Bob sat as serious and solid as the cliff itself. The silence was fearsome. Jonathan fingered the guidebook as Bob began to sort out the gear: *Llithrig. 245ft. Extremely Severe. A very fine route with thin, sustained climbing and an interesting rope move.*

Jumpy with anticipation, they scrambled up to a grass ledge; Bob dried his feet carefully and led off, picking his way methodically across the wall to his right. It was steep and difficult; he felt the doubts begin to pluck at him, and pushed them back. When he reached the edge of the wall and stepped round the arete the sudden exposure sneered: there was a 120ft. sheer drop below him, and then the scree running steeply down to the lake far below. But he was calm, the silent shadows directing his attention to the rock as he wiped his hands and considered the next moves.

He's awfully slow, thought Jonathan, shivering, watching four small figures approach the lake. The rope sneaked out again as Bob inched his way up and across to a small overhang. It was hard: he was pleased to be climbing it well and to be resisting the creepy feeling that the cliff was notorious for, muscles nicely warm as he pulled up to a spike. From a runner on this he was supposed to lower himself down a little and traverse on a tight rope across the feature-less wall, but he saw no reason not to reverse down. From the start of the traverse he saw there were tiny rugosities, fingernail holds, dotted across the vertical wall. He knew it had not been climbed free but it appeared remotely possible, and the spike above was bombproof if he fell. . . He was entirely alone on the vast wall. He decided to give it a try.

"Slack!" he yelled to Jonathan, unseen around the corner, and started to work it out. Detailed, meticulous and nerve-racking, it was exactly the kind of problem he liked; he could not fall far and the challenge intrigued him. But he was climbing harder than he knew he could and it took three attempts, three exhausting fingersapping advances and retreats, before he had the sequence worked out right, knew

which hand went on which tiny hold, knew where to shift his
balance and where to skip feet, so that his final attempt was
smooth and apparently effortless. He reached a ramp and
rested there, relief flooding into cramped muscles.

Jonathan could not understand what was happening. Bob
had been gone hours, messing about. Suddenly the figures
below, who had been watching entranced, started moving
again. Jonathan called: "What's taking so long?"

"I just done it free."

Free! Jonathan could barely believe his ears. That'll make
them sit up in the pub, he thought. When his turn came he
was delighted, for if Bob could do it so could he: seconding,
with the comforting rope ahead, was always a doddle. As he
took the sling off the spike Bob called across: "I'd leave that
on if I were you," for without it there was nothing to stop
him swinging right across the wall below the ramp if he
slipped. But the advice infuriated him: it was not only the
implication that he might not be as good as Bob, but the
echoes of his brother's insistently superior attitude. "I
wouldn't do that if I were you," Richard the righteous used
to mock, secure as his Daddy's darling, and as always
Jonathan continued even more defiantly.

"Up yours," he muttered, and started across the wall. But
it was as intricate as a page of Braille, and he had not Bob's
patient, cautious precision: he rushed it, fingernails
scrabbling off fleabite lumps, fingers cramping up on the tiny
holds, the wall sickeningly vertical when he looked down for
footholds; and then he was slipping, scrabbling, swinging
across the face in a series of grazing bumps. He came to rest
among a chorus of catcalls. *I told you so.* Hating himself, he
started to climb the rope.

When he reached Bob he did not stop but stormed straight
on, embarrassed, soaring over the difficulties in the rush to
leave his shame behind. But it was not hard enough; the
proof was lacking; and although Bob came up more slowly he
was not satisfied. They sat halfway up the cliff on a broad
horizontal swath of brilliant green, a sheepless oasis across
the desolate grey precipice. Bob was frankly pleased with
himself. Below, only two figures remained: girls, waiting for

their fellows to complete some other climb.

"I don't think that one's got anything on," Bob said in amazement.

"She must have." Soft skin on harsh scree: the thought was alarming.

"She will have by the time we get down, any road," Bob said, coiling the rope. Jonathan sat defeated. The silence was broken by the beat of the toy train chugging up the skyline: bevies of city-dwelling troglodytes, pasty-faced and postcard-obsessed, bent on the conquest of Mount Snowdon. Poor old whore, Jonathan thought: pay your money and she'll lie there patiently enough as you defile her, raddled old bag; and then the memory of his fall, and the pain of his bruises, reminded him she still had a sting in her tail. He pulled up the leg of his jeans to reveal a scarlet, dripping ankle, patting his ribs gingerly while Bob, ignoring the train and the tourists, felt the deep peace of the valley echo within him.

"Does it hurt?"

"No, it's nothing. Give us that guide, I want to check. . ." He flicked over the pages, looked up at the Pinnacle looming above. "Yeah, how about a crack at Taurus? I fancy that."

"Taurus?" It was as hard as Llithrig but more dangerous, on rotten, flaky rock with a monstrous drop beneath and poor protection. Oh dear, he's one of those ones who feel they have to prove themselves, Bob thought, but Jonathan was already halfway to the foot of the climb. There was no question as to who was going to lead it.

It was a frightening climb, not technically hard but desperately steep and strenuous, in a hollow-sounding groove that threatened to jettison him at every move. But Jonathan had begun to enjoy himself. He was climbing well again, and he knew it. It was more his kind of problem: I hope it makes him struggle, he thought. At the top of the groove was an overhang. The following few moves went leftwards to a peg which was used as a handhold. I wonder if I'm climbing well enough to do it free, he wondered, that'd even things up a bit.

When he reached the overhang the wall looked horribly steep and holdless, and the rusty peg drooped dismally: not much of a thing to depend on if he fell. For a moment he tried pretending to himself that he had never considered the idea seriously, but then he found himself calling: "I'm going to try this free, Bob," and moving on to the wall. He felt the cold sweat on his fingertips as he reached out to clip the rope into the peg without letting himself grasp it. He was afraid, mistrusting everything — the rock, the rope, the peg, himself — but then he found himself moving forward, committed, and it was too hard but his survival instinct took over and drove him up, fast, round the overhang and up the groove above. He knew his fingers would not last much longer but there was a ledge at the top: he hoped it was not one of those false promises that egg you on and let you down. Hands trembling, he pulled himself up and it was a good one. For a moment he could barely believe he had arrived, but lay there weakly.

He turned to face the valley and was stunned by the sudden airiness of his position. He was perched a thousand feet above the lake, with the bowl of the cwm below him in the sunlight and Glyder Fawr poking its head over the top of the railway ridge beyond the deep cleft of the Pass. Tiny orange figures trudged up the summit track.

"Bloody good lead," Bob called up. Christ, he's got some guts, he thought, it's a holy terror of a climb. He was surprised at what they had managed, the more so when he saw the problem, and the horrific drop beneath. It involved fast moves and snap decisions, never his strong point, and he only just made it. "Jesus, that was hard," he said at the top. Jonathan was content at last. They shot to the top of the cliff and sat glowing with success and sunshine, delighting in the climbs and the view: down the cwm and across the Caernarfon plain to Anglesey, a broad flat patchwork with the hump of Holyhead 30 miles away; over Llyn Cwellyn with its precipices and dark blankets of forestry to the Nantlle ridge running away; across Cwm Silyn and over to the swift lively outlines of the Rivals, way out on the Lleyn. Sea sparkled and a buzzard wheeled upwards on a thermal. Bob felt it settle into him, its calm grandeur soothing him after the delicacy, the exertion, of the climb; Jonathan wanted to fly out into it, soaring and rolling like a raven; both, at that moment, were utterly happy.

Jonathan drew in a vast lungful of the limpid air and dissolved into coughing. Ripping his jersey up he discovered his ribs, on the right, raw and seeping.

"Look at that. I never felt it before, only my ankle."

"Adrenalin."

"Yeah. It was hairy, wasn't it?"

"All the way."

They sat side by side, together, far apart. The train came slowly down the ridge: the conquistadors' return. Slowly they coiled the rope and started along the top of the cliff. The other two climbers were just finishing.

"Wonder what they've been on," said Jonathan.

"Sheaf, I'd reckon. Something like that."

Only a Hard VS, thought Jonathan, nothing like as difficult as we've done, and strode forward confidently.

Elated, they jogged back round the lake and sat on the boulders to look back at the cliff in the fading old light: the interlacing lines of the climbs, the rearing slabs, their routes up the centre. Jonathan was as excited as a young colt up on the gallops. "Look at Woubits, what a lovely line. Tell you what, let's do it tomorrow. The Left Hand's got three points of aid and we could do it with two, I bet we could."

"Let's see what the weather does," said Bob, turning the other way to point out the banks of cloud rolling up in the west, tinged with the sunset.

People were hurrying purposefully to the pub when they pulled up outside, and Jonathan felt a shiver of anticipation: maintaining face in the pub can be as delicate as balance on a cliff, and as important for some. They both unconsciously paused for a moment, as if mentally squaring their shoulders, before Bob pulled open the inner door. Heat and noise hit them like the blast from a furnace: they delved into the thick of it and were swallowed up by the suffocating fug of beer and cigarettes. Door-watchers turned to see the latest arrivals, taking in Bob's glow of inner satisfaction, noting the tall dark bloke's nonchalant swagger, so obviously assumed as to be laughable. They pushed their way through the barrage of excited, gesticulated conversations.

". . . Then you reach up round this corner and there's this massive great jug. . ."

". . . grabbed this bloke's leg and just sank his teeth in it, honest. . ."

". . . and you're hanging on this manky old flake with no protection. . ."

The whole bar boomed as if everyone were trying to prove he had more life in him than the next one while the landlord, whose unruffled tolerance made such exuberance possible, chatted in a corner unperturbed. Jonathan, awaiting his pint, recognised Carver again.

"Have a good day?" He was eager for the opportunity to be asked what he had done.

"Yeah, nice. There weren't too many up there. What did you think of the Clog, then?"

"Big," said Jonathan, and waited, but the question never came.

"'Tis, isn't it?" Carver said, nodded, and moved on, leaving Jonathan stranded. Tall enough to see over most of the heads, he eyed the group round the darts board, the only place where there was relative space and calm. Reverence held the mediocre back, for this was the inner sanctum of the Masters, from whose august lips pearls of wisdom and wit might be heard to drop. Joe Brown threw his third dart. Necks craned. It bounced off the wire and fell to the floor. "Bugger," he said.

Bob was holding out a pint; Jonathan took it, said with a jerk of his head: "Seen who's there?"

"Brown and Whillans?"

"Think they've heard?" Llithrig was one of Brown's routes, and Taurus Whillans's. To eliminate the aid from one of their climbs was qualification for promotion to Olympus.

"Shouldn't wonder," Bob said and, catching Jonathan's worried expression, dissolved into laughter and disappeared.

Jonathan stood alone for a while. He wanted to leap on the bar and cry: "Hey, I freed Taurus today" to a sea of upturned faces, but that was not the form: you had to wait until others mentioned it, and then be off-hand. It was Bob's natural manner, and they accepted him willingly, but Jonathan's very keenness seemed to debar him. He tried to catch the eye of one of the Sheffield lads, but they were vying for attention among themselves and ignored him. Ostracised, he tried to insinuate himself into conversation with a girl whose hair looked attractive from the back, but she turned out moon-faced and stupid, and had not even heard of Cloggy. Watching Bob, eyes alight with amusement, listening to the Himalayan epics of one of the minor gods, he felt miserably lonely.

Bob woke to the sweet smell of sawdust and the drum-roll of rain on the van roof, cursed dispassionately and tried to sleep on. The din defeated him: he leaped out, ran across the road and dived under the Boulder to join Jonathan.

"WOUBITS!" he bellowed, and the humped sleeping bag convulsed, groaned, and excreted Jonathan's head. They sat in the hollow under the great rock and watched gusts of rain sweeping up the valley, swirling over dripping crags; discussed and dismissed the possibility of Tremadoc being dry enough; smoked and read guidebooks until Jonathan's spirits rose high enough to get him up, and drove down the Pass to the cafe.

Bob parked on the opposite side of the road and they ran to the door in the sudden downpour.

"Sounds like bedlam in there," Bob said, peering through the steamed up window. He opened the door and ducked suddenly. A flying egg caught Jonathan full in the chest.

"Oh, *shot*!" came a cry above the hubbub. Jonathan clawed the remains of the egg off himself, threw it futilely towards the counter, and was elbowed violently out of the doorway by a woman: Tourist type II, with yellow hair, red lips, porcine hips and a small dog in her arms. As she reached the door it burst open again and a sodden yolk-smeared figure clutching an arsenal of eggs crashed against her. She moaned as the products of their brief union spattered on the floor.

"What a lovely dog," smiled the intruder, sheltering

behind her as a fresh volley of eggs hit the doorjamb and plopped softly over them.

"Looks like bangers for breakfast," Bob said, but Jonathan plucked two passing eggs from the air and showed them to him nonchalantly:

"There's eggs if you want 'em."

"I like it, I like it," cried a tough-looking little woman at the table beside them. "Well who's your friend, you scummy Brummy? Don't be shy, lad."

Jonathan dropped to one knee and presented her with an egg. "Oh, it's Cool Hand Luke, is it? The fastest egg-catcher in the West?"

"The very same."

"Then mind you live up to it," she said, and left, and he had not only a chair but a name, and a partner, and a future to discuss: climbs to be done, cliffs to be visited, trips to be taken. Grinning, he ordered his eggs fried, with double chips.

The van chugged up the valley between mist-shrouded cliffs: farewell Pass, back to normality for another five days. Luke — he had always hated *Jonathan,* a wispy name — urged Bob to join in the races that were part of the exodus, but Bob would not be moved. Instead he passed over his tobacco tin. "Roll us one, would you, Luke?" Luke resolved he would not be Jonathan again except, unavoidably, at home, and there was only one full day there before he escaped to University.

"See you next week?" Bob asked when he dropped him off to hitch the last leg home.

"Sure," he said, trying to hide his pleasure.

As the door clicked softly behind him, warmth and darkness enveloped Luke. After a moment he went to the kitchen. Flickering striplights illuminated teatowels neatly arrayed, and a note that said: "Saved some apple pie for you, do finish it, hope you had a good weekend."

Mothers.

He wrenched open the 'fridge: polythene containers in aseptic rows, tidy parcels and a row of eggs. He stared at their orderly ranks. Suddenly he couldn't stand it. He seized the remains of a chicken carcass and left the house at a run, slamming the door behind him.

"Jonny?" his mother called sleepily, and he could hear his father's disapproving mutter but he was off like a hare into the moonlight, away from desirable architect-designed developments and into the woods, body buzzing again with the elation of it all. As he slavered over chicken bones he felt that really he should be howling his triumph into some girl: a man, doing the things a man should.

Oh the achievement, the mastery of the thing! We did it, he laughed weakly to himself, leaning against a great beech trunk, we fucking well did it. Perfection. And those old tigers, a bit long in the tooth now, calmly playing their darts as if they didn't know they'd been upstaged. Per-bloody-fection.

He hurled the drumstick at distant lights, felt his ribs twinge and remembered the multiple imperfections of the feat. His elation died down: but for Bob, he might not be there at all. Sobering thought. But then, after the bubbles and the subsequent flatness, came a warm glow.

It really had been an achievement and what was more no mere flash of brilliance like those with which he kept his tutors at bay. Academics could be fooled by cold intellect; sharp wit and elegant theorising scored points in class. But out there on the rock was sheer nakedness, nothing but flesh and blood and the elements. Those cliffs, those men, did not judge so swiftly. They waited, waited for the mistakes. And it was not only that he had proved himself once to those quiet watchers, but also that it would go on, for Bob and he, he felt sure, had the possibility of a perfect alliance. Attraction of opposites, and its consequence, hybrid vigour. That man's a stalwart, he nodded, genuine uranium, valuable stuff, and if I come zapping in there with a few neutrons — that's me, à la Heisenberg, all uncertainty but the punch is there somewhere for sure — if we do that, then we have

$$e = mc^2, \text{ out to infinity.}$$

Bob crawled into bed: 7.00 up, don't forget a pint of oil for the old van, and it's old Wainwright's sodding windows again in the morning. Have to make up for skiving on a sunny

Friday. Good weekend though; pity it rained.

He thought of the calm on the hillside, Caernarfon on fire with the sunset, tired limbs and the pleasure of a great climb. 'Funny bloke: needs his nappies changed half the time, then it's all spark and brilliance. Like a bloody racehorse. We did make a good team . . . wonder if he'd fancy having a go at Surplomb? He'd like to try freeing that first pitch. Then there's that chimney above, that'd be mine, and then the V-groove for him . . . No, that's not right, it's not his style at all. I'd have to lead that . . . or would he get moody if he didn't lead through? Touchy. Have to put things the right way.

He was asleep, smiling at the vision of coiled rope and the soft swell of the mountainside behind.

It was a summer to remember, a summer that even grannies admitted a match for the golden hazy days of their youth, a summer of weathermen's gleeful comparisons; a summer of never having had it so good and I'm all right Jack, when the first of the flower children dreamed into town and jukeboxes throbbed with laments for hard days' nights; when the upland bogs dried out and those sheep that escaped the tourists' meandering cars and dogs grew fat and boisterous while the valleys hummed with haymaking: a summer for girls to grow brown in and old bones to warm in, for farmers and icecream sellers, for lovers and holiday makers, for adders and flies, hotelkeepers and campers.

And climbers.

That summer the cliffs dried out early and people flocked to the high crags in the reek of crushed bluebells, leaving them laced with new routes and abandoned equipment filched nightly by the *cognoscenti*; and while the myth of the peerlessness of the Master and the Villain continued to be disproved even the technical whizzkids of the computer generation produced mythmakers and heroes of their own. They superceded each other as quickly as pop groups. New prizes for old: Cenotaph Corner, that stupendous open-book plumbline, was sweated and struggled up to lose its air of magnificence, while others rose to claim its place as the sorter of the men from the boys.

That was the summer of hot competition and hotter subterfuge, when everyone had a secret line tucked up his sleeve and some of them had whole crags, location veiled in mystery. Scarlet knuckles wrapped pint mugs in the Padarn: "Where've you been?" "Oh, Crag X," Luke overheard the day that he and Bob did Cemetery Gates. It was the Rat Race summer, when Joe Brown cracked the bottom of a line on the giant Gogarth but could find no-one able to follow him up it; the rats picked at the higher pitches, until he teamed up with Crew and polished it off while the sea lashed the rocks below.

It was the summer of outlying cliffs when transport was at a premium, and vans were customised into home-from-home shagwagons, and Black Jack rolled his fourth car in succession on the same Llanberis bend; when PC Jones stopped a lightless scooter on a dark night to find five people and a dog on board; when Sharpe's astonishing Triumph combination, a grim affair with brown paper windows, baulked at a bend and Sharpe baled out, leaving his hapless passenger wrapped in private thought and brown paper to sail onwards into the night; when Evil Ed played chicken along the white lines against all comers for a quid in the kitty and found it a staple income.

That was the summer that Porlock camped for a month under Cloggy existing only on a cauliflower, and Luke and Bob discovered him, emaciated and frantic, trying to talk some poor trog into following him up Slanting Slab. They discarded the trog, did it as a trio, and found it desperate, exhausting, and in retrospect elating.

It was that summer that pegs and nuts arrived en masse, though Tricky Dicky's Big Mistake on the old sea-cliffs at Tremadoc left him wary of such artificial aids. The line had gone free almost to the top, where the lip of the cliff is sheer and smooth: Dicky banged in a peg with regret, popped over the top, thumped in another piton for a belay and brought Jonah up. "Call it 'ard VS and give it a name," Dicky said, swinging off his belay to reach over the lip and knock the lower peg out. But it was his belay peg that came out first. He nose dived down with a howl. Jonah, unbelayed, clung fast to a bollard of rock and prayed; Dicky passed out, fell to the end of the rope and the bottom of the cliff simultaneously and, as the rope stretched, landed gently in one square foot of mud between two great pinnacles of rock, only to bounce up again and hang asphyxiating ten feet higher. He was saved from suffocation by a man who leaped from 30ft. up the next climb, sprained his ankle and ran to take the dead weight off the rope. Dicky's footprints hardened in the mud, a 29 days' wonder for all to see.

Later that summer Bob and Luke returned exhausted and happy from Tremadoc's Vector, a notoriously savage tiger-tester, to find the main street in Llanberis a bloody maelstrom. Harry and Bliss had gone to the chipshop for a tanner'sworth to find themselves jostled by sullen eyed local heavies. Bliss objected. "Twll tyn bob sais" came an incomprehensible jeer, and suddenly the air was full of fists, chips, grunts, blood, glass and boots, a lively expression of international relations. PC Jones arrived in time to find Dafydd Emlyn on the floor, and two of Harry's teeth, but no more.

Harry never cared: three days later he and Fenby were on the upper wall of Llech Ddu trying a steep new route. Harry was belayed about 40ft. above the halfway terrace to a rather frail-looking tree. Fenby was 30ft. above attempting to traverse a ramp which looked the key to the whole climb when a hold broke off. His two runners pulled out immediately and he fell past Harry and hit the terrace as the strain came on the rope. Harry held on but the tree snapped under the strain and he was catapulted into space screaming, falling past Fenby. The pair cartwheeled down the lower face and eventually thudded, with sickening finality, into the grass slopes at the base of the cliff, 400ft. below.

It was that summer that Bob and Luke went for Surplomb, stopping in a crowd at the bottom of the Grochan to watch Evil Ed's half-hour search for an abandoned and salvageable peg on Sickle. Unable to find it, he went on up, but slipped on the second pitch and plummetted over an edge to an audience cheer that turned to a gasp as one of his ropes cut through. "NO!" he yelped and went on down, but his second rope held and he was brought up sharp to sight gold: "Hey, guess what, I've found that peg. . ."

And it was late in the summer, when the weather finally broke, that Luke and Bob were taken aside at a party: "Don't make a noise about it, but there's three guys stuck out on Gogarth in a rising tide and Brown's getting a team together for a rescue: you on?" In the storm-lashed small hours they drove to the sea-bound cliff: RAF trucks, soldiers, and the official rescue team, all as lost as sheep. Brown organised his irregulars rapidly. Silently they crept off, the lightfingered armed with RAF flares and other gear, and tiptoed after him across the dark wet wall where the gale brought waves crashing 60ft. up. Down below three numb bodies endured the thrust and pounding of the sea over their heads, gasping for breath ever more weakly as the sea sucked back and the Master put all his cunning into plucking them out of the teeth of it, swinging down through the storm to reach them and hoist them back to life. Three souls, as grey as the dawn: the mediamen clamoured, but they all drove home while others did the talking. "Thank God," thought Bob, and fell asleep while Luke pinched his tobacco and celebrated the fact that they had Arrived: that long summer of achievement had not gone unnoticed.

CHAPTER 2

No Satisfaction

"You're late."

Bob set his mug of tea on the table and sat down. "I was busy."

"Well you might've let me know. I've wasted an hour festering here." Luke pushed a magazine across the table, stabbing at it with a grimy finger. "Look at that." A pillar with the proportions of a matchstick stuck out of the sea, lone and frail. "Old Man of Hoy. It sounds really good. How about taking a week off and going for a look?"

"Don't need to take a week off." Bob delved into his pocket and produced an envelope which he tossed on the table with an air of finality. "I'm jacking in my job; going self-employed. Got a cottage here."

"You wha'?"

"Got that cottage next to Ed's."

"That's not a cottage, it's a ruin."

"Lot of work, yes. But they give me a long lease for peanuts if I do it up."

"What on earth started this?"

"I've been trying to get one for yonks."

"I never would have thought of it. You, I mean: I don't see you as part of this scene — parties, living on the dole, fights —"

"It's not the scene. I don't give a damn about that; you can keep your egg-fights. And I won't have to live on the dole because there's always work for a carpenter. . ."

"Not here. You'll be down the Bru with the rest of them. I don't see it; it's not you."

"Not me? What am I then, only fit for trotting to my boss like a good boy and living in the middle of a human muck-heap?''

"I didn't mean that.''

"You bloody did and you know it,'' Bob said without rancour. He rolled a cigarette, lit it, spat out a shred of loose tobacco and went on: "Well I've had enough; I'm sick of it. I'm sick of living in a row of rabbit hutches where you can hear the neighbours fart and I'm sick of trundling to work in my little metal box in everybody else's exhaust fumes and I'm sick of breathing stuff that's been in and out of forty bodies already. Weekends is the only time I come alive. It's not the work; I quite like that. But I'm not going to live in a prison all my life.''

"I know what you mean.''

"You don't. Yeah, I know, cheap student digs in Manchester and all that, but for you it's all a game, isn't it? Solidarity with the workers? Don't give me that crap.''

"I'll have to earn my living same as you.''

"Not the same, lad, not the same. Where I come from you go to the secondary mod and you leave when you're 15 and get a job, and then you get married and knock her off every Saturday night if you're lucky, and between the kids and the telly and the beer that's it. Work, booze, telly. Great. And once you start wondering what it's all about you're finished. It's either the fantasies of the pools or you start bleating about oppressed masses and going on Union marches with you lot.'' He grinned suddenly. "My old man wouldn't let me work in a factory, you know. 'I haven't raised you to spend your life lining other people's pockets', he says, and he sends me to learn a trade so's I could be independent. To be your own man, that's the thing: man's got to have his pride. Mind you, he wouldn't have heard of me staying on at school and aiming higher, either. 'All that fancy book-learning' that was. Not for the likes of us, we know our place. I'm proud to be a gamma, I wouldn't want to be one of those stuck-up alphas. . .''

To his shame, Luke found himself surprised that Bob knew the reference, but Bob went on: "Well I am my own man, sod it, and I'll bloody well lease a ruin if I want to. Plenty of fresh air, anyway.''

"Power to you, squire. What are we waiting for? Let's go
and see it."

As Luke had foreseen, they made a perfect climbing team.
Any climber has his characteristic areas of strength and
weakness, but cliffs present their difficulties haphazardly,
calling now for thoughtful consideration, now for sheer
nerve; or for brute strength, or delicacy, or determination, or
deviousness, traits which would be incompatible within one
personality. Between them Luke and Bob had every talent
and trick a climber could need, with the additional advantage
that there were two of them to fire each other to greater
achievement. Each by himself was a good climber; together
they were unstoppable.

Throughout the weekends that they climbed together,
raising their standards each time they touched rock yet never
apparently reaching the limits of what they could achieve,
their functional complementariness gave rise to more than the
usual working partnership. Mutual respect deepened into
friendship.

Initially Luke's intellectual arrogance led him to view
Bob's taciturn steadiness as dull and unimaginative, though
useful: if you fell he and his belay would hold you, if you
arranged a meeting he would be there, and he never ran out
of tobacco. But increasingly he began to admire the strength
of Bob's personality, his quiet but unshakeable determination, as well as his ability. The realisation that lack of
verbal exhibitionism concealed depth rather than stupidity
demolished his last doubts: he abandoned himself to trust,
and grew wings. Relegating responsibility to Bob, he climbed
ever more brilliantly, frolicked ever more wildly, dancing, as
it were, on the stage of Bob's friendship.

Luke's feeling for Bob was hidden beneath a welter of self-
deception and preservation of public image; Bob, however,
would have had no shame in admitting deep fondness for the
boy. "Boy"; they were the same age, yet Bob was the older, a
man already. Luke's dashings and posings, emotional
turmoils and extravagancies, would have confused a less
integrated soul: Bob saw straight through them, regarding

him with a tolerant affection that was tempered by his admiration for Luke's intellectual superiority. Luke dazzled him with ideas and made him laugh; Luke needed him, and although Bob could never have seen that he nevertheless found himself exploiting his own strengths further and, amongst other things, climbing harder and more wisely than ever before.

Such an explosion of potential over a few months made them both long to test themselves further afield before they both settled to winter seriousness, Bob to his interminable ruin-restoration and Luke to his final year at University. Hoy's lone finger beckoned, and they set off for a week in Orkney.

Luke did the research, piling into the van with a mountain of salvaged equipment and papers: magazines, articles, photos, notes, which he thrust under Bob's nose at inappropriate moments.

"Look at this, the Baron on that Tyrolean on Yesnaby. Look at that sea, Bob! You have to swim across that to set up the ropes for the others. . . Look, here's that one of the Old Man. Where does the tricky bit come?"

"Crack after you traverse round the corner, that's the crux. . . I can't look now, you berk, take it away."

"You're not going to drive all the way, are you?"

"No, you can have a go later where there's nothing to hit. You haven't got a licence, have you?"

Worn out by excitement, Luke slept like a child, waking cold and stiff in the dawn light. "Where are we? I was going to drive. Why didn't you wake me up?"

"Thought you might manage that by yourself. Give us a beer."

They changed places in silence as the sun came up over a golden sea, lighting the little houses clustered in the bay below and warming the dark moorland that rolled away to the west. But Bob could not sleep. The road unfolded inexorably in his mind's eye, corners and dips and rises and more corners, and then it became grey rock that he had to climb. It soothed him though he lay awake, feeling the tiredness seeping through his limbs. When they had finally driven aboard the ferry in Scrabster the warming engines rocked him to sleep while Luke fidgeted impatiently, sallying ashore on a bun-hunt that nearly lost him the boat.

The St. Ola swung out into Pentland Firth, that eternal battleground between the long Atlantic swell and the North Sea's fury, and plunged towards Hoy's dark cliffs dancing nauseously on the horizon. The waves were mountainous. The boat pulled in close to the western shore round Rora Head and there it was.

"Bob, Bob, come on out, you've got to see."

They stood in the cold wet wind, warmed and smiling at the sight of it, a slender pillar rising nearly 500ft. sheer out of the wild sea, standing alone, proud and absurd, impossibly slim and tall: the Old Man of Hoy, a gallant and fearsomely obstinate individual unmoved by the spray that lashed its base or the gulls that wheeled around it. Yet even it was dominated by the huge red cliffs that formed its backdrop, the massive vertical bulwark of St. John's Head rising three times as high, grim and frowning.

"There's no routes on those cliffs," said Luke in a whisper.

Bob gazed, and then swung his eyes back to the Old Man now towering over the ship.

"That's our baby. Imagine standing on top of that."

"Tomorrow."

They grinned in delight at the craziness of that fragile climbers' dream. The boat wallowed past it, leaving it behind as lonely as a lighthouse facing the Atlantic, and turned into Scapa Flow.

"Good God!" said Luke. "What's that?"

Rusty-red iron hulks loomed out of the rising swell. "It's the ships they sank in the war to stop the German subs," said Bob. "I didn't know they were still here."

"What were German subs doing here?"

Bob explained about the natural harbour of the Flow, and the way it was used as a basis for naval operations in the war. Luke found himself impressed by his detailed knowledge, and by those extraordinary relics of a time so near yet so far away. Orkney meant seastacks and crofting, not North Sea convoys in weather so bitter that if you touched the guardrail it ripped the living skin off you, or men creeping fearfully along the seabed waiting for the depth charges to crush them to oblivion. And yet, as he told the story of the U-boat that slipped in and sank the Royal Oak, Bob's vision was not of the events themselves but of himself as a small boy, playing draughts with his father before the heaped coal fire in the days just after his mother had died and the old man could not face going out. Bob would run to the pub at the corner for bottles of Guiness and, eagerly rolling black shag cigarettes for his dad, sit all evening listening to the stories, half-bored and half-thrilled until the names themselves became imbued with romance: Murmansk and Lofoten, Holy Loch and Scapa Flow. I must tell the old man about this when I get back, he thought, noting the hulks' positions carefully, he hasn't talked like that in years. Damn the telly.

They had chosen Yesnaby's smaller stack as a warm-up before the Old Man and so from Stromness, where the boat docked, they drove north-west under an immense sky, past little white crofts in their patches of treeless pasture and plough, stopping in an old Army camp on the headland. Melancholy pillboxes squatted on the cliff's edge, windswept and desolate. They walked over to look at the stack.

It rose as high as the cliff, only a hundred feet or so, a two-legged structure of sandstone slices literally stacked on top of each other like an inverted Y. Guillemots and seagulls swooped off its ledges. After the Old Man it looked small, ideal after the long drive. But between it and the cliff lay 50 yards of surging, boiling foam.

"The climbing looks good, at any rate," said Luke, grinning.

"You're the swimmer," Bob said, licking the salt off his lips. "Thank God."

Luke was delighted by the challenge and they abseiled down to the bottom of the cliff. From there the position looked alarming. The swell rose and fell not so much in waves as in great seething masses of water. In the wind he felt thin and cold as he stripped off his clothes, donned a waist harness and tied the rope to it. Shivering, he tried to look for a good landing place on the stack, but every time he thought he had seen one it disappeared under ten feet of raging sea. Bob noted his sudden silence with amusement. "Well?"

"The timing's the thing," Luke muttered. "You've got to get out as it goes out and land off the top of it." He stood hesitantly, clutching his arms, watching the sea rise and fall.

"Good luck," said Bob politely.

"Sod off."

As the water rose again he leaped out into it, submerging completely in the white foam. Bob paid out rope. As the swell rose the head reappeared, too near the cliff: the surge drove him back on to it and he disappeared again, coming up choking ten yards to Bob's left. He swam out strongly on the ebb, but it turned and snatched him and tossed him, swallowing him up and spitting him out until Bob recognised a howl of distress and heaved him back on a rising swell, landing him neatly alongside on the ledge. Luke spluttered and slapped himself.

"Christ, that's no joke. It chucks you about all over the place. It's like being in a washing machine." He stared at it sullenly, watching the patterns of the eddies, and moved further along to the right. "Now don't let me drown."

He tried three times in all, but each time he could not quite reach the top of the returning swell and was driven back on to the rocks again. The fourth time he had a distinctly angry glint in his eye and jumped apparently far too soon, but he was clear of the rocks when the water next poured in, fighting his way out, vanishing from time to time and reappearing in the tumbling seas as Bob paid out rope. Near the stack he vanished for so long that Bob was seriously worried, searching the heaving foam for the dark bobbing head until to his surprise he saw the long white figure clinging to the rocks at the bottom of the stack. It crawled to safety, clearly exhausted.

Bob jumared back up the abseil rope to the top of the cliff, taking Luke's clothes and his end of the rope. He found four young islanders on the top. They nodded and smiled.

"We saw your van. Here's where you tie your end."

When Luke gave the signal they clipped the rope through

several pitons at the cliff edge. Each took up his place as if they had rehearsed the moves, and together they heaved until the rope was as tight as they could pull it, sparkling with drops down to Luke's anchor at the bottom of the stack.

Bob hoisted up the rucksack full of gear, clipped it on to the rope, and launched it. It slithered dizzily down to the stack. When Luke was clothed again, Bob put a safety harness round his waist and buttocks, clipped it on to the rope and let himself over the edge. As on an abseil, the first moment of going over was the worst: the knot settled so that the rope seemed to sigh, and he thought he was in for a repeat of Tricky Dicky's stunt. His heart thumped hard, but the rope was as firm as a wire. As he lowered himself hand over hand above the turbulent sea the wind snatched at him, rocking him crazily, and he tried not to think of the breaking strain of the weak, stretched rope. He could not swim in a swimming pool, let alone fully clad in a raging Atlantic. But he reached Luke safely.

Luke was still blue with cold. "I smashed myself to bits one way and another. Banged my knee up. What a way to start a climb."

"If you feel bad I don't mind leading," Bob said, choosing his words carefully. "That was a hell of a swim."

"If you want to take over the lead go ahead."

"No, like I said, I'm still knackered after that drive. As long as you feel up to it."

They untied the rope from Luke's anchor, clipped it into Bob's harness, and tied themselves on to another rope. Luke began to climb.

The rock was sheer and unexpectedly difficult. First he traversed into the crutch of the Y, then swung out again and went straight up. Already he disliked the climb: the holds were small and sharp, too small for the angle of the rock and spaced out awkwardly so that there seemed to be no way to use the best ones. When he looked down to see where to put his feet the surging movement of the sea below upset his sense of equilibrium, so that the difficult balance moves became alarmingly strenuous. He clung closer to the rock, hampering himself further. He knew that he was using far too much strength, sapping himself unnecessarily, and cursed himself for climbing so badly. On the clifftop opposite the little group of watchers had grown and uncharacteristically he did not appreciate their presence.

He climbed awkwardly and crossly, not with the anger against external difficulties that drove him to succeed at all costs, but with a violent self-disgust that destroyed him even further. The rock steepened mercilessly, blank smooth section after blank smooth section, and his legs began to shake on the tiny holds. He had never disliked a climb so much. He simply wanted to be far away from it, but there was no easy way out now. This technical climbing was Bob's forte, he whined to himself, and began to hate Bob for not leading it — a hatred that rapidly gave way to more self-destruction as he realised that only his own pride had put him there. The sea below was frightening where it should have thrilled him, and the thought that they had driven all that way for such a disgusting display of fear and bad climbing depressed him still further.

Sullenly he went on, climbing slowly. Near the top was a hand traverse with no footholds. He got halfway along it and knew he was not going to make it. Somehow he scrabbled back, shaking.

Bob worried. He had seen Luke climb badly before, but never for so long. Usually there was a sudden explosion: Luke's lips would tighten, his head go down, and he would flash brilliantly up whatever obstacle was challenging him. But here he was climbing worse and worse, and seemed unable to go on. The difficult part was that there was no way back if they failed: they had to get to the top, and Luke would not retreat at this point and let Bob lead. But if he fell and hurt himself. . .

The figure high above started to move again. Oh God, Bob thought, barely able to watch as Luke slithered across the hand traverse, contorted with over-tension, feet slipping where they should have been braced confidently against the holdless rock.

Luke was so frightened that sweat poured from his hands, making the small flat holds even harder to grip, but he

reached the top of the stack and collapsed there. It was a
small platform. A gull hovered over him, peering anxiously
down with round eyes. He swore at it, banged in a piton for a
belay, and brought Bob up.

Bob was surprised by how hard the climb was but once he
had accepted its standard he thoroughly enjoyed it, climbing
thoughtfully and lightly, pleased by its trickiness. The nature
of sandstone is such that even more than most rock it grows
harder the more you cling to it, but a powerful, unfrightened
climber can make it appear simple, as it did now. The hand
traverse was a delight: he braced his feet firmly against the
rock and watched the sea between his legs. Pleased to have
climbed well despite its savageness, he crawled over the top
and said cheerily:

"Well that was hard. Why didn't the bastards warn us?"

Luke sat down and faced America. Bob cleared the rope
away and sat to roll a cigarette. "That overhanging bit was
desperate," he said, passing the tobacco to Luke. He had to
nudge him twice before Luke turned to him with an
expression of such violence on his face that Bob nearly fell
backwards off the stack.

"I don't need your bloody sympathy or your bloody
tobacco."

Bob shrugged and put the tin in his pocket. "It *was* hard,"
he said stubbornly.

"Why don't you say I climbed it like a spastic camel and
get it over and done with? Come off it, Bob, I'm not a bloody
kid."

"You climbed it like a spastic camel and get it over and
done with. And if you're not a kid for God's sake stop
sulking and have a smoke. Lack of nicotine makes you hell to
live with."

Luke set his jaw, but then, as if he were a high-flying gull
himself, he had as it were an aerial view of the two of them,
tiny figures perched on top of this ludicrous elevated platform, living together. He grinned and held out his hand for
the tobacco; but it did not help, and his despondency
returned, and throughout the long process of hauling up the
rope that was still attached to the cliff top, and fixing up the

ropeway from stack to cliff, and making the Tyrolean traverse itself, he remained monosyllabic.

As they drove down to Stromness he complained bitterly of starvation, and Bob had hopes for a food-induced recovery. But it did not work. Bob headed for the nearest pub. It was crowded with small, tough Orkneymen with weatherbeaten faces and old clothes. Luke towered above them, his face drawn and tense, his lank dark hair dull with salt.

"That's O.K.," said Bob, appreciating the flat strong beer. He was bored by Luke's childishness. "Let's go to the Old Man tomorrow."

"Yeah."

Bob sighed and made investigations. They were recommended to search the pubs for a man named Ginger. In the fourth one they ran him down. He was a sandy man who was keeping a crowd well amused.

"Ginger Brown?" Eyes flicked silently over Bob, as if appraising his strength. "Would you take us over to Hoy?"

"When?"

"Tomorrow morning?"

"Are you sure you can wait that long, laddie? Not in any rush at all?"

"I thought you looked busy just now," Bob said, glancing at the glass in Ginger's hand, and won their friendliness.

Ginger had to run people out to Fara and collect his lobster pots, but he agreed to meet them at one o'clock next day. Bob quizzed him about the hulks, and they were soon busy swapping stories while Luke sipped his beer alone, restless and unhappy, sulky because they would not be able to climb next day. Like the sea he had swum that morning he was heaving and swirling, going nowhere except round in eddies.

They drove back to Yesnaby headland to park in the lee of the pillboxes and Bob slept while Luke stalked the windy clifftop in the dark, hearing the sea crashing below.

Laden with supplies they sat on the dock and watched Ginger Brown fiddling with something way out in the harbour until Luke was so impatient he went to buy whisky. The ride to Hoy was exhilarating, the open boat chugging through the swell as they passed the bottle round, but on landing Ginger seemed reluctant to leave them until they had finished a second half-bottle he produced out of nowhere.

"Now, if you see Moses at the Post Office he'll drive you to the hostel at Rackwick for a few shillings, and I'll be back to fetch you the day after tomorrow around nine. If you're still alive," he said finally, to Luke's relief. Bob was in no hurry either, and it was afternoon before they had found the farm with the hut key and installed themselves. It was a long narrow building, an old schoolhouse still haunted by the echoes of children's voices despite the bunks and the pot-bellied stove. There was no-one else there.

Luke dumped the gear on a bunk. "Let's get out and see it properly; if we get a move on we can take a look at St. John's Head as well. Maybe we should have told him three days: I bet we could find a route up there."

"Maybe."

They walked over the moors to the Old Man. From the clifftop, so vertiginous they could not approach the edge, it looked quite small but still elegant, and it was not until they had scrambled down a gully and along the causeway of broken rocks that linked it to the mainland that they could appreciate its impressive verticality and height. Like Yesnaby's, its sandstone slices were stacked neatly on top of each other, but it was a regular, square pillar, like the tallest sliced loaf ever imagined. They stood with their backs to the cliff, looking up the corner between the south and east faces and picking out the route. The line was a vertical crack splitting the east face, but at the bottom of the cliff that face was undercut by the sea, affording no access to the crack.

"Up the arete and over to the left to the big ledge on the south face. That's obvious enough." Luke traced it out. "Then that downward traverse to the right, round the corner to the crack, and straight up."

"That's where the difficulty comes, they say," Bob said. "Getting over that little roof above the ledge is supposed to be hard. And then where you go straight up the crack above, you're on top of that bulge where the undercut is, so you can't abseil down again. You'd be hanging about 30ft. out from the rock if you went straight down. I reckon you'd have to anchor a rope at the bottom of the pitch, before the traverse —"

"And take it up and fix it at the top so you could use it as a guide back round to that face? Yes, that'd work. Nobody said anything about that either."

"Maybe they reckoned that if you had the nous to get yourself up here in the first place then you'd work it out," Bob grinned. "Looks a good climb."

Luke stared gloomily up the stack, and Bob wondered if he was going to sulk all day: but then the familiar set look came over his face. It would be all right.

"Yes," said Luke. "O.K., let's walk along the beach a bit and take a butchers at those cliffs. They look really superb."

They started northwards along the base of the cliffs, but "beach" was as euphemistic as "walk". Between the soaring red cliff and the huge waves was a collection of jumbled boulders as big as houses, and there was no way through them except by climbing laboriously up and down. Often they were forced to backtrack on finding the way down was a 40ft. overhang, or that the water had made the rock slimy, or that they had met another holdless overhang. After two hours they had gained perhaps 300 yards.

"This is ridiculous," Luke said, sitting on a rooftop to look back at the Old Man. From that angle only the unclimbed north face was visible. "Hey, look at that, Bob. Do you see what I see?"

From the right hand edge of the north face a ramp ran up the pillar like an outside staircase on an old house, reaching the middle of the stack about a third of the way up it.

"It looks possible," Bob agreed.

"Possible? It looks a doddle. Can't be hard at that angle. Then from the top of it that crack runs all the way up. That must go. Interesting. No-one's ever done it. . ."

"Let's do the east face first, eh?"

But they sat awhile and scrutinised it carefully until Bob sprang up. "If we don't go now we won't be back off this heap of junk before it goes dark, and it's another hour to the hut."

Getting back took even longer, because the tide had come in, playing with the scores of bright orange creel buoys that were trapped in the rocks. Bob collected a dozen of them for Ginger and they walked back to Rackwick in the dark. There was a light in the window of the hut. Luke nudged Bob.

"See that? Wonder what they're up to. We didn't leave the light on, did we?"

"No. It must be someone else. But they may not be climbers."

Luke hesitated before the door, then flung it open. A pile of rucksacks and sleeping bags lay on the floor. On top of them were climbing ropes. A lanky fair-haired lad turned from a bunk.

"Oh, hello," he said, "we wondered who the stuff belonged to." He spoke in faultlessly unaccented English. "Hope you don't mind, we're staying here for a couple of nights. You're climbers too?"

"That's right," said Bob, while Luke stood bristling like a dog discovering another on its territory.

"The others went down to the beach; they'll be back soon. There's three of us. We're just cooking. D'you want some? It's spaghetti and we seem to have enough for an army."

"We're O.K., thanks, we've got grub," Bob said.

"No, seriously, have some of this. Kate always makes far too much." There were voices outside the door. "That sounds like them now."

The door burst open and a lad and a girl came in. He was small and sallow, an advanced acne case, and stood puffing and blowing while he took his jacket off.

"Oh," he said. "We wondered who you were."

"Sorry, I don't know your names," said the lanky boy. "That's Peter and that's Kate and I'm Dave."

"Bob."

"Hi."

"Hi."

"Hi."

"That's Luke."

"Come and have a look in this pot, Kate. It seems to be boiling awfully fast."

"That's O.K.," she said, and moved swiftly to the gas burner. She had auburn hair and looked fit; what an arse, thought Luke, longing to get his hands on it, with a surge of lust that was almost embarrassing. As she bent over the pot, face flushed by the wind, he thought: what's a girl like that doing with a couple of creeps like these? She was not particularly pretty, but they were not in her class. He wondered which one of them was her boy friend.

"Are you guys eating with us?" she demanded, waving a wooden spoon at them. "I saw your gear so I made enough."

"Didn't you wonder who we were too?" Luke challenged.

"Not much," she said, chin high, and started to set the plates out in a manner that made Luke want to throw her on the floor. The clank of the plates on the metal draining board, the slurp of the hot spaghetti, the chink of forks on china made an appalling noise in the sudden silence after she switched the burners off. Bob produced a loaf and butter.

"Cheese?" She handed him a bowl of grated cheese.

"Salt," ordered Peter, scratching a spot with one hand.

"Did we remember to bring any pepper?" Dave queried, and silence fell again. Luke felt like screaming.

"Christ, you could cut the atmosphere in here with a knife," Kate said fiercely. "What's the matter with everybody?"

"Good spaghetti," mumbled Bob through a mouthful, and winked. Forks clattered like dull cymbals.

She sat back for a second and watched them in turn. Bob caught her eye and shook with silent laughter.

"I don't suppose you've come to climb the Old Man by any chance?" she asked.

Bob nodded and went on chewing, but otherwise all movement ceased. Peter froze with a forkful of spaghetti half-way to his mouth, whence it slithered slowly back on to his plate.

"Of course, you got here first," said Dave.

"We've been on the island all day," Peter said, "if it comes to that. Anyway we aimed to start really early, so there ought to be enough time for us all, surely? But if Dave says you got here ahead of us then I suppose it's your right if you want to go first.''

Bob continued to wrestle with his food, but Luke had finished and wiped his plate round with a piece of bread.

''Great spaghetti, thanks.''

''More in the pot if you want it,'' she smiled almost con-spiratorially, a wicked warm grin after her aggressiveness, and Luke winked back.

''I will, yeah. Anyone else for more?''

He returned with his plate piled even higher than before, and Dave and Peter gasped.

''You can't eat all that.''

''Want to bet?''

For a moment, it seemed, they were all united, but then Peter started up again: ''Well what are we going to do about this climb?''

''We'll sort something out,'' Bob said easily, rolling a cigarette. ''No rush.''

''Yes, but what? You first, or us first?''

Kate rounded on him. ''Oh, for Christ's sake leave off. You've been a fucking pain in the arse all the way up with your bloody moaning.''

Bob disliked obscenity from that soft wide mouth, and turned away.

''Well, he has,'' she said. ''Tell you what, we asked that taximan if there was a pub here, and he said he'd pick us up on the way down. That'll be in —'' she pushed Dave's sleeve back to look at his watch — ''about ten minutes. Why don't you come too, and then we can talk it over there? Arguing at mealtimes might give a man indigestion.'' Another wicked glance at Luke.

''He can't hear above the noise of his chomping,'' Bob said, and they dissolved into laughter while Peter sat stony-faced, defeated.

It was not like a pub, but a long room with benches along the sides, trestle tables to sit at and a counter at one end. Small grey men looked up with lively interest as they went in, and Moses displayed them with pride, as if great honour might accrue from claiming acquaintance with visitors from so far away. Kate, the only woman present, attracted a good deal of attention and it was with relief that they all fled to a table.

"Anybody'd think they'd never seen a female before," Kate complained. "That fellow seemed to want to peer up my nose just to make sure I couldn't drink through it."

"It's the pint," Luke said, slotting himself quickly beside her. "They'd probably never seen a woman drink pints before."

"It's not a male prerogative: there's nothing magic about it. Nor's rolling ciggies: do you think your friend would let me have one too?"

"Sure. His name's Bob." Luke pushed the tin over and watched her small strong hands manipulate paper and tobacco.

"You're worse than them: I'm not a performing monkey," she snapped, and smiled her thanks to Bob. He was listening to Dave.

"Maybe we could toss for who goes first. Pete's always anxious for a really early start, but that seems the fairest way if you'll start early if you win." Peter looked doubtful and rubbed his acne. "They're bound to be faster than us, Peter. In fact, maybe it would be better if they went first anyway because after all we haven't had a chance to look at it and the route description's pretty vague."

"It's an obvious line," Bob said, wondering how long they could keep this up.

"Yes," Peter said. "I know. And we're all fairly fast climbers. I can't see that we'd be that much slower."

"We'd be bound to be," Dave said, "with three of us." His clear voice penetrated Luke's conversation.

"Are you climbing too?" he asked Kate.

"You don't think I drove all this way to demonstrate my culinary skill, do you?"

"It's quite hard."

"So I hear. I'm looking forward to it."

Bob had risen to his feet and collected the glasses. "Pints all round?"

"I'll give you a hand," Luke said, and struggled out to

help. He managed to keep quiet until, treacherously avoiding Moses' eager gaze, they had reached the bar: "Well? What do you think?"

"What do you?"

"I asked first." Bob rarely gave opinions unless pressed.

"I'd sooner be on a cliff with an old age pensioners' Sunday outing."

"They seem O.K.," Luke said, to provoke him.

"They don't know where they're going, and in the limited time they had they pissed about cooking and running around on the beach rather than take a look at the cliff. There's three of them. The public schoolboy's all right, but somehow I wouldn't think he could climb much. Spotty's a disaster area, and personally I wouldn't take a woman up there."

"You're prejudiced about women climbers anyway. She might be the hard one."

"They told me they climbed mostly on gritstone. She's got no scars on her knuckles and her nails are too long."

"Just call me Watson."

"And anyway you'd rather have a crack at the north face, wouldn't you? I'm sure she'll give you a hero's welcome on the top."

"She's done nothing but snarl at me so far."

"Playing hard to get, sonny. She's all goggle-eyes when you're not looking."

"Bullshit," said Luke, collecting pints. "North face, then?"

"Yeah, and I bet when you peel off you'll be glad that it's me at the bottom holding you, not some eight stone woman. That's not prejudice, it's sense."

They went back to announce their decision.

"Thanks very much," Dave said. "That's good of you."

Peter grunted and started to make arrangements; Bob ignored him and tried to conjure up a picture of the north face, while Luke leaned back and started to work on Kate. He was not sure what his approach should be: she was prickly and hypercritical; there was as much of a challenge in her as in a tricky new climb, and he felt as nervous as he did standing below an unknown cliff.

"This your first trip north of the border?" he asked.

"'Tis for me, yes," she said, watching Peter lecturing Dave. "How about you?"

"Never been this far north before. Where do you usually climb?"

"Used to be Derbyshire and Yorkshire when I was at College, but now I'm back home I'll have to find new stamping grounds. Or a job somewhere good."

"Why, where's home?"

"Cheshire."

"Oh, funny; I come from Chester." For God's sake, Luke, he nagged himself, you must be able to do better than this.

"Really." She went on watching Peter. She had not looked at Luke once. He said:

"You'll have to come over to Wales for a weekend. It's really good there, as long as it doesn't rain."

She glanced at him quickly. "Is it? I've never been there either."

"Oh, it's great: terrific scope, lots of cliffs, lots of parties, great climbing, good scene." He launched into an embellished account of the Llanberis climbing fraternity and their nefarious doings, playing to her giggles, watching and evaluating and deducing as carefully as if she were an unknown in one of his experiments. Gradually their heads drew together over the crowded glasses: not exactly hooked yet, but she's definitely nibbling, he thought, and she obviously likes a good time. Quite a find. He said:

"Yeah, come on over some time. We're doing up a cottage over there: plenty of space. They'd bring you over, wouldn't they? Which one's er —?"

"Christ, give me some credit." She drew back, and he poured scorn on himself. "Just because you see me with a couple of blokes does it have to follow that I'm going with one of them, or whatever your cruddy terms of analysis are? I don't need a chaperone." She looked over at the pair again. Peter was arguing, Dave placating. "Oh, Dave's all right; we're friends really, But Peter's a little shit. He can climb, though."

"Really?" He glanced at the sharp scarred face.

"He leads Extreme," she said with pride, and Luke nearly burst out laughing. He longed to tell her what he and Bob had been doing all summer, but thought: never mind, she'll see us in action tomorrow. He wondered how he could work the conversation round to the fact that he was not a nobody, that he was the white hope of Manchester University's physics department and the fastest-rising young star in Wales, that his father was a rich stockbroker but that he, Luke, disdained his filthy lucre; but he knew she would savage any hint of an inflated ego. When they piled back into the taxi he felt as exhausted as if he had done a three-hour exam., and cursed himself for having been fool enough to think it was worth it, but when she pressed against him it set up waves of electricity that even Bob in the front seat could feel raising the hairs on the back of his neck.

In darkness Bob and Luke woke to the clatter of Peter's preparations, and turned and slept on. When Luke woke again it was light and smelled of frying bacon.

"Come on, Casanova," Bob held the pan under his nose. "We've got a climb to do, remember?"

When they reached the Old Man the others had reached the ledge on the south face and Peter was starting the traverse round the corner. They watched for a moment. Kate waved; they waved back.

The pillar stands with its south-east corner facing the rocky causeway that links it to the cliff, its south, west and north faces rising from thin strips of broken rock while the east is undercut by the sea. To reach their ramp on the north-west corner they circled leftwards over the rocks, glancing up at the vertical tower rising proudly above them. The rock was more weatherbeaten than on Yesnaby, older and more crumbly but with bigger holds as far as Luke could see, and he began to feel optimistic about their chances on the north face. But when they rounded the corner in the gusty wind, the ramp ahead did not look as easy as from their vantage point the previous day: true, it was at a kind angle but it sloped outwards and was worn smooth by the buffeting winds and winter's high seas, while there was no helpful crack where it joined the wall.

"Technical," muttered Luke, holding out one end of the rope to Bob. "That's the sharp end."

Bob led off obediently. After the first few feet he found he had no more holds and had to backtrack, making use of far smaller irregularities to climb further. He found it absorbing, so intricate that he had to think very hard to solve the problem of where to go next. The ramp was some 20ft. wide and he found himself weaving from one side of it to the other, sometimes using holds on the walls above or below, reversing and trying again every few feet. Luke watched his drunken snail's progress keenly, trying to curb his impatience and remember where Bob had gone, but from where he was the ramp looked so featureless, and Bob's advances and reversals so frequent, that he found it practically impossible to memorise what had been a successful probe and what had ended in retreat. He was reminded of one of those toy cars which when it meets an obstruction reverses a few inches, turns through a few degrees, and tries again.

Bob found himself climbing more and more slowly but he could not hurry: the ramp seemed to have placed its only good holds in tempting dead ends quite deliberately, and he could almost hear it chuckle every time he fell for one of its lures and found himself in an impasse. It took him two hours to climb 120ft., and he made a rather unsatisfactory belay on a couple of nuts stuffed into a crack. When Luke reached him, after a slow seconding, Bob said:

"Sorry to have taken so long. It's interesting, though."

"We'll just put it in the guide book as 'Climb the ramp' and then sit on the boulders and watch 'em sweat. You always were a devious sod, but that was really a peach." He looked up the ramp ahead, and sounded doubtful suddenly: "Well, here we go."

Luke climbed on with barely a pause, deciding to try different tactics. If the rock was going to play games, he thought, I'll play them too. But that did not work either, and he found himself in the same fretful meandering. He could find nowhere to put a protective runner so he was not able to make a mad upward dash but had to submit himself to the wiles of the rock. He had just managed to forget about time and begin to enjoy the problems when he found himself at the bottom of the vertical crack. There was no helpful ledge for a smoke and a think: he had to move on. Unprepared, he started climbing up it in the same slow, thoughtful manner but found the technique outdated and had to reverse quickly but there was nowhere to reverse to and he had to go up again.

The crack was a disappointment, too wide to jam a clenched fist in, too narrow to get into, and shaped like a shallow bowl so that it seldom offered any help. Delicacy and thought went out of the window and he forced his way up, grunting.

"It's a pig, Bob," he yelled down. "It's a manky old thing that you can't decide what to do with." Bob, who had been wondering at his prolonged silence, lit a cigarette and grinned. "Bloody hell, I'm hanging here with my elbow stuffed in the thing and a seagull's just shit on me." He continued to add his comments to the gulls' falling offerings. "There's a bit here you have to bridge. No, cancel that, I'm coming down, and um —" There was a pause, then: "you just sort of thrutch it. Hell, this stuff's chossy. No protection."

"Stick a peg in," roared Bob.

"Up yours. This stuff's like old soap, dithery old soap. Doesn't know what it's doing. Old woman. Big hold out to the right here —" There was a sudden hush and then a yelp, a crash, a slithering. Bob held the rope tight. "Take a look, I just passed it down. That was a bit close."

Raging and fuming, he gained height steadily until Bob had to remind him there was little rope left.

"There's a ledge just above me; I'll belay there. If I can reach the bugger." After a long silence came the chink of hammer on peg. "O.K., when you're ready."

Bob found the crack puzzling and hard, and it was after four o'clock by the time he reached Luke, who sat with one cheek of his bottom resting on a small sloping ledge, tied to a piton wedged in a dirty crack behind it.

"Great, that looks fantastic," said Bob. Luke shifted over. "Have an inch."

They hung and smoked, watching the breakers crash against St. John's Head, white against the old blood red rock. The wind snatched at them and they felt dispirited; they were both beginning to realise they might fail. The possibility depressed Bob, but it made Luke vacillate between wild optimism and miserable self-disgust.

"Maybe it'll get easier," Bob said, and set off up the next pitch. But it did not: the crack was no more help than before, the surrounding rock was looser, there was nowhere to put a runner, and it grew steadily more overhanging. He took an hour to climb 50ft., and found a solid place for a good runner. Ten feet above was a loose, overhanging bulge. He retreated to the runner and lowered himself back down to Luke.

"If we go any further we'd have to get to the top or we'd have a hard job getting down," he said. "Do you know, we'd have been all right if we'd had ice pegs: they'd stay in this rock."

"Yeah, but we haven't," said Luke, breaking off a lump of rock and hurling it into the sea. "Shit."

Bob sensed his impotent rage, but could say nothing. Silently they abseiled off, and collected the gear from the ramp. It was cold; they moved quickly over the rocks round the base of the tower in the gathering dusk. The wind had risen alarmingly, making tendrils of sea reach out as if to claim them from the dark pillar.

"Wonder how the others got on."

"They're probably back at the hut by now stuffing themselves on more Cordon Bleu cooking. A celebratory feast. Hell, and we'll be eating humble pie."

"That's the way the crookie humbles."

They rounded the south-west corner in the teeth of the gale and stumbled on, Luke feeling worse and worse as he thought of the scene in the hut, with that little creep Peter full of himself. The south face loomed above, implacable and bare.

"Do you think they all got up?"

Bob, ahead as they reached the causeway, turned back.

"Tell you something, they didn't all get down."

"What do you mean?"

Luke turned the corner into the wind and they looked across the east face. Hanging on a rope level with the traverse ledge but a good distance out from it was a figure, Peter, they thought. The wind kept dragging him even further out from the face so that he swooped and swung above the rolling sea. Breakers crashed into the undercut below him, shooting an explosion of spray up round him. As they watched he seemed to be shouting upwards to the two figures crouching far above him on the belay at the top of the second pitch.

"Oh, the silly little bleeder," said Luke. "He'll never get in."

There was no rope running round the corner to link the top and bottom of the second pitch. Evidently Pete had thought he could abseil down without it, but he could not reach the rock. Luke and Bob watched in dismay as he wheeled in the rhythmic showers of spray.

"How the hell are they going to get down?"

Bob had dropped the sack and started to unpack the gear. "They're not," he said. "We're going to have to go up and get them."

CHAPTER 3

Tell Me You're Coming Back

The wind howled, coming in solid blocks of air to bang against them and the stack, whipping the sea even higher. Luke slowly levelled every obscenity in his considerable repertoire at the three in the deepening gloom.

Bob sat down to change his boots. "Here's what we do, I reckon. I don't think there's any point in trying to throw him a rope: the way the wind's blowing we'd never get one to him. The only way is to climb right up to them and trail a guide rope like we said. He'll have to get back up to them and start again. Now that second pitch, up the crack, is the difficult bit. It'll be completely dark by the time we get there but with any luck they'll have the sense to work a rope a bit of the way down for you."

"For me?"

"I'll do the first pitch if you do the second. You'd do it better than me."

As they stood there in the dusk, unhurried in the rising wind, Luke knew, in a moment of honesty such as he seldom permitted himself, that however much harder than Bob he might climb he would never have that objectivity.

"O.K., Chief," he said. "I'll see if I can get the message across."

As he hallooed and gesticulated Bob arranged the gear methodically and led off, climbing first up the corner itself, and then beginning to swing left on to the south face. He could only just see the holds and the rock was steep and loose; the wind pummelled at him as he worked his way up slowly, and he became worried that it would prove too difficult in the appalling conditions. The knowledge that there was no way down for the three trapped round the corner kept him going, but it was hard reaching the ledge and he disliked the foolhardiness of it. Edging leftwards along the ledge he found that it ended in a big pillar plastered against the sheer wall, forming an angle where he could make a good belay and wedge himself in partial shelter from the cold wind.

Waiting below, Luke paid out the rope agonisingly slowly into the wild darkness and he was relieved when, at long last, it was snatched out of his hands. The slack whisked upwards and then he was climbing as fast as he could, forcing himself to take risks in order to save time and maybe the last of the light for his hard pitch. Bob, who sensed his haste and the reason for it, kept the rope tight and for once Luke was shamelessly thankful for its help. Nevertheless by the time he reached the ledge it was dark.

"That git on the abseil seemed to have disappeared just before I came off the arete," he said, feeling round Bob. "I think he's prusiked up again but maybe I just couldn't see him any more. The other two could see me O.K.: I think they caught on. Hope so, they certainly couldn't have heard me in all this lot. Here's the other rope. I can't see your belay: what's it like?"

"Dead solid. No problem."

Luke started to giggle wildly, then pulled himself together. "When I get to them I'll give two sharp pulls on my rope and you can haul the guide rope tight. Then we'll send 'em down one by one."

Bob nodded, and Luke was gone. He traversed rightwards easily on the big ledge but when he turned the corner on to the east face the wind hit him much harder. Every hold had to be felt, for he could see no features, only the rock, blacker than the night, stretching upwards. Spray whisked upwards into his face, and his hands were wet with it. When he reached the bottom of the crack he nested a group of pegs and clipped his climbing rope through them, leaving the guide rope free. Then he launched himself at the crack.

"Like Brant Direct," they had said, and he laughed

weakly, remembering the hot day he and Bob had got breath-
less running up Brant. This crack he could not climb. At the
first attempt he failed to get over the roof above him; at the
second he got halfway over the bulge, lost his nerve and came
down again in a rush. The third time he was seriously
frightened and could not reach his previous high point. Alone
in the darkness he blamed himself bitterly, leaning his forehead against the cold wet rock while the wind slapped and
thudded at him. His fingers were cramped and he stretched
them, rolling his shoulders to relieve the tension in them.
Bob'd agree it was a silly risk, he thought, and they'll surely
survive the night. He knew perfectly well that Peter might
not, in his sodden state, but it was not that that made him
swerve from the thought of retreat: it was the possibility of
failure, failure, failure. Leaning against the rock he turned to
face the sea, and remembered.

He remembered a night wilder than this, seas running high
and rain lashing down, on the giant Gogarth, and the small
sure man who had pitted his expertise against it. He remembered the catlike precision while the other rescuers slipped
and slithered and hauled each other up again; Brown had
looked as calm as if he were supping a pint, taking his time,
making each move easily, beautifully balanced, never letting
the urgency of the situation drive him but rather holding it in
the back of his mind, and Luke had been struck by his
complete, cool control. That's beyond me, he thought, that
just isn't in me.

He turned to face the rock again, and it was as if the self-
dispraise of the last few days — disappointment, failure and
the double admission of his inferiority — combined to
destroy the image of himself that he normally held, leaving
only the dark wet cliff. He began to climb it, slowly and
carefully. Usually he climbed in a series of rushes, making
rapid out-of-balance moves and relying on his quick co-
ordination and sinewy strength to pull him out of difficulties.
In the darkness, feeling for holds, he had to pause on each
move to grope for the next weakness in the rock, so that each
move had in itself to be perfect, a complete entity independent of its predecessor or follower, a statement of equi-

librium. Several times he reversed carefully and tried again. Absorbed in the task, he was unconscious of the fact that he was making the best lead of his life. He only felt the rock, and the wind tugging at his ropes, and the cold damp air against his face.

Up on the ledge the three cowered and shivered.

"They won't," Peter said, shuddering. "It's well over two hours since you saw them and they can't still be trying. Anyway no-one could climb in this lot."

"They said they would," Kate said. "He waved that he was going to."

Dave said gently: "They'll have gone back by now, Kate. But they'll be back as soon as it gets light, I'm sure. We'll just have to sit it out. If it's any comfort I bet they did try, but they're only human. Look, let's try to get this better arranged."

"Piss-artists," said Peter.

"Bloody hell, are we going to have to sit here all night listening to you swearing at people who've tried to save your snivelling little life?"

"But they haven't."

"So they will tomorrow. Anyway it's your fault for not thinking about how to get down."

"They won't tomorrow," Peter said. "Because I'll be dead."

"Don't be like that," Dave broke in. "Here, let's get ourselves organised, then we can get warmer. We'll get you in the middle, Peter, and see if we can all sit down in a huddle."

"I am sitting down," Peter said, "and if you want me to move you'll have to do it. I can't feel my legs. They don't work." He was not afraid any more, only bitter. The fear that had gripped him for so long on the abseil had passed, as had his exhaustion after prusiking up the long, swaying rope, and now he accepted the death that was creeping up his legs. It did not hurt, and he no longer cared. Dave passed a hand over him.

"My God, you are cold," he said. Peter did not reply.

In the darkness Bob huddled closer in his corner and held the rope lightly, feeding each inch out with faith and warmth, an umbilical contact between himself and Luke.

Kate screeched: "I can see something, I swear I can. Look, Dave."

Dave peered down into the dark. "Oy, down there!" he yelled.

Luke could not hear them, for the wind whisked their words away, but he happened to look up a few moments later and they could see the pale oval of his face for a second.

"Lower him a rope, Dave," Kate panted, "quick, lower him a rope."

They scrabbled for the rope and clipped a couple of karabiners into it. Dave lowered it over the edge into the gusty blackness. The wind snatched it and the weights hit Luke's head, dizzying him so that for a second he thought he was lost; it was the first time he had thought of himself since the ledge. He bellowed, as loud as he could, a vivid instruction to desist, and after a while he was with them.

"If you didn't want rescuing you might have said so instead of trying to kill me," he said. "Clip me into that belay, will you? Where is it?"

Five minutes later he had them organised, Bob had pulled the other end of the guide rope tight and it stretched diagonally round the corner to him.

"O.K., you first, Kate."

"Send Peter first, he's in a really bad way."

"Makes no difference, we'll all get off the cliff at the same time. Anyway if he goes last I'll be able to help him. What's up, Pete?"

"Exposure," said Kate. "He's soaked and this wind's really cold if you stop moving. It was brilliant of you to get here: I don't think he'd have lasted the night, he's already very chilled."

"People are tougher than you think. Never mind, the walk'll warm him up. Here, you clip on to the guide rope, Kate — no, this one, feel — and give me your rope and I'll lower you. O.K.?"

Kate stepped bravely off the ledge, feeling his rope firm and strong, and vanished into the inky gale. Luke paid out the rope, chatting gaily to Dave, until there seemed to be no more weight on it. She must have reached the corner and be holding the guide rope to slow herself down round it, he thought, and paid out more slowly.

Dave put his mouth to Luke's ear. "I'm really worried about Peter: he seems to have given up."

"Here, you pay this out — slowly, mind — and I'll see to him."

He shuffled round Dave and bent over Peter. "Come on, Pete, let's get you warmed up."

Peter's head lolled and he did not speak. Luke rubbed and massaged him none too gently and after a while Peter muttered: "Le' me alone. 'S no good."

"Come on, you've got to make an effort. Move those arms around, move 'em. Wriggle about a bit, then you'll get your legs back." It seemed to take hours to provoke the despondent Peter out of his inertia. When Luke straightened up he said: "Now keep at it. O.K., Dave, let's get you down."

"She hasn't arrived yet. There's no weight on the rope; I don't know what she's doing."

"What?"

"Here, you feel."

Out in the darkness Kate swung helplessly on the guide rope, jerking like a great kite as the wind caught her. When Bob had tightened the rope it had snagged in the corner so that there was still slack above it, and when she had reached the corner the snag had worked free. Then the wind, increasing suddenly, had plucked her away from the pillar, whisking her outwards with such force that it supported her weight and blew the guide rope out like a bowstring. From her to Luke it sloped upwards, and she could not pull herself back towards him, while the part of the bowstring below her ran vertically downwards, and naturally it did not occur to her to turn upside down and pull herself towards Bob. The wind swept her out from the wall like washing on a line, 200ft. above the boiling seas tumbling over the rocks in the blackness below. She could not see even the stack itself: there was only the rope holding her from being whisked to oblivion, and the darkness and the mighty wind.

At first she could not understand what was happening and was startled, but her confidence in Luke after his magnificent climb was complete and she trusted that this was part of the plan or if not that he would get her out of it. But as she hung there for minute after minute, battered by the gusts and occasionally even smashed back against the stack, fear overwhelmed her. By nature she was not a timid girl and like many girls had never placed herself in positions where she learned about fear and how to control it; climbing did not frighten her since she never got a chance to lead. Even that day, climbing above her limit, she had not been particularly afraid. She had simply found parts of it too difficult, and Peter and Dave had given her tight ropes, and she had been extremely cross with herself but not particularly frightened. Out there in the chaotic night she knew what real fear was for the first time. And she could not cope with it.

At first it came in bouts, sweeping up to choke and freeze her, and in between times she screamed and tugged at the ropes; but the one from her to Dave was slack and the other was taut and no-one could hear her. But then the bouts came closer together and ran together, engulfing her, and it was as if she lost consciousness: she became nothing but a senseless ball that fear washed over like the ocean that lashed the rocks below. She did not think or move. Alone in the darkness she hung paralysed, wrapped round the rope in a foetal position, while the wind played with her mercilessly, tossing her against the cliff and out again, patting her and bouncing her up and down. Up above Luke waited for something to happen, and down below Bob waited for something to happen, and nothing did.

Bob waited patiently. The fools must have got their ropes in a knot, he thought, and gave Luke enough time to have sorted it out and sent one of them down, and then doubled it, but still there was nothing. He ran his hand up the guide rope. It was taut but —. He climbed a couple of feet up the pillar and felt it again. It ran vertically, not diagonally. He climbed down to the ledge again, and thought. Finally he tied himself on to its trailing end so that he was on about 20ft. of rope, and climbed to the top of the pillar in the dark. He could hear the guide rope humming out in space. He peered and saw, far out and above him, but downwind where there should have been nothing, a kind of solidness in the night, like some gigantic hovering bird. He roared at it, again and again. He went on shouting for minutes before his voice penetrated Kate's stupor and, as if fighting her way back to consciousness, from deep sleep, she realised someone was there. She shrieked back again, but he could not hear her.

Once she knew there was someone there she could fight back but it made her even more afraid and she started to cry. He did not call again; she knew he had gone away and she felt abandoned. She wanted no more, she wanted to be out of it, a simple straightforward girl doing the things girls are supposed to do, not alone, near death, and scared. She sobbed helplessly, then stopped suddenly. There was his voice again. Then came a thud on the rope that made her cry out with terror. When she looked, there was a second rope wrapped round the loops of Dave's. He had climbed down for it, come up again and thrown it out from the pillar.

She knew she had to pull it in to her despite being buffetted around, though it was terrifying making herself let go of the guide rope and swing wildly in space. She was afraid, too, that it would jerk loose from the coils and they would have to repeat the whole process. Shuddering, she pulled it towards her inch by inch; suddenly the wind caught her again and swept her nearer to him for a split second so that she could hear him clearly.

"Clip in! Clip in!"

A gust swept her against the cliff again and she made a grab for the end of the rope and caught it just as she smashed against the cliff face. But she was not afraid any more; she clipped the rope in to her waist as she sailed out again, and shrieked back to him, and went on shrieking until he understood. Within minutes he had pulled her down to the ledge.

"You O.K.?"

She shook uncontrollably.

"Here, give me your rope and we'll send it up too, then I can pull the others down. What went wrong?"

"Guide rope's too slack. I can't unclip this, my hands are too cold."

He unclipped it, tied it to the end of the abseil rope, gave a couple of sharp tugs and paid it out as it went snaking into the dark; then he untied the end of the guide rope, pulled it mightily until it was stretched taut, retied it and turned to her. In the confined space he could see her face shattered with emotion and for the first time felt sorry for her.

"It's all right now."

"I was scared," she said.

"I bet you were. I'd have been totally gripped."

"You wouldn't." She was not prepared to believe that anyone else knew what such fear was. "I was so scared I couldn't do anything."

"There wasn't anything to do. If there had been you'd have been all right," he said, pulling Dave down.

"How do you know?"

"Maybe not, then: I don't know you. But it tends to happen. Some people are better when they're gripped. Luke's like that: he's always best when he's terrified. Mind you don't stand on that rope. Here comes your mate."

Shivering in the dark, she thought of her fear, and of Luke's climb, and thought him magnificent.

On the long walk back to the hut Dave and Bob helped Peter while she walked ahead with Luke, carrying the gear. Peter seemed to be recovering, though he was silent. She asked:

"Do you think Peter's all right?"

"He'll be fine," said Luke.

"He was so shattered he couldn't move. I thought he was dying of exposure."

"Exposure!"

"What do you mean?"

"Oh, he was cold, but he could have worked his way out of it. He'd convinced himself he was going to die. Gripped."

"So was I," she said after a pause.

"Yeah, but he's not a woman, is he?"

"Oh, hell," she yelled, swiping at him with her rucksack

but he caught it and had her down on the ground in seconds, both of them giggling helplessly in their tangle.

"What's up?" Dave stood above them.

"It's a woman's privilege to be gripped," Luke spluttered, suiting action to word until she howled about her bruises.

Back at the hut she made food.

"Moses's supposed to be coming for us in the morning. Early," Bob remarked. "Ta very much, Kate."

"No," Luke said. "No go."

"He'll be here at half past eight."

They looked at each other.

"What the hell," said Bob. "We'll just give him that quid and ask him to tell Ginger —"

"And get to the top of that bloody stack."

"We'll take your lift," Peter broke his long silence.

"But we were going to stay two days," Kate protested.

"I don't care what we were going to do. The plan's changed. We're getting out."

"You rotten little —"

"Oh shut up Kate, I've had enough of your bi-"

"Had enough of me? Well I've had enough of —"

It was a full-scale slanging match. Bob and Luke went to bed.

There was a commotion in the morning but they both turned over and took no notice; by the time they woke properly the others had gone. Sun streamed through the windows on the empty bunks. Luke and Bob got up lazily, savouring the silence.

"East face in the light, eh?" Luke mumbled through a mouthful of egg.

"Before anyone else beats us to it, Luke me lad. God, what a crew."

"Spotty faced berk. What was it you called him, a disaster area?"

"All three of them. Funny thing is, I bet none of them would've seemed so bad if they'd been with other people."

"No, he was bad news anywhere. He was scared legless up there, you know: I've never actually seen what the expression meant before.''

"So was the girl.''

"That was different. I'd have got the wind up myself —
hey, that was good, wasn't it? I thought she did O.K. I mean,
he was supposed to be prepared for that kind of situation;
hers was one of those freak things you'd never think up in a
million years.''

Bob shot him a perplexed look. "What you mean is that
you fancied her arse.''

"Yes, that's true. But I liked her too. She wasn't going to
stand for any claptrap from that idiot.''

"Sooner you than me: I'm glad to be shot of them.''

Suddenly Luke realised he had lost her. She had gone,
flown, vanished, and he did not know enough about her to
find her again: only that she had been brought up in a boys'
school, and was a trainee journalist. He did not know her
surname, nor where she was going. Had gone. Hell and
damnation, he thought, bloody stinking hell. He felt cold and
angry, as if he had been tricked by whatever fate had put her
on the cliff for him to rescue in the first place.

"Let's go and beat up that stack. Come on, let's go, don't
hang about,'' he raged, tearing a mug of tea out of Bob's
hand.

Out there it was blustery and sunny, a glorious day, and the
Old Man rose proudly out of the sea to mock him. But he was
clean, empty except for a streak of pure anger that drove as
sheerly and defiantly as the rock itself. He climbed fast and
well with nothing to hold him back or confuse him, flying up
the first pitch and yelling impatiently at Bob to follow. Bob
led the traverse and the crack above, finding it serious even in
the sunshine and reaching the stance above astonished at
what they had managed in the night. Luke howled and
screeched his way up, singing snatches of song that the wind
hyphenated. The next two pitches were easier, though loose,
and finally they were both on the top where Luke did a
windswept wardance. He seemed half-crazed, throwing rocks
off into the sea, and even Bob was thoroughly triumphant.

"Stuff you, Old Man.''

They lay flat on the soft turf of the top for an hour,

chatting and watching the Atlantic roll and swell, until they both dozed off to wake cold and stiff.

Next morning Moses knocked on the door at half past eight exactly.

"Your friends said you were a day late," he said. "I heard you had a wee spot of trouble. Is that tea you have in the pot?"

They regaled him with a hyperdramatic account of the epic to add to his extensive collection, paying great attention that he understood the mechanics of it all, and said goodbye to him with real regret as they ran down the jetty to meet Ginger.

"So you're heroes, I heard," he said, "and what's more, you seem to have won a peedie trophy for yourselves." He held out a box to them. "The lass was most concerned for your future."

It was a whole bottle of Highland Park, wrapped up with a note: *Thanks for my life. Kate.*

On the back was her name, and address, and telephone number.

"What a player," sighed Luke, and then noticed Ginger's slightly expectant air.

They were half a bottle down before they set off for Stromness. Ginger seemed to have taken a fancy to them and fed them with snippets of information in a manner that hinted of myth and mystery. As the whisky took effect in the sharp, sparkling air the sea seemed vast, pervading their thoughts: they were taken over by the sensations of it, the rhythmical never-ending motion, its paradox of harshness and softness, the inner whisky-glow and the fresh breeze on their faces.

"Anywhere we can catch fish?" Luke asked. "I'd really like some fish."

"Aye, laddie, I've just the place if it's fish you're after," Ginger said, turning the boat slightly towards the sea. "There's something else you might like too."

He headed for one of the hulks lying at the mouth of the Flow, and soon its bracken-red sides loomed above them. It

lay aft-down, the sea washing over its decks, though its front
half reared up clear of the water.

"Can we go on it?"

"That's what we're here for."

Ginger pulled in and tied the boat to the rusty iron ladder
running up its side. They climbed up carefully, surprised by
the sudden lack of motion under them, and strolled around
on the sloping deck. From the very front they could see the
land much better: Mainland flat, with the sunlight catching
on the windows of tiny houses in Stromness, Hoy higher,
rugged and majestic. The hulk was scaling and rotten, stinking of old sea, a maritime ruin ripe for exploration. Luke
stepped into a corridor leading between the cabins on the
foredeck.

Inside, it was dark. He could feel the walls on both sides of
the narrow passageway constrict him as he crept along in the
slimy stench. Doors led off into cabins or rooms on both
sides and through them light trickled. The smell was over-
powering, lending a cavernous feeling to the eerie half-light.

"Weird," he said aloud, his voice echoing against the rusty
iron bulwarks. Outside the sea whispered back and then
gradually changed, muttering and threatening louder and
louder until it was thrumming and pulsing in his ears.
Bewildered, he stood as if petrified as the sound crashed
about him. In the split second before the drumming overwhelmed him he had as it were total simultaneous recall of all
the extreme emotions he had experienced within the last two
days: elation, despair, fear, control, sickness, lust — and in
the last welcome crescendo of noise he threw himself down as
the ship exploded inwards in an eruption of birds.

A thousand birds streamed from the cabins into the
corridor in blind panic, surging and beating against him while
he crouched on the floor, their wings shushing through the
darkness in a cataclysm of white noise, soft harsh feathers
slicing the air as they poured out, bursting into the sunlight in
a cloud. They blundered into the walls, each other, his body,
in an endless spew of terror pouring outwards. The rush went
on for minutes, the strange thrumming of their wings beating
louder and softer, swelling and dying in the darkness only to

trickle away altogether. When it ended he crawled to his feet and staggered out into the sunshine, trembling.

"You disturbed the pigeons, laddie," said Ginger, holding out the whisky. Unable to speak Luke gulped it down, watching the birds wheel and flutter in a cloud of indecision about the ship.

"My God, did you see that?" he said finally. "There must be millions of them. They just went completely mad. It was like being run over by a train or something. The noise! Did you hear it? They all bashed right into me, they were so frightened. Boy, what a thing to happen."

"Pass the whisky," said Bob with a wink.

Ginger related the ship's history and suddenly they were off in the little boat again. "Fish," he muttered heading out to the open sea, and they journeyed on in silence, each his own little boat on the fertile ocean of thought. After a while Ginger appeared to wake up and take his bearings, looking first at Hoy and then Mainland, then back to Hoy again, lining up two secret points. Then he stopped the boat.

They rocked in the big seas, passing the bottle round until they had finished the last drop. Luke began to feel foolish.

"What have we stopped here for?"

"You want fish, don't you?"

"Are we going to catch fish here?" There was no sign of a line, or fish; they swung and rolled in a marine desert. Ginger looked at the sky, at the sea, at the Mainland, at Hoy, sighed and launched into another wartime tale. There seemed no point in asking him more; by now both Bob and Luke had realised that they were in the presence of a kind of Orcadian (or is it Arcadian? Luke mused drunkenly) Tom Bombadil into whose fantastic world they had somehow blundered and who held them trapped as he led them down his inexplicable fairytale path. Questions were pointless, since they could not provide understandable answers.

And so they listened, and waited, and suddenly the sea was full of fish, fish zigging under the boat, fish leaping each side, the sea white and boiling with them so that they foamed out of it, glistening in the sun, exploding as had the pigeons yet with more direction, heading only God and Ginger knew

where. The water seethed with them: Bob could see their eyes
open and serious as they flashed by, while Luke stared openmouthed as if hypnotised.

Ginger, still talking about the scuttling of the German fleet
in 1919, reached under his seat and produced a line with 12
hooks in it. He dropped it over the edge, jerked it a couple of
times as if beckoning the shoal, and hauled it in again. Eight
fish writhed and flapped. He unhooked them, dropped them
into a cardboard box, and repeated the process. Eleven fish
leaped to his call; the third time the whole line was full of
them dancing and spinning, drops of water flashing off their
silver skins.

"How many can you eat?"

"Are all of those for us?" Bob peered into the squirming
box. "Stop, stop."

Ginger started the engine and headed for home. "Can you
clean them?" he asked. He bent down, grasped a still
flapping herring, stuck two fingers splayed in a V into its
gills, ripped, squeezed, and its innards plopped softly over
the gunwale. He tossed it back into the box where it fought
staring eyed. "There, you try," he said, but Bob diverted him
on to an account of herring behaviour.

Luke was dazed. He had realised that giants and witches
surely existed, that Noah had built his Ark, that plagues of
frogs and seas running red were possible in a world which
could produce Orkney's extravagances. Dimly he tried to
recall that there were people stepping grey-faced off trains,
working in offices, being deafened on assembly lines, watching television for hours, but he found it hard to believe. This
island of unreality was nonetheless real, a Homeric world of
paradoxes where nothing was mundane but all extreme: no
fish or millions, gales and storms or sunshine, disaster or
vivid success sprang in rapid and violent succession so that no
man could live amongst it and remain sane and yet men did,
and not only survived but could speak to him warmly and
offer him a drink, nudging him and making him laugh.
Extravagance of extravagances, they were not blind to it but
delighted in its extremity. As he thought about it, he knew
that he and Bob should go deeper into it and also that it

would remain an impossible memory as long as he lived, so that every now and then he would be forced to contact Bob and ask: "Do you remember Orkney? The birds? The Old Man? The fish? Ginger? Or has my mind run away altogether?"

Bob was shaking him.

"Ginger says that if we're up to it we could find his son and go out after lobsters with him this afternoon. I don't know about you, but I fancy that."

"Lobsters?" Luke had a vision of ten million lobsters, and started to laugh.

"Are you pissed?"

"No — yes — no — it's not just the whisky. . ." He waved an arm at the sea, the sky, the boat.

"You've got to go for it, though."

"Who's stopping?"

Abandoning past worlds, they went on, and Orkney laid more marvels in their path as reward. In a dark crowded pub the landlord showed them a newspaper cutting:

News that climbers are once more assaulting the stacks on Yesnaby and Hoy has prompted the question: what will they tackle next? Our picture by Gerald Meyer Jr. shows a little-known rock pillar, known variously as Stack o'Roo Castle of Geo Stick or Louston, situated about two miles north of the Bay of Skaill. Is this the next stack to tempt their efforts?

The photograph showed a nightmare stack. Shaped like a golf tee only convex at the top, it rose out of a stormy sea with cliffs in the background. On all sides it overhung monstrously.

"Where's the Bay of Skaill?"

Then there were lobsters, blue-black knights in armour, bright eyes roving uncertainly on their stalks; there were huge waves that drove them towards the rocks below St. John's Head while they fought to haul up the pots, and their Old Man again; there was a sunset fish-feast and a bitter morning; a stack-hunt punctuated by calls at each little farmhouse with its inevitable fiery wee dram; there was the stack at last, ludicrous, a bulbous narrow-stalked wart, disappointingly not as high as they had hoped and defended by a fierce sea; and finally there was triumph, pure and unalloyed, as they lay with aching arms on turf where no man had ever been and watched the gannets wheel and plunge into the tumultuous sea below.

CHAPTER 4

I Just Want To Make Love To You

Luke sat in the University refectory despondently stirring his cup of sludge and gazing at the girls being pasty-faced and interesting. Leaflets on the table announced a meeting of the Radical Marxist League and an avant-garde French film as forerunners of the term's delectations. He had spent all morning shuffling along corridors to collect his grant, arranging to sleep on the easy-going Andy's floor until he found digs for himself, and checking his timetable. A sense of greyness, enhanced by the vivid splashes of plastic brightness dotted hopefully and futilely around the concrete, pervaded his future, and he realised with sudden horror that he no longer had an easy lift to Wales.

It was hard to readjust. When he had first come to the University full of hope, determined despite family opposition to pursue a brilliant career in research, it had seemed that academic achievement and student bonhomie would provide a satisfying alternative to the materialism of his father's world. Rejecting a place in the firm or a business degree ("something *useful,* dear", as his mother called it, as if pure science were mere frivolity) he chose his own challenge: there would be scintillating essays, wild parties, night-long debates, girls. . . a full life. But it was not like that. He was surprised to find his fellow-students dull; there was no enthusiasm, so that the work became monotonous; the parties were boring, and he had found few friends. It was climbing, with its pains and glories, ebullience and quick-wittedness, that had occupied his energies throughout his second year. It could not continue. He had to get the best First or there would be no point. He vowed to work hard all week and let off steam on occasional weekends.

"Hi there." A thin dark girl arrived opposite him, slopping an indeterminate grey-brown liquid into her saucer. She wore a long brown leather skirt, black stockings and a long shapeless knitted garment. Hair crawled over her shoulders. "You still alive?"

"Funeral's Saturday."

"I know, isn't it awful. Same old drag, same old smell, it does make you feel dead already. I'll be glad when this year's over, except it means Finals. I'm dreading them already, aren't you?"

"M'm."

"'Course, you don't have to worry much; you'll get a First anyway." She stirred her liquid dreamily and Luke found himself wondering, not for the first time, what it would be like to be inside Annie's head. "Good vac.?"

"Fabulous."

"What did you do? Anything interesting?"

"Went climbing."

"What, all the time?"

"Except when it rained."

Annie had locked into the mesmeric activity of stirring, a messy process, until Luke put out a hand to stop her. "Sorry, I was thinking. What do you do it for?"

"Nuclear physics? It's the only place to be at the moment: a new particle every week."

"Don't evade the issue: you know perfectly well what I meant. Climbing."

"Oh, God, Annie, what does anybody do anything for? Why has Ross got an obsession about bikes? Why does Bullard play rugby? Why do you go around trying to see how many junior lecturers you can screw?"

"Just as charming as ever, aren't you? Why do you have to be so bitter? Do you think it makes you more masculine or something?"

He shot her a brief glance, slid his chair back and rose to his feet. "Got to see the Prof. See you, Annie."

"Don't run away: I came to ask you to a party on Saturday. My place. As you know, I don't confine my activities entirely to Junior Faculty."

"Thanks, I'll see if I can make it." He strode away, wishing he had never got drunk enough to crawl into bed with her one night over a year ago, lured on by the magnetic attraction of those gaunt wide hips so that he woke next morning to the spread of her hair on the greying sheets and the inevitable feeling of self-disgust. Why was it that women came in three categories, he wondered: the ones you couldn't get your hands on, the ones that everybody got their hands on, and the ones that you had to promise undying love to before you could get your hands on.

And Kate.

He made for the Library.

Dear Kate, he wrote, *sorry I haven't written before to thank you for the whisky, which was unneccessary but fun. We did the East Face —* He read it over. *Unneccessary* looked wrong. He tore it up and started again:

Dear Kate, Thanks for the Highland Park. Does everybody who rescues you get one? Seriously, though, I was wondering if you'd like a weekend's climbing in Wales some time.

Dear Kate, University Libraries are the most uninspiring places in the world and I long to be back in Orkney drinking your Highland Park —

He dashed out, found Ross and two hours later had spent most of his grant on a five year old Gold Star with a small end rattle.

Dear Kate, Thanks. How about that weekend in Wales? I can pick you up next Friday (a week from the day you get this) at about 6. O.K.? Luke.

The cottage stood aslant on the hillside overlooking the Caernarfon plain, with a view from the blank east wall up to the mountains. It was older than most, an early eighteenth century peasant longhouse rather than a nineteenth century quarryman's cottage: a long low building of two rooms with a barn on the west side and a scullery out back. There was no water, nor electricity; slates were missing from the roof and the thick walls were greenish-black with damp, the plaster crumbling off in great chunks. The massive range in the west wall was smashed, heaped with soot and jackdaw's nests. On one side a small staircase curled up to the windowless attic space under the eaves; on the other a door gave on to the steps down to the barn.

For days Bob stayed there alone, seeing no-one, clearing out rubble, sweeping and scrubbing, tearing out the range and lighting monster fires to dry the place out; most of all these days were spent in feeling the cottage around him and waiting for plans to grow. When he looked at the amount of work to be done it was depressing: he preferred not to think but to bide his time and brew his tea, eating bread and cheese in chilly solitude and watching the clouds roll over the hills opposite.

On the Friday he woke early, tore down the flimsy partition dividing the fireplace room from the central corridor, ate fried eggs and soloed two routes in the Pass. He drove back to Caernarfon, signed on at the Labour Exchange and bought more lead strips for slating. On the way home he made a detour into a deserted quarry yard and took a large flat slab, jagged at one end, that he had been watching for months. Back at the cottage he took two hours cutting three stumps and the slab straight, and had a table, or a bench. Mightily pleased with life, he ate a bacon butty and drove to the pub.

With new eyes he saw the weekend turnaround, the small grey village invaded, its air of closeness and tightlipped poverty overrun by hedonism, its flickering gutteral language drowned by flat, raucous Northern voices. From the towns and the cities they trickled in, faces alight with expectation and settled happily into climbing talk until the pub was roaring and booming under the impassive eye of Clive the landlord. He had seen it all before, and nothing moved him. Sally Fabian pushed her way through the crowd:

"Hear you've come to join us, Bob. Another convert."
The Fabians lived above Llanberis: Josh taught climbing and Sally raised children.

"I didn't need converting; it's the cottage that needs that."

"Which one is it?"

"Cae Ganol. Up past Ed's. It needs a lot of work."

"When can we come and see it? Having a house-warming?"

"Come up tomorrow night if you like. There's nothing there though."

"What, you mean really nothing? I mean, would a load of old mattresses be any good to you?"

"They'd be wonderful."

Luke, at his elbow, said hours later: "Well, I hear you're having a party tomorrow night."

"Am I? Oh, I can live without that. Still, at least there's nothing to smash."

"Been climbing? Who with?"

"Nobody, but there's some desperate boulder problems straight out of the back door and I've done a bit of soloing. How did you get down?"

"Come outside and see, come on, bring your pint."

Saturday's climbing went superbly: both were on good form, climbing hard and fast, joking all the way. The cafe was in uproar in the evening, and they went to the pub hungry to find everybody keyed up for Bob's party. Ed, breathing garlic over them, muttered wildly: "What about the sounds, man? Have you got the sounds sorted out?"

"There's no electricity."

"You can't have a party without sounds. I'll bring mine if you get the carry out."

Laden with beer, loudmouthed with anticipation, bodies converged like locusts on Cae Ganol. In vans and cars, on bikes and scooters, some hundred blokes and a tenth as many girls swept in with cries, ate everything, raw or cooked, in Bob's meagre rations and licked the crumbs off each other. They gnawed the tops off beer bottles and burned the legs of Bob's bench; they drove Ed's van up to the open door and used it to drive a deafening variety of music; they cavorted and drank, laughed and shouted. Sometimes whole sections of the swaying throng collapsed, cheering; one of them fell in the fire, but did not appear to notice. He was propped in a corner and left to smoulder. The stairs were found and explored; soon there were even fewer women in evidence.

"Where's Dick?" Ed demanded. "Anyone seen Dick?"

"Anyone seen Carol?"

Ed pointed a finger upwards with a quizzical expression, collected a cohort and scrambled upstairs. Shouts, shrieks and thuds added to the uproar. Bonzo Dog was splattered decisively down the stairs; Ed followed, bloodynosed, triumphantly clutching a pair of jeans.

"You should have got hers as well."

Ed disappeared again, to more shrieks and growls from above, and managed to throw a second pair of jeans down the stairs. Outside, somebody was trying to drive a motorbike over a VW Beetle, four people were attempting a girdle traverse of the cottage, and 'Bill' Bailey was exerting his seductive charms on Ellen Pritchard; high blood alcohol levels, rather than lack of persistence, defeated these projects. Those inside were more successful, if less ambitious, in their endeavours to stay more nearly vertical than horizontal and to make as much noise as possible. Dirty Dick re-appeared wearing a T-shirt and tiny socks, flattened Ed and, in the absence of his own jeans, contrived with some assistance to remove Ed's; they were somewhat too small for him and his bare ankles projected sadly out of the bottoms of them as he climbed up the front of the cottage to retrieve Carol's from the chimneypot.

By 4 a.m. there were half a dozen people unconscious on the floor and two more resting outside. Bob sighed, drove his van further up the track and went to sleep in it.

In the morning the house looked as if a refugee ship had been wrecked inside it. Bodies littered the floor; some were in sleeping bags but others huddled in corners, whimpering. The scullery was awash; Luke had started a waterfight with Bob's laboriously collected water before retiring. Upstairs, Carol woke to find him on one side, 'Bill' Bailey on the other, and five hands on her; on examination one of them turned out to be hers. She tried vaguely to remember, but it was too much like hard work.

Bob peered into his home, failed to find Luke, thought for a moment and went to the cafe for breakfast. There he met Carver, who seemed to have lost his woman, and they had a pleasant day on the Mot together. He bought food from the cafe and went home.

It was a cold, stinking shambles. Luke lay in his sleeping bag on one of Sally Fabian's mattresses, reading a guide-book; there was nobody else. All the returnable bottles had disappeared, but no other attempt to remove the mess had been made. It was what he had expected. He kicked the cans out of the fireplace and began making a fire.

"They certainly seem to have had a good time."

Luke grunted.

"When did you get back?"

"Haven't been out."

Bob straightened up, watching his fire. "There, that ought to go. Now for a brew. Christ, this place stinks." He strode out, returning with a pile of logs, a plastic sack and a brush, and noisily started to clear up. Luke ignored him. After a while Bob realised he was sulking.

"What are you reading?" he asked, leaning on the broom-handle.

"Idwal."

"Good read?"

"Yeah."

"Fancy getting off your arse and lending a hand? Or are you going to lie there all day?"

"For Christ's sake, I was waiting for you. I've been sitting here freezing my bollocks off with nothing to eat since this morning —"

"What did you want to do that for?"

"Because we were supposed to be going climbing, remember?"

"You weren't here."

"I was here."

"Well I couldn't find you. I thought you were off at Carol's."

"I was upstairs. I wasn't going to sleep down here in this

pigsty.''

"What's this: accommodation not good enough for you?''

"It was you who wasn't here: where were you?''

"I dossed in the van. I couldn't find you this morning so I went climbing with Carver.'' He shrugged.

"Just like that. I thought we were supposed to be mates, you and me,'' Luke said passionately, and Bob nearly accused him of jealousy. But as he looked at Luke, at that long tense athlete's body, the petulant child's expression, and the hurt in the angry eyes, Bob knew that fundamentally he was right. What was at stake was not merely a date broken, or a day's climbing lost, but a transgression of the unwritten rules of friendship that say that you do not let your mates down, you do not walk off and leave them hanging in mid-air without a second, you hold them when they fall even if it means skinning your own hands to the bone, and you do not betray their trust in you to Be There, for once that trust is broken it has gone for ever; and he liked the child in Luke who could point that out, rather than remaining silent like a cynical adult.

"I'm sorry,'' he said. "I was pissed off about the house.''

"That's what I reckoned,'' said Luke. "Got any baccy?''

"Fine,'' she wrote, "but make it the Queen's in Tarporley at 6 — your hair's too long for Father.'' Luke spent a nervous Friday trying to remember what she looked like, borrowing a spare crash helmet from Ross and having a bath, cursing because as usual someone had stolen all the plugs from the student baths and he had to use a sock.

She was late, and he was angry but concealed it for she was as good as he had thought: not glamorous, not a girl to make heads whirl, but she did have a spark, a fierceness and high temperament that were like electricity to him. He set out to woo her. On the bike he was cautious where he should be and reckless where he could be; when they reached the pub he was attentive but not too much so, pointing out the heroes and recounting the epics, unobtrusively edging closer to those famous enough for her to have heard of so that they would greet him. He could see she was impressed, and when the

ebullient editor of a climbing magazine came in, shouting:
"Hey Luke, come over here a minute and tell me about that
stack of yours, the monster mushroom thing — I want it for
the new ascents list next issue," it was she who dragged him
over while he played nonchalant.

Jack was surrounded by his usual acolytes waiting for the
next verbal swordfight: building and demolishing images was
his speciality.

"O.K., Mr. Cool, let's have the facts, none of your usual
fantasy. Was it hard?"

"Quite. I wouldn't try it if I were you."

"Now then, now then, got to think of our readers.
Responsibility, you know." He turned to Kate, who was
grinning. "That's funny, is it? Who are you?"

"Kate," she said, chin high. "Who are you?"

"I like it, I like it. Do you feature on the crags too,
sunshine?"

"She's done the Old Man," Luke said, generously
neglecting to mention the circumstances.

"Has she now?"

"And he's hoping she'll get round to the young ones
before the night's out," put in an acolyte.

"I'll stick to the ones old enough to shave, though," she
countered, patting his hairless cheek, and Luke was pleased
with her despite the fact that she never did explain about the
rescue for the magazine.

"Hello," Bob said in her ear. "Didn't know your field of
operations extended this far."

"It doesn't usually," she said. "Is it always this
crowded?"

"Only at the weekends. Your friends here?"

"No, I, er — came down with Luke, actually."

"Oh, I see," he said.

"Now don't you start. I just came down for a look at this
much-famed scene, that's all. Perfectly innocent."

"You may be, but sure as hell Luke's not."

Bob had spent the week knocking a hole in the top of the

east gable and installing a window with a view of the
mountains; he had also torn out some of the rotten roof and
put in a huge skylight. These they admired. He then showed
them how to make a bed in front of the fire, claimed he
wanted to wake by his new window, and went upstairs. "I
think I'll try the skylight," said Kate, and followed him,
leaving Luke aghast.

In the morning she sat on his mattress and gave him a
brew. He snuggled round her as she blew on her tea,
describing the topography of the Pass while she in turn
quietly watched the ripple of muscle in his arms as he
gesticulated and wished she had had the confidence to be
bolder. She said she did not want to climb but would rather
reconnoitre, and he was thankful; when Bob yelled: "What
gives?" he returned: "Hangover," but it was not a comment
on his physiological condition.

They drove up the Pass to the Grochan, past the famous
cliffs and the people carrying ropes. Their arrival provoked
interest; when Kate saw what they were aiming at she understood why. It was a broken, overhanging wall which bulged
out fiercely, affording no respite.

"What is this?" she asked.

"Hangover."

"No, I meant what grade? It looks desperate."

"Oh, it's hard," Luke said airily, sitting down to change
his boots.

"Must be Hard Extreme," Bob offered helpfully, and Kate
gaped.

"Tell you what, Bob," Luke said, "how about a variation
first pitch, over to the right of the original start?"

"Yeah, looks as if it might go."

"Give it a whirl?"

"Up you flash."

Luke studied it carefully and led off. It was savage, a
continuous test of arm-strength at an angle so dramatic that
other climbers came over to watch. "Typical Luke," said
one, "can't even have a hangover the normal way," and they
shook their heads while Kate vacillated between whole-
hearted admiration and pride that she should be with them. It

was a brilliant lead, followed with elegant ease by Bob. She
watched until they had both disappeared and, singing to
herself, strolled along the bottom of the cliff to watch the
apprentices getting gripped.

In the pub she was flushed after the mountain air, and it
gave her a hectic look that was corroborated by her dancing
at the party they found in the next village. She flirted, gyrated
and giggled for him; he thought he was home and dry, but
when, after much bribery, he produced a pair of sleeping
bags zipped together, she carefully unzipped them with a coy
smile. Curled beside her, he was unable to sleep.

Bob found them walking towards the cafe in the drizzle
next morning.

"Want a lift?"

"Oh, ta. We were going to the cafe for breakfast," Luke
said, embarrassed.

"I was going climbing. I reckon it'll be fair at Tremadoc; I
fancied a shot at Garreg Hylldrem if I can find a partner.
You're not free, are you? I did look upstairs, but —"

"You miserable sod, don't rub it in," said Luke, clamber-
ing in.

They bombed up the grim, hollow-faced crag overhanging
the road in record time while she sauntered up a river, listening to their distant shouts as she made out the dark outline of
a salmon under a bridge and thought about Luke. Liking him
was not the point: there was simply a sickening attraction,
and she did not know what to do, how to behave. She had
always been one of the boys, and had graduated from playing
football and cricket with them to other, apparently more
grown-up, games when the time came. But this was new
territory, and she did not know the moves. . .

In Tarporley he touched his crash helmet gently against
hers by way of farewell.

"That was fantastic," she said. "Thanks a million."

"Same time next week?"

"Oh *yes*."

They were in the pub, downing a pint before leaving for
Wales. He had managed to phone her twice in the week on

the pretext that the bike had broken, and then been mended; each time she had called him back for a long, giggly conversation. Face to face, they seemed tongue-tied until she said: "What was Bob being so funny about when we met him?"

Without thinking, he said: "Oh, the week before he hadn't been able to find me and he thought I was knocking off some bird — oh, sorry —"

She was laughing. "Oh, come off it, you don't think I'm exactly innocent, do you? A wide-eyed virgin?"

"So why all this playing hard to get?"

"I'm not playing hard to get," she grinned, chin aloft. "I *am* hard to get."

"Oh," he said, suddenly irritated by her arrogance. "Fancy yourself, eh? Well, happy wanking to you." He finished his pint and strode out so that she had to go trotting after him.

Throughout the weekend she treated him coolly and appeared to take more notice of Bob and his opinions — except on Saturday night, when the Rolling Stones sent her into paroxysms of dancing and flirting with Luke. Angry, Luke went out early on Sunday morning with Bob, leaving her asleep, and explored Craig y Llyn, a little-known crag in the next valley. There was no guidebook to it, and few route descriptions had circulated; perched high above the lake in an unknown realm they worked hard at sorting out some good lines, and even some difficult ones. Excited by the cliff and the possibilities it opened up, Luke had forgotten about Kate until they got back to the cottage.

"Hello fellows," she said cheerfully, "had a good day?"

"Fantastic, thanks," said Luke, kissing her on the cheek like a returning businessman.

"Listen," said Bob, "you two lock up behind you and leave the key above the door in the barn. I've got to go to Birmingham."

"Now?"

"I've got to see my old man and sort things out a bit." He seemed preoccupied, but added: "Stay as long as you like, though."

"Well, have a brew before you go," Kate said. "Kettle's on."

"What have you been up to, then?" Luke demanded. "Festering all day?"

"Not at all. I went down to see that bloke in the next house — Ed, is it? Isn't he funny? — and we went trundling boulders in the quarries up there."

"You don't waste any time, do you?"

"Well what do you expect me to do? Sit patiently in the house like a good little woman?" She flung out, flouncing into the scullery.

"Hardly. I wouldn't expect you to behave like a woman at all."

Silence. Then: "What do you mean by that?" She sounded genuinely surprised as she returned with three mugs.

"Just what I say. You're not a woman, the way you carry on."

"What do you mean, the way I carry on? What the fuck are you getting at?"

Bob suddenly said: "Your language, for a start."

"It's no worse than yours."

"I'm not a woman, that's the point."

"I don't see that that makes a shred of difference. Women shit and piss just the same as you do, you know."

"Oh, I know. It sounds bad from a woman, that's all."

Kate was at a loss, unable to decide whether he was baiting her or was genuine. She wavered too long; he said: "Thanks for the brew. Must go. Do lock up properly, ta-ra."

"See you next weekend," Luke shouted at his disappearing back, and they were alone.

"He went quick," she said. "Doesn't hang about, does he?"

"Decisive chap, our Bob; it's one of the things I like about him. He's no messer; he's really. . . mm. . . *solid*. I like that. He's a good bloke."

"Yes, he's nice," she said, surprised at the warmth of his feeling. Then she giggled: "Wasn't he funny about the swearing?"

"No, it's just how he feels, that's all."

Another silence as she watched the mountain opposite; then she turned: "You don't mean to say you've got these Victorian ideas about women too? You? I thought you lived in the twentieth century."

"I do, but I'm a caveman at heart," he said, pulling her towards him abruptly, enveloping her in a bear hug that over-balanced them both on to the mattress before the fire, and sinking his teeth into the side of her neck.

"Ouch! No! Luke! Don't! You're hurting me!" She struggled and giggled, deliberately provocative, until he was incensed by the feel of her under him: he tore at her sweater, pulling it up over her head so that she fought blindly, arms stuck. Amazed at himself, he ripped open her shirt, pinned her flailing legs between his and started to work on her jeans as she threshed about with shrieks that were still only half-serious. Only when he had pulled down her pants and pushed up her bra so that the whole lovely length of her lay before him did they stop fighting. Blind, she waited for a moment, then sat up, pulling her sweater off so that she could rebutton her shirt.

"There!" she said furiously. "Are you bloody satisfied now, you —"

He had taken off his clothes and was waiting.

"Go on, then," she said softly, and bent to take off her jeans.

It was no good, it was too good, being inside her at last and she passive and not so passive, no good resisting, too good, too soon. . . He could not help it.

He lay on her, heart thudding, and she wondered what he would do next: apologise? Or did he think that that was what it was all about? What did he know? She ran through the possibilities as he lay inert, dying to nothing within her.

He raised his head.

"Hello," she said.

He smiled very briefly, got off her, picked up his jeans and went to the scullery pulling them on. She heard the back door bang and smiled.

Funny fellow, what a berk, what a *nice* berk. . . She waited for him to come back to her but after a while she grew cold. She curled up and waited but he did not come. She dragged her jeans on tiredly and went out of the back door pulling her buttonless shirt close in her folded arms.

He was 20ft. off the ground on the monster boulder, hanging by his right hand from the top lip which overhung the base by some ten feet. She held herself and watched as he looked down, decided against jumping and, hanging from the one hand, looked underneath the rock for a placement for his bare feet, feeling around for a second handhold at the same time. He found the handhold, a pinch grip as she could see from the sudden welt of sinew running down his bare arm. One foot clutched a knob with bare toes; the other felt for another protruberance, found one by his knee, and began to lever him upwards and outwards. She saw the muscle stand out on his shoulders and back and thought he had done it, but his right hand gave way and then he was down at her feet in a rolling, grunting ball.

"Shit," he said, and started again. This time she could see the impossibility of what he had tried: right from the start it was a perverse undertaking, throwing him out and on to his hands all the way up. As he reared out under the roof again his feet kept contact with the rock; quickly and surely he reached his previous high point, let his legs drop, pulled up over the lip, threw his right arm high and, scraping horridly against the rock, drew himself up out of sight. A whoop split the air; she responded with a cheer and clapping. He loped into view.

"That was mad."

"That was Bob's idea. What about you doing some? There's an easier bit round the corner here —"

He caught her elbow, jerking her arm so that her shirt fell apart.

"No, don't," he said. "I've got a better idea."

The second time it was better: he obviously did know what he was doing. Well done kid, she thought, that's great, you've got it right thank you very much; but then he went on, insisting at her, and it all got serious and beyond her control because he was past all her defences and nothing like that had ever happened before. It had not for him, either; for a second he was poised, still conscious, realising that this was the whatever it was that had always been missing before, and then he was as lost as she, plunging off on to a sea of discovery where they were both, together, completely, nothing.

A world later, she opened her eyes and looked at the ceiling and said in a flat voice: "I love you," and he rolled on to his back and made a cigarette, pulling her over to keep him warm while he smoked it.

They did not leave until Monday morning, Luke shouting impatiently at Kate, who was fearful of her father's reaction.

A Wimshurst machine, he thought when he saw her the next Friday, that's what we are, two brass balls so charged up that when we get near a spark flies between us, leaping that impossible gap with a crackling snap and a faint prickling smell.

I've fallen in love, she thought, the thing they all dreamed about at school and I thought was an old wives' tale. I've gone and done it. I hope he's nice.

All Saturday it poured down, the valleys heavy with rain, drifts of it beating against the windows. Bob had brought books, a couple of mats and other small furnishings from Birmingham, allaying the starkness of the cottage; Luke and Kate stoked up the fire and made a giant bed in the attic above against the warm chimneybreast, and while Bob stripped the crumbling plaster off the back room and patiently rendered the crevices between the stones they pulled off each other's clothes and spent hours exploring and experimenting, stroking and smoothing. From time to time one or the other would rise to make a brew and toast, finding Bob as absorbed in his labours as they in theirs, and then return to play endless variations on the theme of mutual appreciation as the rain lashed the skylight.

After supper Luke said: "We'll never get to the pub at this rate."

"I'm not going to the pub," muttered Bob from the depths

of a climbing magazine.

"Not going to the pub?"

"I know exactly what it'll be like; I can't be bothered."

"Lend us the van then: I don't want to take the bike out in this."

"No."

"Oh come on, Bob, we'll be drenched. I mean, look at it."

"You can borrow my cagoule as long as you don't fall off in it."

"Big deal. *Big* deal."

Bob shrugged and read on.

"Oh all right then, sod it, you miserable bastard. Where's your cag? I suppose if I take a spare pair of jeans — can I borrow your jeans to go down in? If I die of pneumonia it'll be your fault, you realise."

"Don't take my clean jeans, there's a mucky pair behind the door," Bob said, waving at the door to the back room, whence Luke disappeared while Kate stared out of the window.

The door flung open again. Luke bulged in a red cagoule crammed over his bulky leather jacket. Over his thighs it hung like a skirt, flapping about his knees. Bob's plaster-covered jeans covered the next brief section, to mid-calf; then there was a naked hairy bit, an assortment of socks, and massive climbing boots.

"Like this, you mean? Bloody marvellous," he shouted above their laughter. "Come on, Kate."

"I can't be bothered either."

"Don't you start. Come on, get a move on." He handed her his jeans and went to the barn for the bike. She looked helplessly at Bob.

"Ed'll give you a lift back," he said, turning a page. "If you get there."

But when, in the pub, she arranged a lift back with Ed Luke was angry. He had not spoken to her all night, making a bee-line for his more illustrious cronies, and she had felt glad to have an excuse to approach Ed who, with Dirty Dick, was equally pleased.

"Come on, woman."

"It's O.K., Ed'll give me a lift."

"What is this, a kidnap party?"

"It's drier."

He took her arm, drew her aside. "I don't want you going back with Ed. He drives like a maniac."

"So do you."

"Are you going to be reasonable? I brought you down here."

"And got me wet. I'd rather be dry. I'll go straight home."

"You're telling me you will, you bitch."

She pulled away, angry herself at his presumption, and deliberately spent the last five minutes flirting openly with Ed. When they left she could feel Luke's fury burning at her back. Equally deliberately, she persuaded Ed and Dick to come up to Cae Ganol with their cans of beer. Luke did not arrive.

By the time they had been there for some 40 minutes Kate was on tenterhooks; Bob, watching her, said: "He's only trying to get the wind up you, lass," and she laughed for there were lights coming up the track. But it was not a bike. There came a knock on the door, and a head poked in.

"Have you lost anything? We found this on the road and we thought it might belong to you." He came in, a massy short man, followed by a swaying trio. Kate presumed the middle one was Luke, but he was scarlet and dripping, lolling his crash-helmeted head as the other two held him up.

"Luke!" She ran to him. "Luke!"

"It doesn't *speak*," said the man disdainfully. "Just sort of growls now and then."

She pushed his head up and unbuckled the crash helmet, lifting it gently off to release a powerful smell of beer. There was not a mark on his face, and she realised that the scarletness and the dripping were unrelated: one was shredded cagoule, the other rain.

"Luke. Are you all right?"

"Course he is. I wish the bugger'd stand up properly."

"Luke! What's the matter?"

"Drink," said Carver, staggering on Luke's left.

"He might have a brain haemorrhage or something," Kate

said.

"He might if he had a brain to haemorrhage," said the first man, who resembled nothing so much as the biggest garden gnome in the world. "Drop him over there, lads. Hey Luke, what do you want us to do with those bits of wire and things?"

"Stuff 'em up your —" Luke collapsed on to the mattresses, with a howl of pain.

"Are you all right?" Kate kept asking, brushing the remains of the cagoule off him and trying to take his jacket off. "Luke!"

"Isn't that tender?" jeered the garden gnome, and she whirled round to him in a fury but he caught her in one giant hand, saying: "Now now now, no fisticuffs, I don't want to get hurt. Get back to the Florence Nightingale act, I like watching it from behind."

There were more people. "O.K.," someone was saying, "we've got ale in the van and two packs of cards and one two three four five six seven — play bridge, darling?"

"Strip poker's her game by the looks of things."

"Yes or no?"

"Yes," said Kate, busy with boots, and looked up to find Bob standing over her. "He's just drunk, I think."

"Drunk," echoed Luke happily as Bob picked him up effortlessly in his arms and carried him upstairs like a child.

"Strongest man in the world, Bob," Carver said, shuffling.

"I beat him at arm-wrestling once," said the gnome. "On that rescue on the Ben, last winter, when they were all out for about twenty hours bringing down those kids who'd died of exposure. I thought now's me chance and filled him up with whisky and beat him flat. Do we cut for the bird or shall we raffle her now we've got rid of the opposition?"

More rain, more lying-in; Luke spent the afternoon reassembling the bits into a bike. Most of the damage was superficial — twisted forks, snapped clutch lever, dented tank and mudguards — but the lights were totally smashed. In the downpour Luke and Kate drove down to the village and chased rumours of light bulbs from cafe to hut to cottage, admitting defeat only after dark.

"Stay the night or hitch back," said Luke, picking over the remains of someone's abandoned chips in the cafe. "I can't miss that practical again though: it'd be the second week running."

"There'll be hell to pay if I'm not home tonight," Kate said, glancing at the monsoon and gnawing a fingernail. "And no-one'll pick us up in this lot."

"Hang about, I'll start cadging. There's bound to be someone going to Manchester."

There was one, and his car was full; the rest had left.

"If we get up at five we'll make it in time; it's not that far."

They woke at nine: her fault, naturally.

On Tuesday Luke's professor remonstrated.

"You wanted to see me?"

"Ah, yes, Fry, come in, come in."

Luke sat uncomfortably on the regulation chair. Professor Martin was a thin, nervous man who bit his lips. He should be an income tax inspector, thought Luke.

"I — ah — I've been having a few words with other members of staff — or rather, they've been having a few words with me, ha, ha."

You old bureaucratic creep, thought Luke. "Yes?"

"Yes. Well — ah — that is, to come to the point, we feel — or rather, they feel: as you know I do not actually teach you myself this term — ah — they — let me put it this way: is — ah — is your — ah — your — do you feel your work is going, shall we say, *well*, at this present moment in time?"

"My work?"

"Your work, yes."

"No. I mean, yes: the work's fine."

"Not *the* work, Fry: *your* work."

"My work?"

"Your work, yes."

"Is there anything wrong with my work, Professor Martin?"

"Now then, Fry, I implied no criticism, no criticism at all. In fact, there has been no criticism, either overt or implied, from my colleagues. Your work has always been — ah — erratic, but there has been no doubt in the minds of any of us that you are capable of the very highest standards."

"Well, thank you, sir. If that's all —"

"Sit down, Fry. The problem that is central to my enquiry is: where is it?"

"Where's what?"

"This work, Fry, this work. Where is it? I see nothing. My colleagues see nothing. In fact there is nothing, nothing but a sorry record of lectures missed, practicals — *practicals*, mind you — cut, essays not produced, in short, work. not. done. You are a third year student, Fry. If you think we are going to award you a first class degree on the kind of achievement you have attained this term, you are sadly mistaken. Of course, it may be that you are choosing to pursue your own course at home, or in the Library; but the evidence, Fry, the evidence leads me to doubt this. Tell me, are you in any kind of trouble? Personal trouble? Financial difficulties? Problems in your approach to work?"

Only that I'd rather go climbing and biking and biffing, feeling her warm and smooth, her legs around me. . . To his horror Luke realised he was developing an erection. He turned his mind to the question of his First.

"Er — no sir, I mean, thank you for your concern, but it's not very far into the year yet and I have had difficulty with digs and that, but it'll be fine from now on."

"Ah. Good. Good. I should be disappointed — we should all be disappointed — if you were to jeopardise your career in research at this vital stage. One of our most promising students, we have always felt."

"Thank you, I'll er —"

"Fine. Fine. Well, off you go." Arrogant blighter, thought the Prof. Pity he'll get a Third: those ones never learn until too late.

Nit-picking little pedagogue, thought Luke, sprinting down the corridor. He's got a mind like an animated typewriter: no wonder he was so bad at research they had to boot him up to

Admin. What does he think I am: a third-former?

On Wednesday Luke was a model student, thinking about what he was doing for the first time all term. Once he set his mind to them the problems genuinely interested him beyond the mere satisfaction of being able to master them. He vowed to work harder for the sake of his First and, pondering what he might choose for a Ph.D. thesis, wandered into the refectory at tea time head down, gazing with distaste at the antique buns sadly sweating sugar. He pocketed a plastic-wrapped briquette of mustard coloured cake and paid for his tea.

Kate — impossibility — Kate was there, standing straight and vigorous against the wall opposite, looking every direction but his. For a moment he felt she had thrown a gladiator's net over him; then she turned.

"Kate!"

"Hi!"

"What are you doing here? Do you want some tea?"

"I had to see you," she said when they were sitting as far as possible from the other physicists, and his heart sank. He said:

"It's crazy you being here. You look incredibly healthy compared to everybody else."

She surveyed the earnest girls with their motheaten fur coats and granny glasses. "Healthy? Me? I've got some pretty unhealthy notions at the moment. Listen: I've got a job."

"Oh, great."

"Christ it's horrible being here with this revolting plastic table between us and these revolting plastic chairs and —"

"Revolting plastic students. . ." He caught her hand and dragged her out through endless corridors, up and down stairs, past noticeboards and doors, doors, doors, one of which they stopped outside.

"Hang on a sec."

He dived in. It seemed to be the men's toilets. Re-emerging, he pulled her in and thrust her into one of a series of cubicles. It was a bathroom. They locked the door, turned on the taps, and splashed through his last lecture of the day,

slithering over each other to create tidal waves that rapidly
became too serious and threatened to swamp the whole
University, or the whole Universe.

Later he said: "We'll have to run another one now."

"If we stay here any longer we'll shrivel up."

"I am shrivelled up, look."

"Idiot. You're a sex maniac."

But suddenly his mind was filled with a vision of cliffs, of
Orkney, of the spray-soaked stacks, and he lusted for them as
he had lusted for her. "Hell, what are we doing here? I don't
want to be shut up in this city any more: I know what Bob felt
like. Let's get out, let's just go, Kate, let's go climbing."

"I've got this job. . ."

"Oh yeah, tell me about it."

"Just what I wanted," she said. "Junior reporter on a
local paper. It's grotty pay at first, but I get a full Union
ticket at the end of my indentures."

"Kate the newshound," he said, and kissed her. "Well
done. You'll have to get yourself one of those macs. . .
Where is it?"

"Reading. As soon as I've sorted out some decent digs I'll
let you know, and then you can come down."

"Reading? But there's nowhere to climb. I can't go there."

She felt as if he had turned the cold tap on. "What do you
mean, you can't go there? What — what about —"

Us. He dreaded the thought of her saying it, and tweaked
her nipple in case she might. He had thought her immune
from those turgid female emotions regarding Our Future,
Our Relationship, Us; lest she demean herself he played type-
writers on her knees, pinging bells off her breasts until she
said: "I don't understand. What do you want, Luke?"

"You," he said, and started to make love to her again.
When they left there was a small group of students looking
extremely interested outside the door.

"Having a good time in there?"

"Great, thanks: you should try it some time," Kate said,
and fled, giggling.

They walked for hours in silence through the cold hard
streets before going for a pint. The pub was crowded and

alien, and they could say nothing to each other. Luke wanted to go back to his work, and kept flipping over his beer mat until Kate nearly screamed at him.

It was not a good month. Incessant rain swept the country until land and spirits were waterlogged. Kate, pursuing the career she had trained for, found it not what she wanted now. It was not the prospect of long, irregular hours she minded, but the unexpected boredom of it, the stuffy smoke-laden office, the way she was treated: "Where's that girl? Here, fill this up" — a filthy mug full of cigarette butts to be filled with coffee and two sugars — or "empty this." She was the office drudge, the waitress, *that girl*: a new role, and one she did not appreciate. When, after two weeks, she begged for something to do they threw the contacts file at her and told her to update it. She would walk for hours through the rain to kill time. The brown flowered wallpaper of her bed-sitter made her wonder what she was doing: she longed for action, for the hills, for Luke's knees thrusting hers apart, his hard body against hers. It was confusing.

He missed her too, but angrily, for she had deserted him. He was working hard, and wanted her there to play with at weekends. He felt almost diminished without her. Her fire had aroused the interest of other climbers, and set their girls bristling; in her absence it was the girls, who had not spoken to her, who inquired where she was in tones that barely concealed their mockery. And there was no climbing.

Even Bob was morose. He was sick of the weather, sick of living in a morass of crumbling plaster, sick of never being able to buy what he wanted from people who spoke a foreign language and regarded him furtively. As he came into that damp hovel day after day to find it cold and unwelcoming, with no-one but himself to warm, he wanted to do what he had so despised in others: spend his dole money in the pub among the little enclave of his friends, and not bother. Unaccustomed to thinking about himself, he did not realise he was simply lonely. Luke was no help.

"This place is getting worse, not better," he remarked one weekend, retrieving his rucksack from under the newest leak.

"If you don't like it you know what you can do," Bob
said, coming from the kitchen with a cup of coffee to slump
in the ancient sagging armchair. "I don't know why you
bother to come here in this weather, anyway. What's
happened to Kate? I thought she was supposed to be the
greatest thing since sliced bread: all over, is it?"

"No. She's all right."

Bob nodded, drank his coffee. Luke said: "So what's
eating you?"

"I don't understand you, that's all. One minute you were
mad for her and then you don't seem to care at all. Or is it
that you don't give a damn about anything but yourself
where a bit of effort's concerned? What the hell, it's none of
my business. I wish it'd stop raining."

And I wish she were in my bed, Luke thought fiercely. I
wish she were there now, and my hand on her just there, and
the rain on the skylight. Maybe he's right: we can't climb
anyway, and my grant's run out and she's earning. . .

In the freezing rain of the next weekend he drove to
Reading, cursing.

"She's on a job," the editor said, tucking his pencil back
behind his ear and reaching for the phone. He did not
approve of beer-breathing greasers who forced their way past
his switchboard girl and demanded his junior. It was that
girl's first job, and he would not even have given it her had
the reporter not had 'flu; as it was he would have to rewrite it.
There was no reply to his call. He hated Saturdays. The boy
had not moved but dripped quietly, shivering. "Well, I
suppose you could pick her up and bring her back. That way
we could finish sooner. It's a funeral, St. Peter's."

Luke sheltered in the church porch, gibbering with cold
and frustration. It was so quiet he could hear the rain hissing
off his bike. Two rubber-soled figures, anorak hoods up
against the cold, stopped by the bike, glanced at him and
laughed. It's so provincial they haven't even grown out of
mods yet, Luke thought: come on, Kate, before I die of cold.
As he watched, one of the fellows hooked his foot round the
sidestand of the bike and jerked. "Ponce," said the other
distinctly, as it crashed to the ground.

Kate, hurrying round the corner only yards in front of the funeral cortege, was surprised to see the small crowd at the church gate. It must be quite an important funeral, she thought excitedly. But they were not dressed like mourners, nor were they wearing funeral faces; some were even yelling encouragement to the three figures scrabbling in the mud round the gravestones. Jars of flowers flew into the air; fists flew after them; grunts and thuds greeted the vicar's open-handed welcome as he came out of the church door. She could not see over the shoulders as the fighters rolled in the mud.

"Hooligans," someone said.

"Funny place to choose," said another. One of the figures crawled to its feet, scrambled over the wall, picked up a bike lying in the gutter — *Luke's* bike — and started it. She pushed her way to him.

"Luke? Oh Luke, Luke —"

"You're late," he said through mud and blood. "Hop on. Which way?"

"Straight up, right at the lights, I love you."

They could not wait to get warm but flung themselves at each other and into bed, where they belonged, rejoicing. Neither had realised quite how much they had missed each other until skin touched: the grey day, the small drab room, the limitations of time and space, could not contain their boundless curves of pleasure. Lying in the crook of his arm later, Kate watched the smoke from his cigarette spiral towards the ceiling and thought: I cannot live without this. The past month seemed intolerable as she looked back at it.

"I was supposed to take that story in. I wonder if he's still waiting."

He reached over to stub the cigarette out. "What do you want to do?"

"Come back to Manchester."

"You can't," he said, getting out of bed suddenly. "God, I'm starving: got any grub?"

"What?"

"FOOD."

"No. . ."

"I'm skint," he said, pulling his jeans on. "Damn, these are still wet."

"Well put the fire on then." She rolled out of bed, angry, betrayed. "I'm not staying here, Luke. I've had it. I hate that job."

"Well you can't come to Manchester: there's nowhere to stay. How do you work this fire?"

"Yours isn't the only bed in Manchester, you know. I've got a friend there who'd be glad to put me up. I'll get a job waitressing or something, find somewhere to live. . . Or are you afraid I'll intrude on some scene you've got there?"

"I didn't mean that: you do fly off the handle." He stroked her leg as she stood above him. "I only meant I'm kipping on this guy's floor, I'm working hard all week —"

"You can at least give me a lift, can't you? Then we could go to Bob's at the weekend."

"That's fine," he said. "Come back to bed while these dry." It was easier there. But she could not contemplate it so swiftly; the barriers had to be lowered first. She sat beside him in front of the fire so that her breasts glowed with the heat and said:

"Funny thing is, I bet Father'll be pleased. He'd never say as much, but he's never liked the idea of my being a reporter."

"Why? Not good enough for his daughter? Bit infra-dig in front of the parents?"

"No, he wouldn't mind about that. I think he just thinks it's not a nice job. He doesn't really mind what I do so long as I make the most of things. But — I don't know, I can't help feeling he's not interested, actually. He'd have liked it better if I'd been a boy."

He was silent, staring at the fire, thinking: my father would have liked it better if I hadn't been at all; but he said: "I'm glad you're not. Come back to bed, Kate."

In the morning he was edgy, impatient while she packed, and in her flurry she resented his brooding lack of sympathy. He only wants me as a source of food, cash and bed, she thought bitterly, forgetting her own hunger for him. Wrangling, they fled through the driving sleet, passing a whisky bottle forwards and back in unfeeling hands, losing sensation by the hour. With a numb glow of exhaustion warming him Luke headed into a bend 20 miles an hour too fast. But for Kate's lack of skill he might just have made it; as it was the heavy rucksack overbalanced her, and they sprawled sideways across the wet tarmac in a shriek of metal, slewing in dizzy whorls into dead blackness. . .

Luke came to in a ditch, and he hurt. For some time he lay there unwilling to move, knowing that he had broken his leg. He cursed and moaned to himself, rocking from side to side in agony, feeling unutterably silly and hurting like fury, the pain soaring up his leg and invading his arm, his whole side. He was so cold that he could not even vomit up his hurt; his stomach was frozen into a hard ball. He simply hurt and hurt and hurt, beginning to feel the blood trickling from a split lip, the ooze of it down his leg, the heat from the bike burning him. It came to him that the bike was on top of him, driving him into the cold sepulchrous ground, and he tried to collect his thoughts to get it off him since nobody else seemed willing to do so; there was no-one there, and he was very cold and painful except where he was burning where the machine was driving the two pieces of his leg apart. With a convulsive effort he threw it off him and rolled over. But the pain, despite his gasps, was not more but less, for the bike itself had been causing it. His leg felt flat and flabby, like a beaten steak, bloodsoaked and useless but not in two pieces. He punched at it and clambered to his feet.

It seemed very important to see to the bike, and so he lurched and heaved at it, ignoring his leg now, until he had extricated it from the ditch. The clutch lever had snapped and the handlebars bent but otherwise it seemed mostly unharmed. His left hand began to hurt suddenly and he peered at it in the dusk. When he touched it it felt like wet cottonwool but he could not feel the other hand's touch. It was then that he remembered Kate.

Staggering drunkenly on his steak of a leg he fell down twice before he found her. He had not thought of calling out and it took him by surprise when he nearly walked into her. She was sitting quietly, huddled against the cold.

"Kate?"

She leaped to her feet and, with a howl, caught her head as it was about to fall off. "God, my head. Where were you?"

"Have you been sitting here all this time? You didn't even look for me?"

"I called and called. I couldn't find you and I got scared. Thank God you're —" She took a step towards him, hand out, but he stepped back.

"Are you all right?"

"Yeah, fine really, except my head. It was the rucksack that saved me — well, it was that that got us into it."

"It wasn't that, it was you. If you'd leaned the right way —"

"Are you trying to blame me for that?"

"Jesus!"

They faced each other like fighting cocks in the gloom. For her he had given up his weekend, ridden hundreds of miles, fought among the gravestones, smashed his bike and injured his leg and hand; for him she had lost her job, her lodgings, her security. They screamed like children, Luke infuriated by her lack of sympathy and she by his. They both became violent and were throwing a clod of earth at each other when a car drew up.

"Everything all right?"

"Great, thanks," said Luke.

"We had a crash," Kate said.

"Are you hurt?" The driver, a middleaged woman, did not get out nor switch off the engine; she was leaning across to the open passenger door when Kate poked her head in.

"Will you give me a lift? Anywhere. I can't —"

"Surely."

He was left on the roadside unable to believe her as she grabbed the rucksack and drove off with a farewell V-sign.

It was a wet, cold Sunday, and it took her all day and half the night to reach Llanberis, and another hour and a half to walk up to Cae Ganol.

"Thought you were in Reading," Bob said. "You look

cold; let's have a brew. Where's Luke?'' But she was in his arms, crying her eyes out, worn out, bruised and still confused from concussion, while he was as solid as he had been on the Old Man, a rock himself. He held her awkwardly, patting her back, but she only wept harder and he grew more embarrassed until quite suddenly he found himself hugging her, and she him, with a warmth and familiarity that neither had realised they felt. She stood with her head laid against his shoulder and felt she could go to sleep there; but he pulled away, saying: "I'll put the kettle on.'' As if in a dream she followed him.

With two of them to do it the work on the cottage went better, though it was disrupted every weekend by Luke, Luke who swept in on Fridays to drink and argue and amuse and infuriate, laying claim to mastery of Kate and rock alike. There was something about those few weeks that drove him to demonstrate his ability even more dramatically than before. Gogarth had captured his imagination; hearing of the horrors of Wendigo he craved it, talked Bob into it, and frightened them both. As they had been warned, the vast wall offered not a single decent belay point: the wide ledges were full of muck that would not hold an ordinary piton in a fall, and the psychological reassurance of the poor runners was as crumbly as the belays. It added a dimension neither of them wanted, that of the certainty of death for both if either made a mistake. They huddled together on each belay nervously chainsmoking. There was no way off either, and the sight of Kate merrily hallooing over to them paradoxically made the sweat run down their backs. When they reached the top Bob said, "I don't know about you, but I'm bloody glad to have finished that. Not glad like pleased, not chuffed like after Rat Race, but glad we didn't both go whanging down like those poor buggers off Llech Ddu.''

"I don't know,'' Luke said. "It'd be quite good with a decent belay or two.''

They could not stop: they had to climb every current challenge, forgetting the fear in the elation of succeeding, and the failures in the triumph of being good enough even to try. Luke pestered Bob with plans; he never seemed to notice Kate except at night, and it was never he who invited her on their expeditions. She did not mind: on the quiet she was climbing all week with Bob, who had offered to help Carver with the ground work for a guide book to the Moelwyns. Together they checked out all the easy climbs; he taught her his intricate craft, insisted that she lead so that she gained a true appreciation of the routes, and accepted her as a friend. She could relax with him; her haughty aggression disappeared; and for excitement there were the weekends with Luke.

Suddenly it was Christmas: for Luke, a fortnight in Wales spoiled only by the necessity of spending Christmas Day with his parents; for Bob, a pleasant few days' chatter to his father, who had let Bob's bedroom to a young lad called The Lodger, or Lodge for short; for Kate, hotel work and a cautious letter to her father who, to her horror, insisted on staying in her hotel for three days. And there were parties. There were parties with fights, and parties with Little Red Rooster interspersed with Help! There were parties where the beer had to be fought for and parties where people could not consume it all but swayed soporifically to the floor, parties where cars were 'borrowed' and parties with uninvited guests in blue. By day alcohol-sodden masses, red-eyed and saggy-faced, picked at nauseating chips or threw eggs at each other in the cafe and found excuses not to go climbing, or roared up and down the Pass having waterfights from van windows; in the evening they warmed up for the serious business, the atmosphere in the pub tightening by the minute until, like a plane taxiing down the runway, they were finally airborne and headed for — "Where's the party?" Bob grew bored with it from time to time, and Kate was working, but Luke stuck his throttle full open and followed the merrymakers wherever they went, leaving Kate, duty over, searching the valley for him. Once she was walking home in the icy moon-light after a dreary party where he had been thought to be but was not, when, topping the rise on the north side of the valley, she heard a noise like a car smash. A moment later it came again, and then again, in a long-drawn out series of metallic shrieks that sent shivers down her spine. She started to run, and had to climb a wall. Silhouetted against the moon on the crest of the ridge were two giant earth-moving machines fighting like a pair of prehistoric monsters, their claws grappling together in mechanical fury. As she watched, one was forced sideways and broke away, raising its rear blade high like an angry scorpion. The other one swiftly re-engaged it with its claw but the first bounced up and down, standing on its hind legs, and, by shaking its blade, broke free to whirl round and attack with its own claw midway along the second monster. The din was appalling: the angry howl of their gearboxes rose above the growl of the engines, punctuated by shrieks and clatters as blow parried blow. Moonlight streamed through their great talons. Kate stared in disbelief, then noticed a lone cottage behind spilling light and rhythm. It was only another party.

For Luke, time had become disjointed. He no longer knew what he was going for: he merely went, obsessed by the necessity for staying on the merry-go-round as long as it was moving. Pulsating in a time-warp he travelled at the speed of light from one crowded hullaballoo to another, arriving weeks later at some party that lasted half-a-year and was over in a night. From time to time he was sick; knowing that he was poisoned he rapidly consumed whole dogs' coats. From time to time he became unconscious, whether from alcohol or lack of sleep he neither knew nor cared, and from time to time he met Kate, who seemed to be enjoying herself but made him feel guilty for reasons he could not remember. Sometimes he was asleep beside her, which made him too hot as well as cognisant of the fact that he should be doing something to her, though there seemed little point.

By New Year, when Luke's face had wizened with fatigue, taking on the saggy greyness of an elephant's bottom, Kate's admiration had dwindled to disgust. She was even more disgusted when the next night he came back from a "final" party accompanied by Dirty Dick and a crowd of others all in a state of utter drunkenness and, flopping into bed beside her, puked all over her. She ran downstairs to the bathroom, ignoring the bodies scattered over the floor, and took an hour washing, rinsing and bathing herself. Lying back in the clean sweet water she was furious when Dick staggered in and threw himself at her with a yell. She leaped out of the bath, hit him most unfairly several times, wrapped herself in a towel and ran out, leaving him moribund on the floor. In the kitchen she stopped. She did not want to go upstairs, especially since there seemed to be a migration in that direction, and downstairs she was prey to Dick. Suddenly all this jollity was revolting to her. She went and climbed into bed with Bob.

He was deeply asleep, but stirred when she crawled in beside him.

"It's me. Luke's been sick, the pig."

He mumbled something, put a hand on her bottom, gave it a squeeze and went back to sleep with a happy grunt.

In the morning Luke woke stiff, stinking and lonely. He was even lonelier when he discovered that none of the scattered forms in the attic was Kate's. His head hurt. After a bath he felt, or smelt, better, and wondered where she was. He looked at the downstairs room and felt as if he had landed from another planet: he could not understand what had happened to the past week or more. As he drank mug after mug of tea his puzzlement turned to anger: where was she, the bitch? He sat on the floor, watching Dick's unconsciousness. There was a click and Kate, dressed in one of Bob's shirts, came out of Bob's room.

"Hi," she said wanly, and made for the bathroom.

By the time she came out he was seething with fury. He grabbed her by both wrists, held them in one hand, and made to hit her. But something in her own taut rage changed his mind. He dragged her upstairs and flung her in a corner while he evicted the comatose chrysalids on the floor, whirling at them like a hurricane and throwing them down the narrow stone stairs so hard that they protested dolorously. Kate tried to scurry after them, but he seized her, and when she went on protesting he tied her wrists together.

An hour later he was still angry, and ashamed too, and that made him angry again because he did not like to be ashamed. They had run through a gamut of emotions from extreme hatred to extreme pleasure; violence, tenderness, pity, self-pity, selflessness. . . He released her and stroked her chafed wrists; he was shocked at the strength of his emotion and realised that he was quite capable of murder, even, for no good motive or reason. I suppose I must love her, if she moves me so much, he thought, and he said: "I love you."

"We didn't do anything, you know. I wouldn't, you know that."

"That's beside the point. I love you, damn it, and you behaved like a whore."

"But I didn't. Anyway Bob wouldn't, you must know —"

He put his hand over her mouth and said with determined joyfulness, "I love you, I love you," over and over until she believed him, or at least did not want to argue. But he was still confused, ashamed and angry, and thought he was lying.

When he finally crawled downstairs it was to find Dick and the others still in occupation. Dick had a porno magazine which he thrust at Luke. "Take a look at that. Fancy her, don't you?"

It was a woman in fishnet tights and black suspenders doing things to herself with an expression of glee. Luke could not understand it. He handed it back.

"No use asking him about women: he's in love," cackled Bliss.

"He's not in love," Dick sneered, as Kate came downstairs. "He's just discovered biffing. Whoops, sorry, darling."

"I'm fed up with all this sleet and stuff," Luke said through a mouthful of bread. "I'm fed bloody up with Wales. Let's go grimping, let's go and look for some decent winter, let's go to Scotland. Come on Bob, let's go to Scotland."

"Now?"

"Yeah, now, why not?"

"No reason, really: I can finish Ed's windows later. How long for?"

"I'm working," Kate said. "I've got another four days yet. Anyway, you're supposed to be back at University in a couple of days, aren't you?"

"Not for another — oh, more than a week," he lied easily.

"We could have five days clear up there. You don't have to work."

"I'm skint," she said, not referring to the hundred pounds he owed her.

"Sh, come on. Chance of a lifetime. We need you to do the cooking."

"Pig."

Two hours later they were on the road.

CHAPTER 5

Playing With Fire

Dawn caught up with them over Rannoch Moor, flooding pink light over the snowcapped peaks and making the ice on the road glow ominously red. Kate, driving in silence while the other two slept, pulled up and got out to admire the view; the slam of the door woke Bob, who recognised the stupendous sight and came tumbling out too. It was bitterly cold; the wind whined and clattered in the frozen sedge.

"Well done, half-pint. If there's any more coffee I'll do the rest."

They pulled into Fort William for midmorning breakfast and a supermarket raid, haggard, unshaven and boisterous among the Episcopalian housewives, like extra-terrestrial visitors on Earth for a refuelling stop; then they drove up the narrow wooded valley to Polldubh with the vastness of Ben Nevis towering above them. The van seemed tiny and they impotent, mere cheeky ants, as they crawled below its brooding bulk; but at the roadhead the crags beckoned. A couple of hours' climbing on the steep little testpieces blasted the van fumes out of their lungs; Wales seemed like a foggy sponge in comparison to the massive snowy mountains rearing around them, the black rock of the buttresses formidable against brilliant white.

While there was still enough light they drove to the foot of the valley running up the north side of the Ben and, heavily laden, trudged up the long track to the CIC hut. Halfway up the snow started; higher it was deep enough for snowballs, and they reached the hut in the dusk with snow melting in their hair. Lamplight glimmered from the windows.

"Well, at least there's a lot to choose from," Luke said, jerking his head at the invisible bulk of the mountain heavy above them.

"What do you mean?"

"No repeats of the Old Man epic: argumentative acne cases and feeble females. Kate if you dump that on me you'll be sorry. . ."

The inhabitants were a pair of small ratty Glaswegians who regarded them suspiciously, furtively retiring into a corner to mutter in sullen and unintelligible chirrups. Kate fell asleep while Luke tried to talk to them; they rolled their eyes and made vague hiccuping sounds.

"What are we going to do, Bob? Start with one of those easier gullies and then go for a big one?"

"We'd be better just taking a stroll tomorrow: I'd like to see what the snow's like, and anyway there's Kate."

"Ah, hell, we're here to climb."

"Well, we could do an easy gully and go to the top of the Ben and all the way round."

"I s'pose it'd wear her out. Yeah, O.K.," Luke sighed.

It was brilliant, the snow shockingly bright in the sunshine, the air bitingly cold. They turned to the dark brooding face sweeping up for 2,500ft. above them, its black buttresses jutting powerfully out between the broad white vertical slashes of the gullies: a zebra mountain.

"Zero, Point Five, Number One — that's Gardyloo veering off to the left at the top there — Number Two, Number Three," Bob enumerated, checking off the gullies from left to right to Kate. "That's Tower Ridge running down between One and Two, and the Pinnacle at the bottom of it. We're going to do Number Three." The mountain looked enormous; she longed to be up on it.

"The Scotsmen must be going for Zero," Luke said, squinting at the two small dots high on the face. "Hard stuff." He shook his head knowingly.

They climbed steadily up the slope, Bob instructing Kate in the practice of kicking steps, to a small corrie where the sweep of the mountain came to a brief hiatus in its downward plunge. "You're walking on a lake," Bob said as they crossed the flat bowl, and watched Kate try to tiptoe.

Above, the gully reared steeper and they roped up, belaying on ice axes and gaining height gradually up the broad band of snow until the hut was an infinitesimal dot against the white sweep of the valley. It was nothing more than a tiring plod, though near the top the view broadened with every foot climbed: even Luke's boredom vanished as peaks started peering over ridges and the folds and moulds of the land were revealed. Kate delighted in the drop below them until she suddenly became aware of their precariousness. There was almost nothing to stop them whizzing all the way down, and although that was unlikely, and the gully was anyway at an angle easy enough to stop on, she was aware of the fundamental inadequacy of their anchors. Steeper snow would be really dangerous, she thought, and turned back chastened to find Luke singing and dancing above her.

At the top of the gully the overhanging cornice had been broken away by previous parties, and once above it they were on the broad summit plateau in an icy wind. They turned left, traversing across the tops of the other routes, to reach the summit itself and see for half a hundred miles in all directions. A riot of white and all shades of darkness leaped and flowed about them, the grey-blue ribbons of the lochs stabbing inwards from the grey-grey sea. The vast slash of Loch Linnhe, running into Glen Mor and Loch Ness, led the eye north-east between the jumbled plethora of peaks to the Cairngorms, round and glistening in the distance. To the north range upon range of mountains stretched boundlessly away; to the south the deep chasm of Glencoe erupted into the Three humped Sisters, and then there was the sea and the scattered islands, the promontory of Ardgour bearing its mountains boldly out and, on the north-west horizon, Skye poking its Cuillins defiantly out of the sea. The space, the freedom, were overwhelming, the hugeness of the cavorting land shrinking the excesses of humanity into insignificance, draining the small things from them and leaving them simple and wondering, tiny passing dots on a vast and timeless landscape. Kate and Bob huddled against the cold in stunned silence at the revelations of perspectives of time and space; Luke jigged restlessly and retreated to the ruined building nearby to roll unenjoyable cigarettes for all of them.

They trudged on, munching chocolate, along the ridge which swept in an elegant curve round the head of their valley. It was narrow, and heavily corniced; on each side a sheer drop swept vertiginously down so that they seemed to be crawling along a tightrope with the wind howling up from below. Round the other side, past Carn Mor Dearg, a smooth slope jutted out, inviting descent to the hut two thousand glistening feet below.

"Glissading time," said Luke, and, trailing his ice axe and pointing his feet forwards like a skier, whizzed down the slope at alarming speed.

"Keep your feet forwards," Bob told Kate, "and your weight on your heels." There was a yelp from below as Luke tumbled, went flying, regained his feet briefly and disappeared into a flurry of snow. "If you want to stop, dig your ice axe in and turn sideways. It's quite easy really."

Bob and Luke were the tortoise and the hare, Bob moving steadily, though at a fair speed, without mishap, while Luke alternately shot past him and then broke through the crust to flounder and cartwheel in the softer snow beneath. The long hectic slide down the featureless slope prevented the mind's usual descent to mundanities on the way down from a climb: there was only the harsh crust of snow, the crunch and hiss of boots, and the gargantuan mass of the Ben opposite, demanding attention in the crisp air.

Scrabbling the cellophane off a packet of rice later, Kate remembered with vivid clarity the gap that had separated her from the Fort William housewives in the supermarket, and knew that whatever happened she could never return to the company of people who had no idea of dimension.

In the morning the taciturn Scotsmen had again beaten them off the mark, and were visible nowhere as Bob and Luke walked up to the base of the north face. They went to the bottom of the hard climbs, and were impressed: Zero's icy ribbon shot straight up for 1,500ft., smooth as velvet between the comfortingly wrinkled ribs of rock, with the Scotsmen's footprints dotted up it like the rungs of a ladder to heaven; Point Five's first 150ft. were vertical ice, a frozen waterfall. Even Luke was daunted.

"Fair enough," he said. "Not today."

Bob made his way to the foot of Number One gully, and they set up its easier angle together, kicking steps. Luke disliked the sheer labour of it, and knew why he had not been lured into ice-climbing before. At the top the gully split into two; they took the left fork, Gardyloo, and put crampons on, for the ice was steeper and harder. Already the drop was impressive and as the gully closed in on them, its dark walls squeezing them claustrophobically, Luke felt as if he were climbing into a funnel. The buttresses flanking them leaned closer, enclosing them in a cold and sepulchrous chimney where the ice gave out. They scrambled clumsily in crampons, chimneying up the gap on ice-glazed rock with distaste.

"Anyone who enjoys this needs his head seeing to," Luke said, scrabbling in his borrowed crampons. "Nasty, brutish and long. These flipping crampons don't fit properly. Horrible, horrible." A few feet later the ice started again, and after a steep haul they were at the top under a roof-like cornice. Luke belayed Bob, who crept under the hanging ice and started to tunnel upwards. Back-and-footing up the hole he had made, he chipped away at its roof until he burst out into the light and space above, revelling in the exposure after such a confined climb. Luke continued to moan.

"Thought you were the one who wanted to do ice routes," Bob said.

"Yes, but not vile ones. Let's keep out in the open. This stuff's good and hard: we could do a face."

"We could try one of those ones going up to Tower Ridge. I don't know where they go exactly, but we could find something, I'm sure. Sort of mixed rock and snow stuff."

"Lead, on MacDuff."

They swung rightwards to the top of Number Three, slid through the gap in the cornice and glissaded down the gully at terrific speed. Halfway down Luke shot over a small bump, cartwheeled over, and came to rest with a yell which he followed with every obscenity in his repertoire.

"What's up?" Bob slid to a stop beside him.

"Lost my bloody axe. The wristloop snapped and it's gone

zinging off down there somewhere.'' He pointed vaguely to
the left. Bob peered over. ''Oh, you'll never find it: it was
going too fast. Still, one's enough, isn't it?''

''Mm.'' Bob considered. ''I suppose we can manage with
peg hammers for the second. It's bloody annoying though.''

''Well we can't go back to Wales just for that.'' Petulant,
Luke kicked steps down to the little bowl at the bottom of the
gully, and they started working out a route back up to Tower
Ridge; they picked an exposed line that alternated snowfields
with rock buttresses, a long enjoyable-looking mixed climb.

The first snowfield was pleasantly steep, the snow in
perfect condition, and after the confines of the gully the
shimmering sweep was exhilarating. Its very featurelessness
added to the feeling of exposure, and Bob was even more
than usually careful. At the top, where the rock started, Luke
took the axe and the lead and climbed slowly up the arete of
the buttress. Towards the top he started traversing gently
rightwards on to its flank, which was undercut beneath him
so that he seemed to be on a long airy staircase, with nothing
below for 300ft., and then only the patch of snow running
down to the corrie.

''This is the stuff!'' he yelled down. ''None of that manky
speleological thrutching: it's great up here.'' He reached the
bottom of the next snowfield just as Bob was beginning to
calculate how much rope there was left. Excited chatter
drifted down from above; Bob could not hear it but its gist
was that there was nowhere to belay. Deep snow piled the
top of the buttress, affording no hold for an ice peg, and the
rock offered no help either. Luke climbed on to the wall of
snow and started digging. Ten minutes later he was deep in a
bucket-shaped hole he had excavated, with the ice axe buried
in the slope above him. He leaned over the lip and yelled to
Bob.

It was pleasantly sheltered in his hole, exposed to sky but
not wind, and he dug it deeper while he was waiting for Bob.

''What a brilliant pitch. What a brilliant hole, too,'' Bob
said in delight.

''Good, isn't it? Are you going to lead this snowfield?''

''We ought to get a move on: it's quite late.''

Luke emerged from his lair and glanced up. "Not very steep, is it? Can't we move together up there?"

"Yeah, but stay close." Bob coiled the rope in one hand and, peg hammer in the other, started straight up the smooth slope. "My crampons are better than yours: you keep the axe."

The boring upward plod began again. Luke's ill-fitting crampons slowed him down, and instead of walking up like Bob he had to kick steps. By the time they were 80ft. up he was considerably behind, and fretting again. He started complaining, first *sotto voce* and then in an increasing whine.

"Bloody hell, man, slow down, I can't keep up in these stupid things."

Bob looked up. There was only another 20ft. to go. I'll get up there and belay him, he thought; better not to rush. He turned to tell Luke to wait, and as he did so the strap of the crampon on which he was standing snapped. He did a nose-dive down the slope.

As he whizzed past Luke in a flurry of arms and legs Luke saw him desperately slamming the peg hammer into the slope, but it would not hold him. He let go of the coils of rope and accelerated rapidly down, hurtling towards the yawning drop. Luke drove the ice axe in above his head and prayed, but he knew it was futile: there was no way he could stop that precipitous fall. Hours seemed to pass as he waited for the inevitable, and then Bob shot over the edge of the 400ft. cliff at terrific speed. Next moment Luke was wrenched off his small stance as the weight hit the end of the rope.

"No- o — o," he screamed, slamming the axe into the slope, but Bob's weight hauled him inexorably downwards. As he slithered down in a flurry of snow, heading it seemed infinitely slowly towards the abyss, he tried desperately to think of a way out, using anything he had to slow the fall; but like a man dragged to the scaffold he could not avert disaster. The edge yawned. He clung to the ice axe, hunching his shoulders futilely. Twenty feet, fifteen, ten. . .

He stopped. Right at the edge, he stopped. At first he barely realised it; then, in the silence, he could feel the rope bouncing, tugging at his waist while he still clung to the ice

axe with both hands. Under his feet was solid snow. He had
gone into his snow hole, and it had saved him. He was not
going to die yet.

For a moment he could not move or even think: it was as if
his mind had glued its eyes tight shut, but then he forced
himself to breathe. It made a cloud in the cold air. He was
shaking like a leaf. He called: "Bob! Bob!"

There was no reply. He could feel the rope swaying gently
and dreaded to know what was at the end of it. Carefully he
braced himself, drove the ice axe in to a better place, belayed
himself to it and peered over the lip of the hole. "Bob! BOB!
BOB! Answer me!"

A faint cheer drifted up from below. Luke felt like singing
the whole of the Halleluja chorus.

A hundred and fifty feet below, Bob swung in the void,
barely able to believe that the nightmare had stopped. He felt
very woozy, but he had only seconds to get the weight off his
waist. His right arm would not work, and although it did not
hurt he knew he had broken it as he smashed into the top of
the cliff before shooting over the edge. With enormous
concentration he took a sling from round his neck, tied a
prusik loop on the spinning rope, stepped into the sling and
tied another above it. He did not allow himself to stop, but
inched gradually upwards. Yells came from above, a frantic
plea for information.

"I'm O.K.," he shouted as loudly as his bruised ribs would
allow. "Broke arm. Prusiking. Keep still."

It took hours. Managing the knots with one hand and his
teeth was incredibly difficult. He felt sick and, as the light
faded, extremely cold, but he forced himself to think only of
the rope, the slings, and his movement upwards. He was
sweating heavily, with a thick, oily perspiration like stinking
grease smeared over him. His right arm kept flopping into the
way and his left freezing up: he had to put it under his
clammy armpit to warm, but there was no warmth there. The
rope seemed a mile long. By the time he reached the rock it
was almost dark.

"Can you pull me up?" he called. "I could walk up the
rock if you pulled me, but go gently."

Luke, half-frozen, said: "'Course I can. No need to yell, you're right below me. You ready?"

Seconds later they were together.

"What a jammy sod I am," Bob said. "You'd never think you'd get out of that one alive. Don't touch that one, it's broken. I've done my knee in too."

"Does your arm hurt?"

"Not much. Yet. It's just starting. If we tie it up it'll be better."

Luke did so and waited, watching a trickle of blood run down the side of Bob's face.

"Fine," Bob said after the pain had passed. "O.K., you lead that pitch — but for God's sake go slow. With any luck the moon'll be up in a bit."

"You all right to move?"

"I'll be worse off if we don't." Shock, exposure: unless the weather lasted he would not.

Luke climbed very carefully, taking his time, and it was not until well after midnight that they completed the snowfield and the rock pitch above.

Kate was frantic. She had started worrying an hour after dark, and had forced herself to read for another hour until the Scotsmen came in. It was a bright night and they, knowing the mountain like the backs of their hands, had used every minute of daylight before coming down. When she heard them Kate ran to the door and nearly flung her arms round the first one before she realised who it was.

"Have you seen Bob and Luke?"

They shook their heads. "Where were they?"

"I don't know exactly. Where were you?"

They muttered something she could not translate, and then an interrogative ditty which, oft repeated, turned out to be: "Are they on the Ben?"

"Oh yes, but I don't know where. They were going to do Gardyloo and then something else."

They did not reply, but slowly made themselves a gargantuan meal. Every half hour Kate wrapped herself up and went to stare at the dark mass of the mountain, but there was no sight or sound of humanity, nothing but the whistling of the wind echoing forlornly round the valley. She wanted to talk to the Scots, about anything at all, but her inability to understand them made her feel silly. Instead she pushed biscuits at them with a smile they did not return. Lost in their own thoughts they dozed in front of the stove, clucking to each other like contented hens going to roost. At ten o'clock one of them got up, stretched, took his sleeping bag and stuffed it into his rucksack. It was followed by ropes, pegs, slings, a hammer. The second followed suit. They handed her a Thermos flask.

"Tea."

She brewed up, found chocolate and more biscuits, Bob's torch. . . When she turned back they were ready. The first one held a mug which he pushed into her hand. It was half full of whisky. He pushed the bottle into his rucksack and they vanished into the night.

Luke was lowering Bob down Number Three when he first saw the lights coming over the lip of the corrie below. "Look, Bob, there's a light."

But Bob could not distinguish it from the other pinpoints of light that danced about him. His arm hurt dreadfully after the shock had worn off, and every tug on the rope jarred it so that the broken ends of bone grated on each other. His knee sent howls of hot protest up his leg at every step. He longed to stop but he knew that he must not: he had to keep moving or die in the savage wind. Luke kept up a continuous flow of meaningless chatter that comforted him; from anyone else it would have been irritating but it was Luke's way and he was grateful for that small warmth in the aching cold. He did not want to leap at the idea of rescue in case it might make him give up; but ten minutes later he saw a flash of light too, and in the agony of each step he hoped fervently that they would find him. They would have warmth. He was fading at every step.

The Scotsmen stopped at the edge of the corrie. They wondered, and turned their thoughts over quietly, and added up every shred of evidence: their knowledge of the mountain, its ways up and ways down, and the time factor, and the weather; the conversation they had overheard the previous night, their impressions of Luke and Bob as climbers and as people; the fact that they had not returned despite the superb conditions; their own physical state and ability; and they crouched and smoked silently as the possibilities sorted themselves out and led them to a number of conclusions. Taking the most optimistic, they headed towards the base of Number Three.

Half an hour later they heard Bob's piercing two-fingered whistle above the whine of the wind, and an hour later had reached him. But the moon was setting over Carn Mor Dearg as they came slowly down from the corrie. Bob said: "You go ahead, Luke, and tell Kate. And get the kettle on."

"She'll be all right."

"She'll be out of her mind. I can't go any faster even if you're here."

Late next afternoon he was in the casualty unit in Fort William hospital, surrounded by brisk nurses and the smell of antiseptic. He looked as old as Lewisian gneiss. He propped himself against Kate and she stroked his matted hair.

"Your Luke was brilliant," he said, "and don't forget the whisky for those lads." He fell asleep.

CHAPTER 6

Here It Comes

It happened the next weekend.

"You ready, Kate?" asked Luke, eager to go to the pub.

"I'm not coming."

"Why not? You always come."

"I don't feel like it tonight."

Bob was reading quietly. Luke looked at him and back to Kate. "Come on, misery, it'll cheer you up."

"I don't need cheering up," she said. "I just don't want to go out, that's all."

All week, he knew, she had been nursing Bob, revelling in being attentive, and Bob liked it. Luke felt a sudden surge of anger at that studiously downturned head. "We could take him too if he'd lend us the van — lend *you* the van, I should say."

"What's the matter with you? Jealous or something?" He thought: if there were no reason to be, she wouldn't think of it. She went on: "I just don't want to go out and get drunk, that's all."

"You don't have to get drunk, do you?" he bellowed.

"Nor do you, but you always do," she said.

"Goddam it, what's turned you so holier than thou all of a sudden?" He was incensed. "You're not so pious when you get your clothes off, are you? You'll be begging for it —"

"God, you've got a filthy mind. Do you have to see everything in terms of your prick?" But she was shaking, betrayed again, for it was true: the way he touched her, pinched her, teased her, heated her up until she howled for him to be in her.

"Why, does someone else's matter more now?" he roared.

"Cut it out, you two," Bob said, without looking up.

"D'you hear that? Cut it out," she said.

Luke took a step forward and for a moment they were frozen in a dramatic charade: Bob reading as if nothing were happening, Kate shrinking back, one hand on the back of his chair, as if seeking reassurance, Luke, one foot forward, one arm aloft, poised in mid-action. Luke gazed at Kate; at Bob; at Kate; then he turned and slammed out. They heard the roar of the bike.

Racing down to the pub he overtook a lorry on a blind bend. As he was hammering down the wrong side of the road the headlights of a car suddenly appeared, coming straight at him. Luke pulled back towards the white line and the car flung towards the kerb, avoiding him by a few inches but cannoning into the high kerb with its nearside front wheel. The tyre exploded and the car slewed round and turned over twice, hitting a telegraph post with a crack that broke the driver's neck. Neither Luke, exulting in the fact that he had escaped again, nor the lorry driver cursing at him, heard the smash and it was ten minutes before anyone else came down the road. Peering through the gaping hole of the windscreen, Ed and Dick saw the driver. It was Carver, and he was dead.

Sharpe reached the pub just before closing time numb with shock. He pushed his way to the bar and ordered a large Scotch, which he threw down and reordered.

"What's up, Sharpe: seen a ghost?" someone asked.

"No. Worse than that. A stiff." Heads turned. "Carver's got the chop. I've just seen him. Carver. Dead as a doornail."

Within seconds a group had gathered to hear him recount in dull, frightened tones how he had seen Ed by the roadside, and then Carver's wreck, and had seen Carver dead. Dick had gone for the police, and Sharpe's Triumph was so illegal that he had pressed on. Ed seemed all right by himself but Carver was dead, he said. There was an inquisition into where it had happened and Luke listened petrified, with cold torrents pouring down his back. He stood mesmerised as others pushed around him to hear the news and to spread it, and it was he who was in front of Sharpe when Sharpe said finally:

"I looked in through the windscreen. Poor sod, he was there with his face poking through the steering wheel, all cut to pieces by the glass but his eyes were all right and he was like looking at me, staring at me, as if he was saying, why did it have to be me?" He gazed at Luke. "Just like I'm looking at you: he was staring straight at me like that. I wish to God I hadn't gone and stuck my nose in."

Luke was elbowed out of the way by a crowd of enquirers, and stood frozen with an image of Carver's bleeding, staring face, staring at him with eyes lit up like the headlights of a car. . .

He walked slowly up the wet street to the railway, climbed over the fence and on to the railway line, and started to walk up Snowdon. The light drizzle, and the constant reiteration of the interval between the sleepers, turned him slowly into a mindless mechanical thing, cut off from all sensation, stepping rhythmically from one block to the next: left, right, left, right, left, right, left. He did not want to think about it because he knew what he would have to think if he allowed himself, and so he walked on up the mountain, left, right, left, right, left, right until the images stopped coming at him and at last, near the top, where the drizzle turned to small, light droplets of snow and he was walking on the track, he was simply a man on his way up a mountain. He was cold and tired and he turned back.

By midnight Kate was wondering where he was. "I hope he hasn't crashed again," she said, turning for the fifth time to the window. "Or do you think he's trying to make me jealous?"

"He's not that calculating," Bob said. "I should think there's a party somewhere. You can take the van and go and look for him if you like."

"Here's lights," she said suddenly. "Not a bike, though. Maybe it's Ed. No, they're coming up here. Hell, I hope he's not in little bits in the back."

It was Ed, with a bottle of whisky.

"Hi, Ed," Bob said. "Are we celebrating?"

"Hardly. Sorry about this, but Carver's got the chop."

Bob sat and stared at his hands in silence for a long while.

Presently he said simply, "Oh. Carver."

Carver had been a well-liked man, quiet and reliable, no great entertainer but pithily humorous; before Bob had taken up with Luke they had always climbed together, and he had remained Bob's most respected friend. He said:

"Well, come in, Ed, let's hear about it. Get some mugs, will you, Kate?"

They sat for hours drinking the bottle dry, talking first about the accident and then about Carver, retelling tales of what he had climbed and what he had said, elaborating a sad appreciation of his qualities. Kate was struck by their calm acceptance of Carver's death, which she could barely believe; after a while she realised that for both of them it was far from the first time that they had faced a friend's sudden death. If Bob had not been so lucky, she thought with a shiver, we'd have been relieving the pain by talking about him like this. For the first time in hours she remembered Luke.

"Ed, d'you know where Luke is?"

"No idea."

"He'll be off somewhere getting pissed," Bob said. "With all those cops on the road he can't have come to any harm without us knowing by now."

"You'd think he'd come back though."

"He won't want to see me," Bob said.

Ed said: "Why not? Carver wasn't a particular mate of his, was he?"

"No, but you know what Luke's like. It's all a bit more Technicolor for him, and he'll be wondering if I'm all cut up or whatever." He drank more whisky.

In fact at that moment Luke was climbing into bed with Carol.

"Don't talk, just take me to bed," he had said when she opened the door and Carol, who had been trying to do that for a year, obeyed. Hating himself, he pounded away mechanically at her in the rhythm of his pace on the railway track until he was so bored and exhausted he fell asleep.

At six in the morning. Kate, who had not slept, crawled downstairs to Bob's bedroom. He was lying on his back, open-eyed.

"I can't sleep," she said miserably. "D'you want some tea?"

"No." He threw aside the bedclothes for her, and she climbed in beside him and put her head on his chest. He hugged her with his good arm; she could hear his heart beat steadily, strongly, and was comforted, as was he.

Late next morning when they woke up he touched her body with wonder and pleasure, like a child having a superb Christmas surprise, and made love to her. She was pleased, because she wanted something nice to happen to him.

Luke took to drinking heavily. He did not do it at first but his nerves let him down. He became a truly appalling driver, partly terrified and partly even more reckless than before. He ceased to be able to work. He knew that his lecturers had been watching him since the Prof's warning, and he knew they were spying on him in practicals, in tutorials, in the corridor. Chance meetings with members of staff, who had always found him one of their brighter students and worth talking to, took on a sinister significance. As the pressure of Finals mounted and references to the exams and their possible outcome increased even the most lackadaisical students started working seriously. Luke tried, but his mind seemed fragmented and he could not pull it together to concentrate on anything. When he stared at a book, or a blank piece of paper, the image of Carver's bloody face with its staring headlight eyes would form and shift leerily about the page. Andrew's flat or the library felt oppressive and imprisoning, but as he strode about the city streets the Cat would follow him.

The Cat had developed gradually. He was not sure it was a cat; it was merely a black shape that he could see out of the corner of his eye. It stalked him, not all the time but increasingly often. At first it only came every couple of days but after three weeks it appeared several times a day, unnerving him. When he whirled round to see it properly it was not there. It only came when his guard was down, sneaking up on him like a child playing Grandmother's Footsteps until his jitteriness increased and he felt worn out by the constant

battle of trying to maintain his sanity in a world where everything and everybody peered at him and persecuted him.

It would have been better if he could have slept, but he
could not. The moment he lay down in bed he was wide
awake. Formulae rushed through his brain, snatches of music
tormented him, teasing him with the inanity of their words;
tiny memories, like snapshots of scenes and faces, whizzed by
as if whoever was the projectionist had gone mad. When he
finally did sleep it was to be attacked by a dismembered pair
of jaws armed with sharp teeth that snapped at him, sailing
up from behind a bush or a cupboard or even out of somebody's mouth to buzz around him like a mosquito, darting in
with its hideous white teeth while he flailed and squirmed out
of its way, waking halfway across the floor in a sweat. Then
there was a train that appeared out of nowhere down a street
or across a field, startling him at first and then panicking him
as he realised that his foot was caught between the rail and
the sleeper and he could not get away. Hooting and puffing,
it bore down on him gleefully. His previous dreamless
unconsciousness was a thing of the past, but even without
sleep he did not feel tired so much as clenched up tight like an
overwound clock spring, sending out undirected panic waves
of energy.

Two things helped: drink and climbing. When he started
drinking he got hopelessly drunk night after night, so that he
slept at least a few hours before the nightmares got him. Then
he pulled himself together, realising that he would never get
any work done that way, and took to sipping whisky in the
evening while he studied. It seemed to work: the images left
his pages and he knew that in a little while time would
eradicate the horror and it would be all right. He longed for
the evening so that he could begin the slow process of
inebriation, until he saw in an inspired moment that there was
no reason not to calm his nerves in the daytime too. He hid a
special bottle of Scotch for the mornings and had another tot
or two at lunchtime in the student bar — or three, or six,
since there were always friends there. His hypertension
erupted in a flood of speech; he talked wittily, sarcastically,
until there was always a crowd of admirers ready to buy him a

drink so that he would amuse them with an outrageous monologue interrupted by demands for more. He missed afternoon lectures but it did not seem important since he was working at night; the Cat, too, lost its importance and although it was constantly there it no longer made him twitch and start. In fact he felt liberated from pressures, social and intellectual, finding that he could do almost anything he wanted without fear of the consequences: shoplifting became so easy as to be ridiculous, and he borrowed money freely and lied incessantly. He was having a lot of fun.

At weekends he went to Wales. At first that was extremely difficult and he had to get very very drunk. He no longer wanted to talk to Kate but he still desired her immensely, and satisfied himself vigorously; she did not complain and he told himself that the old adage about the way to a woman's heart was true. His new-found witticism went down well in the pub: "Hell of a character, that Luke," they would say, impressed not only by his command of speech and capacity for drinking and playing but also by his climbing.

Just as in Orkney Luke had realised that the supernatural could exist, and that anything was possible in those Biblical islands of famine and plenty, so now all things became possible not only morally and socially but on the rocks too. As barriers to behaviour slipped away physical fear shrank to nothing. Imagination no longer held him back and he led a charmed life, taking risks even he would previously have abhorred. Since Bob could not climb with him he soloed. His lone figure could be seen on impossible positions on impossible routes; anyone who chanced to meet him on one of his soloing bouts found him incapable of communication, with the frenzied, glittering air of a man in a high fever. Admiration and amusement turned to censorious disdain, for his unwillingly captivated audience felt he was tempting fate too far. And so they watched, and waited, and he simply climbed harder and harder.

Kate was terrified.

"Bob, do you know what he's doing?"

"The word gets around."

"I don't understand it; he must be off his head. I don't

understand it, Bob.''

"Yeah, he's making some kind of breakthrough all right.''

"Oh, Bob, *please*.''

He put his book down. "Please what?''

"Tell me. I mean, what he's doing, what he's playing at. Since Christmas he hasn't been the same. It's not just the climbing, it's —'' She stopped, not knowing how to tell him of their savage, cold nights of frantic coupling, the greedy excesses that she hated and could not resist. "Oh, *Bob*, don't you find him changed?''

"So have circumstances. What does he say?''

"I haven't spoken to him for weeks.''

"Well ask him then.''

"Luke?'' she asked that night after he had thrown her on her face and banged away at her until they were both slimy with sweat.

"Mm.''

"Luke, listen to me a moment.''

"Tell me in the morning, I'm knackered.''

"No, listen, I've got to sort this out.'' He sighed heavily and reached for a cigarette. "I don't understand what's going on. I mean, what's up? What's the matter?''

He said nothing, watching his smoke.

"Luke?''

He sighed again. "Nothing's the matter. Nothing's 'up'.''

"Luke, I'm trying to talk to you.''

"Talk to me? Talk to me? That's not talking, it's just trying to pick me to pieces. You're just like everybody else, everybody — 'why are you doing this, Luke? Why are you doing that, Luke?' Pick, pick, pick. Can't I even have a moment's peace in bed?''

"Oh, come on,'' she said. "You know what I'm talking about, love. It's just a question of which gets you first, isn't it, the drink, the driving or the climbing. But what for? Luke, I love you, can't you understand, I love you. I don't want anything to happen to you.''

"Oh, I love you too, if that's what you're worried about,'' he said, so disdainfully that she hit him with her clenched fist, as angry as a squirrel.

"What the hell's the matter with you, woman?" he roared. "I've just fucked you for an hour and you've still not had enough, eh? Well get it up again, then, go on, you put a bit of effort into it." He grabbed her head and thrust it between his legs, but she bit his thigh. He clutched her hair, swung her head back and slapped her as hard as he could, again and again. Then he threw her aside. She crawled away across the room, coughing, and crumpled in a heap. After a while she reached out for her T-shirt and put it on.

"Yeah, I'd run off to Bob if I were you," he sneered. "He's still fresh: he'll give you a jump."

"You bastard! You lousy stinking drunken bastard! I told you before, I —" But it was no longer true, although it had not been for the reasons he thought.

"Go on, say it. Even you can't, can you?" He rose slowly to his feet, coming at her while she crawled about looking for her jeans. He reached down and took hold of the front of her T-shirt, pulling her up to face him. "Go on, tell me that my dear good friend, my great mate Bob, never stuck his little nasty up you."

He was breathing heavily, the muscles standing out on his shoulders and neck, but Kate was spitefully angry. She pulled at his fist. "Let go of me, you great ape, let go. He was a bloody sight better than you in bed, anyway."

"Bitch," he said, and hit her. "Whore, liar, bitch." He let go of her and punched at her with both fists, hard, slamming into her small body and pounding her face as she collapsed against the wall. When she fell down he kicked her several times until she stopped moving. He stood back and sniffed majestically.

"Bitch," he muttered, and went to the window. In the moonlight the snow-capped peaks loomed enormous and clear. Clouds drifted across the moon, which sailed along picking out one mountain after another. He watched the shifting patterns until he grew cold, and turned around.

She had not moved.

"Oh no," he said. "Oh no, oh no no no no no."

He could not go up to her. He strode down the room,

switched the light on and, shuddering horribly, went back to her. Her face was lying in a pool of blood. He dared not touch her. As he watched in terror a bubble of blood by her mouth moved in and out. She was breathing.

He threw the sleeping bag over her and ran downstairs. Shaking so much he could barely coordinate his movements, he found a saucepan and, clattering it against the tap, filled it with warm water whose temperature he tested carefully. In the bathroom he found a flannel, soap and a towel. He took these and the saucepan upstairs. She had stirred and was gradually pushing herself up into a sitting position.

"Here," he said, and helped her. He washed her face carefully, removing the congealing blood from her while she tried to turn her face away, and then rinsed the flannel and started again. She took the flannel from him and did it herself. He patted her dry with the towel and sat back.

She looked terrible, with blotches of red already beginning to appear and puffy lumps swelling on her cheekbones. He kissed her on the forehead, which seemed the only safe place. He started to shake violently again.

"Luke," she said miserably, and he knelt closer and put his arms round her and said, "I'm sorry, it's all right. I'm sorry, I'm sorry." She leant her head against his chest and he held her to him, feeling her crying hot on his chest, and he rocked her to and fro in his arms, his face turned up to the skylight and the infinity of stars outside so that she could not see the tears that were pouring down his face as he rocked and rocked her.

He barely slept, listening to her heavy breathing, and when she stirred so that he could see her face he was again appalled at what he had done. He slipped out of bed and got dressed. He found she was watching him. He came to her and said: "I've got to go away for a bit."

"Don't go."

He touched her face. "I've got to. I've got to get things sorted out. This is ridiculous, you know that."

They were close in a way that they had not been for weeks. She said: "Don't go. It doesn't matter, I —"

"It's not really to do with you." Her forgiveness was one thing: Bob's would be another.

"It's not just because of me and Bob? It was only because he was sad, honestly. Is it to do with your work?" She had seen his papers, full of unintelligible symbols and words that had taken on secret supernatural meanings: charms, black holes, injected charges. To live see-sawing from that world to this must encourage schizophrenia, she thought.

"Well, yes, really," he said, relieved. "That's why you can't help. Pressure of Finals and all that. I've got to get my nose down for a bit, that's all. I'll come back in a few weeks. But, er, don't feel too sorry for Bob in the meantime."

"Idiot."

Bob took her chin in his hand and swelled silently, like a toad. Kate had never seen him angry before. He turned her face from side to side. "Why didn't you call for me? Why didn't you shout?"

"I never thought. It doesn't matter."

"It bloody does. I'll kill him."

"He's gone," she said. "For a bit, anyway. He said it was better, but —"

"You're telling me it was better: he knows I'd have crippled him, even with one arm in plaster. Sneaked off like a rat, that's what."

"Please Bob, don't be cross with him."

"The bastard," he said, touching her face gently all over with his lips.

He had left with a terrible air of finality. As he turned to look back once more at the cottage the Cat was behind him, and then he felt it settle lightly on his shoulder and realised it was not a cat, it was a big black Crow.

CHAPTER 7

Paint It Black

In Manchester, Luke went briskly to the library, found the books he had been working from, and settled down to reread the last sections he had been revising and his notes on them. He could not understand a word: it looked like complete gibberish. He went further back but it was still double Dutch. He tried and tried, but after a while he realised that the noise he could hear was the Crow on his shoulder laughing triumphantly. He stormed out in a fury, went to an off-licence, chose half a bottle of vodka, changed it for a bottle, locked himself in the nearest toilet and had a couple of large tots. He felt much better and, knowing that vodka would not smell, quite safe. He spent the afternoon in a bookshop reading Hemingway, to the Crow's enjoyment.

It was not difficult, once he had worked it out. Obviously cutting it out all at once deranged the system: you had simply to drink a little less each day, and not in the pub or you got too drunk. However since the watchers were watching it had to be vodka. He learned to get it in half bottles that fitted snugly into the inner pockets of an anorak he had picked up in the refectory, and could nip to the lavatory without anyone suspecting. It was easy. It was also easy to deliberate for hours over a bottle of cheap wine and filch two halves of vodka at the same time. Everyone was happy, and he was managing quite successfully. It was all under control. He did not count the bottles.

But when he reached Friday it got a little out of hand. He promised himself he would work, but Andy seemed peculiarly hostile to his hanging around the flat all weekend, and the cronies who had missed him dragged him out for a night's pub-crawl. By closing time he could not remember

where he had left his bike. He walked back drunkenly, found
he had forgotten or lost his key, and had to drag Andy out of
bed to open the door. During the next ten days he was picked
up for drunken driving after a chase involving high speeds
and red lights, Andy threw him out of the flat, and he ran out
of money and people to borrow from. He sold the bike at a
loss, returning to the student bar to watch the proceeds
disappear from his hands into those of his creditors. In a fit
of panic he thrust the remainder at the barman and asked him
to look after it. He slept on floors and lost his things, ending
up at the sluttish Annie's shaving with the razor she used for
her legs. But he was not unhappy; in fact he was devoid of all
feeling except for the terrors at night.

When Luke had not turned up the first weekend Kate was
distraught, and tried to think of convincing reasons for being
so. She wanted to go searching for him but Bob dissuaded
her, and so their pleasant life together continued uninter-
rupted. They found each other's company easy, and
gradually developed a domestic familiarity that made the cafe
society put two and two together and come up with five. In
fact it was not until the second weekend that Bob's quiet
hopes were realised. Kate was again keyed up on the Friday,
wild-eyed on Saturday morning, miserable in the pub and
lonely in bed, and again Bob found himself 'comforting' her.
To him it was pure delight. He had had little sexual experience
and every revelation was a wonder to him: her small, perfect
breasts, her soft shoulders, her flat belly and sudden hot
passion made him realise his manhood in a way he never had
before, though he thought only of her; and his pleasure made
her melt with sweetness that was a revelation to her too.
Where Luke was tempests and high seas Bob was honey and
cream, a fortress of strength. As Sunday melted into
Monday, Tuesday, Wednesday, she slipped into a kind of
holiday fantasy, a backwater of peace. But on Thursday she
was frightened and bewildered. By the evening she had
concocted a plan.

On Friday afternoon, after a couple of hours' searching,
they tracked Luke down coming out of a lecture he had dozed
through. He stopped dead when he saw them.

"You look rough, squire," Bob said, and it was all right.

"Working," he said. "God, it's good to see you."

Kate hugged and punched him with little squeals. "We're a press-gang," she said. "We're going to drag you off. Bob's been practising all week without his plaster."

"Where to?"

"The Lakes. Weekend in Keswick'll do you good. Your PA's are in the van, it's all fixed, you've got to come."

"Hey," he said, shaking his head, "just like old times, eh?" He thought of the Old Man of Hoy with the gulls shrieking round it, and of the magical northern light, and the shoal of herring, and his spirits lifted like the clean Atlantic spray.

"That's what we thought."

"We," thought Luke, what's this "we"? As they clambered into the van he was suddenly aware of the easy way they talked together, of Bob's automatic rolling of cigarettes for Kate when she drove, of the way they combined to relate things that had happened in Wales so that he felt more, not less, of an outsider. He felt passed over again, and although this surge of jealousy was not based on any sexual doubts — he was sure he was the better in bed — it revealed a closeness between them that led him to misery, and he hated Bob's complacency.

Luke insisted on stopping for several pints, and monopolised the conversation noisily so that when they piled back into the van again and he pulled Kate into the back with him she understood why. She cradled his head in her lap and he slept like a baby while she talked softly to Bob. It was early in the morning when the van coughed itself to a halt just outside Preston.

"What's up?"

"Don't know," Bob said. "Sounds like petrol starvation."

Kate scrabbled for the torch, disturbing Luke who woke cold and petulant. Half an hour later Bob had stripped the carburettor and cleaned it, and they were chugging down the road again; but the same thing happened 30 miles further on. For Luke it was the last straw in a camel-load of strains, and he swore bitterly at Bob's incompetence. "Oh, shut up,"

they both said finally, as if in chorus, and their laughter sent
Luke diving for the beer they had brought, wishing for something stronger, wishing for it all to stop, wishing simply to be
out there on the rock which would make it come right.

They reached Shepherd's Crag late in the morning. Ideal
for the morning after a bad night, the small crag reared up
from the roadside, with an interested group of loiterers sitting
on the wall to watch the action on the shiny, slatey rock.
They booed, cheered, whistled and cat-called: a critical
audience.

"Let's do something not too hard at first," Bob said.
"Give the old arm a chance to remember." He rotated his
wrist, gazing up the rock.

"Oh, yeah, I forgot. How is it, anyway?"

"Surprisingly good. I've been bouldering all week. Not up
to scratch, though."

"Let's do Conclusion then."

Kate sat on the wall while Luke shot up the corner-crack
with impressive ease, which made her smile and the audience
start to watch. Bob was far slower, without his usual power,
and as the interest dwindled she felt like defending him
angrily.

"Are we going to get you to perform?" Bob asked her,
while Luke nodded at an old acquaintance suddenly eager to
renew their friendship. "Any secret ambitions?"

"Little Chamonix?"

Luke looked extremely bored, but Bob took the rope from
him and handed it to Kate. It was not until they reached the
bottom of the climb that Luke realised she was going to lead
it.

"Three up's a drag," he said. "I'll just solo a bit." He
strolled off, leaving Bob and Kate trying not to laugh.

Little Chamonix is a classic delight, an airy wall and ramp
with good holds, a testpiece of vertigo more than hard
climbing. Kate nipped neatly up it, revelling in the exposure
and failing to notice the crux while Luke soloed the climb
round the corner, pretending to fall off, swinging one-handed
off big jugs, traversing round to peer at her and finally
bawling "K-K — K — Katie" in a passionate baritone. They

enacted a melodrama of lovers parted by an unbridgeable gap, swooning and sighing while the watchers scratched their heads and wondered. Bob took the role of village idiot, interrupting with howls for a tight rope, and doing most of the moves back to front. "Golly, I was gripped there," he announced when they were back on the road. "Are we going to do another one?"

Luke pointed. High at the top of the cliff next to Little Chamonix was a savage overhang jutting out above the road. "Bludgeon," he said.

"You would," said Bob.

"It's your boulder problem, only higher up," Luke said. "Watch."

As Luke started up the wall underneath the prow, nudges and nods rustled between the idlers. Climbers walking down the road stopped; climbers on the cliff found resting places and waited; Kate found herself holding her breath. Plastered against the overhanging wall was a broad pinnacle. Going out to it Luke faltered for a moment, then found the moves. Wedging his leg behind it he reached up, a long stretch and felt for the finger jams in the crack that split the overhang. As he worked himself out slowly no-one else twitched. Mouths agape, they watched as he started moving faster, found a jug on the rim, pushed away from the pinnacle and swung on his hands. For a second he dangled there, feet hanging, and then, reaching up with the other hand, hoisted himself grunting up the crack. Ragged applause followed his disappearing feet.

"Immaculate," said the man next to Kate. "Looked a complete doddle."

"He's improved one hell of a lot since last year," said a thin fellow, leaning across. "Really found his form, hasn't he? Who's the other one?"

"Dunno. One of the Welsh mob," the first said, and they left before Kate could explain.

When she saw Bob struggling hard, with Luke shouting as loud as he could about tight ropes, she was ashamed for him, and cross with Luke.

They went to the cafe nearby, Luke talking nineteen to the

dozen, Bob silent. The fingerjams had left red hot runnels of pain streaking up his arm, and he was concentrating on not showing it. There was a small but perceptible stir as they walked in, and Luke strode aloofly ahead, nodding briefly to those he knew. The sychophantic bastards, thought Kate: that's what it's all about half the time, not the romantic clap-trap about man and the naked elements, and pushing yourself to the limits, but an ego-gratifying supremacy struggle with those below licking the boots of those above. And Luke's making sure they know he's on top, even if it means standing on Bob's face to be there.

"How's Wales, then?" they asked Luke as he sat down. He grinned modestly, as custom decreed, and a small grizzled man pulled up a chair beside him.

"You been practising, young Fry? That was a tidy lead." He rolled a cigarette. "How are you doing?"

"Great, thanks."

"Fit?"

"Not the way I drink and smoke."

"You should take a crack at something decent, looks like." Kate realised from the rapt way that Luke was listening that his informant was a Hallowed Being of some stature. "Castle Rock, say. Bit of size, it's steep, serious. . . Try one of the hard ones there, see what you think. Quite like Welsh rock, that."

"Never climbed there. What do you recommend?"

The grizzled man stared at his cigarette and pretended to consider. "Oh, something like, say Rigor Mortis'd suit you."

After a moment Luke realised that the noise he could hear was the Crow chuckling to itself.

In Keswick, Kate said: "I told them we'd meet them in the cafe."

"Who?"

"Dave and Belle. The people we're staying with."

"I want to go to the pub," Luke said.

"We can go to the pub afterwards."

"Well you go and meet them and bring them to the pub, O.K.? The Packhorse? Bob'll go with you, won't you,

Bob?''

"I don't need a chaperone," she spat out, and flounced off.

Bob dropped Luke by the Packhorse, bought a bottle of wine and went to the Lamplighter. A cafe down a side street, it was packed with climbers gorging themselves, pinching the waitresses, playing darts, fighting over table football and singing lustily to the accompaniment of a guitar. They drank wine and tried to ignore an out-of-tune rendering of Wild Rover until Dave and Belle appeared.

Luke was not in the Packhorse when they arrived, nor the Vaults; he had been sighted in the George, but had been adopted by a group of hard-drinking Lakeland climbers who were christening him the traditional way: a pint in each of Keswick's 26 pubs. They were pleased with their find: he seemed to transmute alcohol into pure energy, and although they had not achieved their aim by closing time he wanted more.

"Threlkeld," they roared. "There's a good band there. Got any boots?" They bundled him into the back of a van and shot off towards Threlkeld while Bob, Kate and the two others were leaving the Packhorse.

"We could try the Pavilion. . ."

The Pavilion's big dance floor was lined with bouncers watching the gyrating dancers with intense disapproval and glancing up to the balcony to anticipate any trouble. But 20 minutes later a figure streaked past them, leaped on to the stage, seized the microphone and burst into a version of "Blue Suede Shoes" far more purposeful than the previous gutless rendering. The singer stood politely back with a smile that enlarged as portly bouncers encroached upon the stage. The Elvis fan was cornered and, while the band played on, escorted down the hall. With a whoop of 'Geronimo' two figures swung off the balcony to floor the two leading bouncers, but they were sadly outnumbered and ended up on hands and knees gazing at the feet of the policemen ranged outside.

"Well he must be in Threlkeld," Kate commented, "or he'd be fighting."

"He'll be fighting there," Dave said. "That's all anybody goes there for. Except the birds: they go there to be fought over."

Five miles away tension reached a head. In the packed barn the climbers had stomped and shouted, grabbing the few girls and whirling them round in an aboriginal stamping circle until one section lost its hold and flew off at a tangent. The locals lining the walls were crushed. It was the 'go' signal. Within seconds everyone was at it, swinging punches that missed wildly or connected with sickening thuds, scrabbling and wrestling on the floor as the girls shrieked and teetered out of the way. Boots fought shoes in a pitched battle; rock-scarred knuckles opened gushing noses and the doors were flung open so that the fighters went outside without disturbing the band's euphony. As the punches crashed into beer-laden bellies it grew distinctly messy, but nobody minded. It was a great Saturday night.

Luke only stopped when he found to his disappointment that the opposition were all flat on the floor or writhing off into the shadows. He had fought long and hard and nastily so that he should not get hurt, and felt good. The night breeze blew chill against his face; he threw back his head and howled like a wolf into the dark.

When Bob woke up with his arms round Kate in Belle's spare bed, he said: "Do you know you're beautiful? Every time I've woken up next to you I've thought it was the best thing in the world."

Luke was finishing breakfast in the Lamplighter when they found him.

"You fit?" he asked. "Let's do this Rigor Mortis thing; it's supposed to be quite good. Your hand all right? Got the gear?"

"Tiger, tiger," said Bob with a wink.

The crag looked horrific, like a compressed Gothic cathedral, all ribs and fluting spires, towering and dramatic. It was also leaning like the Tower of Pisa, as if someone had pushed it gently from behind with a giant hand. As they walked up through the plantation they could hear voices; as they arrived someone fell off into space, amid boos. They roped up quietly.

It was hard, savagely steep, and Luke climbed the first pitch so fast that he was not sure he was going the right way: he was simply climbing to avoid the fierceness of it. Bob, following slowly, found it enormously difficult since he often could not use his right hand but had to fiddle about finding ways to use his left. He knew what Luke was doing to him and did not particularly care after the previous night, but he wondered whether he was going to get up it at all.

They sat on the stance flicking ash at the group watching them from below. Luke said: "What's all that about?"

"The interest? I don't know: you know how they like to burn Welsh climbers off. I guess it's some kind of test piece: the crag's always had a reputation for seriousness."

It was exactly the right note. Luke waited some time, his head sinking into his shoulders with the familiar determined look. Then he sprang up.

He went 20ft. up, stayed a long time, and came down again.

"It's hard. It's really hard, Bob. Steep. Nasty." He rubbed his wrists, looked down. "I couldn't work it out up there."

"Take your time."

"You can't: it's all on your arms."

He went up again and got stuck at the same place. The watchers craned their necks; Bob could not see him, but he was holding himself in to the rock with one hand and feeling desperately for the way up, feet on almost nothing above a clear drop. He retreated again, a little abashed.

"Got to have a rest. I think I can see how to do it, though, but I was knackered getting there." He explained the moves carefully to Bob, gesticulating the holds, competition forgotten in the interest of the problem. "O.K., third time lucky." He paused for a moment in concentration and then shot up again, past the sticky point and onwards. Bob paid out rope and admired the valley spread below, the lake ruffling in the breeze. Sixty feet of rope went out and Luke was stuck again at a shallow overhanging groove. His strength was ebbing; he could not do it. He knew that if he reversed to a resting place he would be even more sapped the next time up, for the rock was so steep. Furious, he draped a sling around a spike and stood in it.

Immediately laughter and cheering broke out below.

"O.K., you bastards, how are you supposed to do it?"

"Like that. You're all right, the sling's allowed," they called.

"Any more of that?"

"No, no, just keep on climbing," they shouted airily, but he rested awhile.

Kate, realising their game, asked: "How much more aid is there?"

"Put it this way: three points is normal, and two's good. It's lucky he didn't know about them: he's done without the first one. You know the bit he found hard? Most people use a sling there. And then there's a tension traverse above him, across that blank bit."

It was obvious that Luke was about to fall off at any moment, yet somehow he did not, and skated across the tension traverse without the tension. Bob had to use both the slings and climbed fast, with a reckless air that did not suit him. As Luke started up the next pitch she walked down to the van and went to the pub. Luke's a selfish pig, she thought, and bought them both cans of beer.

But Luke would not stop; for the first time in weeks he felt good, and just as he did when he got drunk and danced, he wanted to go on and on until he collapsed.

"Triermain Eliminate?"

"You'll have to pull me up it," Bob said grimly. "That's one of the Villain's jobs, remember?" But Luke had gone.

The first pitch was not difficult; the second did not look it, and Luke set off jauntily. He returned appalled, declaring it desperate. On his second attempt he left a sling.

"It's really steep, Bob. Doesn't look hard, does it? Hell, that sling's not hanging straight." He flicked the rope but the sling still hung obstinately out sideways from the rock.

"Nothing's straight," Bob said. "Look." The trees below

grew slanted, the lake sloped. . . They readjusted. When the
sling hung vertically and the trees grew upwards the cliff
overhung monstrously. "I said it was steep."

Luke had to have several attempts, but finally he powered
up past the sling with fierce determination. Above, a groove
swung over from the left and a second came to join it to form
a horribly overhanging chimney. As it narrowed to a crack
there was nothing for his feet, and small fingerholds for his
tiring hands. He was exhausted, his arms screaming for mercy
up the relentlessly overhanging wall above. With the last of
his strength he reached a belay, his hands so tired that even
unclipping a karabiner hurt. For 60ft. he had carried his
weight entirely on his arms.

In normal circumstances Bob, being the more powerful,
would have found it easier than Luke. As it was he should
have refused to second it. As he watched Luke disappear up
the next pitch, he wondered why he had not. He had been
hauled, shouted at, and submitted to blazing agony that
would not go away. His right hand felt white-hot, searing;
despite the far easier pitch above he still could not do it and
Luke had to pull again. But for Bob the public failure was not
the disaster it would have been for Luke. He did not have to
make a good showing, like Luke: for him the competition
was internal, a battle of himself against what he set himself,
and if others happened to see and not be impressed that did
not concern him. Thus he was never driven to Luke's reckless
extremities; yet marooned on a desert island he would have
gone on climbing. Luke would not.

When they went to the pub Luke was afire with enthusiasm;
he seemed too large and energetic for the bar's refined tone,
planning assaults on new cliffs all over Britain.

"It's got to be good for us this year," he said, "I can feel
it, even better than last year. Let's go away in the summer,
let's go and do something really big. I want to do something
massive, a bloody great monster of a climb. Or two, or three,
don't you?" Bob nodded. "It's time we stopped pissing
about on all these little routes: crag rats, that's what we're
turning into. Hell, we're climbing hard enough for almost
anything. I'm fed up with 250 footers: I want to climb

something ten times that size, something that takes days, not hours. Britain's too small: let's go to the Alps. Or the Dollies, that'd be better, the Dollies.''

Bob nodded again. He's too quiet, Kate thought, and saw he was grey and drawn. She went to the bar and asked for painkillers; they had none, so she bought a triple whisky.

"What's that?" Bob asked with difficulty.

"Medicine. Analgesic."

"You'll have to drive."

"What's that, whisky?" Luke demanded. "Where's mine? Give us a whisky, Kate."

"When you break your arm maybe I will. You can buy your own now."

It was some time before they could get Luke out of the pub, and he insisted on staying in Ambleside too. He did not want it to stop. It was ten o'clock when the van first broke down, and then it stopped every ten miles or so.

"Petrol pump, I reckon," Bob said. "See if we can limp as far as Preston and see to it in the morning." Luke cursed roundly. "You'd be better off hitching, there's still traffic about."

"No, I'll stay with you. You might break down in a bad place and not be able to push it. Bloody drag, though, I'll be late for my practical."

"Not if you're up early."

But he found time for a leisurely breakfast and helped with the van before leaving for Manchester. It was like re-entering a prison. It alarmed him that he should hate it so much. He got drunk again and wondered where his few remaining possessions were.

Exhaustion, pain and alcohol had inebriated Bob too.

"I think you ought to go to hospital to make sure."

"Butchers. Nothing the matter with it. Right as rain in the morning."

"You are a fool. What did you want to let him do that to you for?"

"Was good for him, that weekend. Good for him. He's my mate, old Luke. And I know I love you but you are his bird."

On the Tuesday morning Professor Martin asked to see

him. Red-eyed, unshaven since Friday, Luke swayed slightly as he stood confronting the professorial desk. His tutor and one of the senior lecturers formed flanking offensives.

"Sit down, Fry, sit down."

Luke sat. The Prof. continued to scan the file open before him, then placed his hands together precisely. The desk seemed to advance and recede, and when he spoke his voice echoed.

"Next year's research openings promulgate Ph.D. quanta in particulate muons ah — capabilitise the probabilitise the mutabilities infinitely." He beamed. "Conditional upon conditional upon conditional upon the — er — forty ninth parallel, mustn't it?"

"Mm," Luke said enthusiastically.

"The Copenhagen interpretation," smirked the lecturer.

"Many worlds?" asked his tutor.

"Fuck off, the lot of you," he shrieked, backing against the bookcase.

His tutor smiled happily. "E to the i pi is minus one, and then what'll you do with Schrodinger's cat?" He advanced, arms outstretched like a great dark wizard, and Luke hit him.

"What am I supposed to do, lie on your couch and tell you my parents didn't love me?"

"If you like," said the student health psychiatrist, "but I could take it on trust." Luke rather liked him. "What seems to be the problem?" He appeared bored by students and their problems, which was true: he wanted to finish early and meet a special one.

"The usual bullshit," Luke said. He rolled himself a cigarette slowly, lit it, and went to the window. Britain's hopes for the future walked past, chattering. He waited for a long time in silence. He thought, what the hell. The clock ticked on, and he said: "I don't know."

"They could have you up for criminal assault," the psychiatrist said.

After a while Luke took a deep breath and said: "Funda-mental instability triggered into paranoia by a succession of untimely events: accidents, bad ones. Pressure of work.

Expectations. Insomnia. Nightmares. Inability to concentrate. Hallucination. Lack of communication between the emotional and the rational. Inability to express emotions that grow increasingly powerful." He wanted to say, help me, for God's sake help me, but when he turned round the psychiatrist said: "Here, have one of mine," and passed him a cigarette.

"Drink," said Luke.

"Money?"

"Not a problem." He waited. The psychiatrist said:

"Look, how are you at the moment?"

"Fine."

"Not feeling like hitting anyone else?" Luke grinned. "Can you come back in — let's see — three days? Can you hold on that long?" Luke nodded. "I had to see you, they said it was an emergency; but actually I'm on my way to a meeting. . . I'll give you a prescription. Three a day, start them tonight, and cut out the drink. I'm sure we'll be able to sort this thing out."

"Yeah," said Luke, taking the paper. "Thanks."

He was never able to remember the next few days.

On Saturday evening he was in the pub looking, Kate thought, terrible. He smelled grey and tired.

"Where the hell have you been? You look like the bottom of a dustbin."

"Shut up. Lend me money." He pushed at her, his eyes ringed with scarlet. She fumbled in her pockets and produced a ten-shilling note.

"That's all I've got. You haven't had another crash, have you? Where's the bike?" But he was pushing his way to the bar.

It poured with rain all Sunday. He could not stay in Cae Ganol, but when he was laughing in the cafe all problems except climbing ones disappeared. Only the Crow on his shoulder, looking at people in a way that scared him, reminded him that other worlds existed.

In the city he went to one off-licence after another but

could not strike lucky. He went to Andy's and found some
gear; then he bought a paper. It was raining over the whole of
the north of England but clear in the south. He hitched to
Bristol and spent all week climbing on the great limestone
cliffs at Avon, sometimes with a partner and sometimes solo.
He enjoyed getting to grips with the new rock, angular and
disconcerting. Shoplifting and a fund of stories bought him
food; it was not difficult to find floors to sleep on; he kept
moving, and it was easy apart from the nightmares.

Easy except for the nightmares except for the nightmares
the nightmares the nightmares. . .

He was back in Wales on Friday full of life, ignoring Kate
and getting horridly drunk. Notoriety's gone to his head,
Kate thought: he burns off a few Lakeland climbers and
thinks he's God. Even if he did not others certainly did, and
perhaps indeed it was the adulation that made him feel too
big for Wales, bored with the familiar myths and cliffs, the
weather which still prevented climbing on Clog, Bob's
placidity, Kate's hurt looks and the same old faces in the
same old pub. Perhaps he really is through with me, thought
Kate the next morning when, still ignoring her, he leaped out
of bed to persuade Bob to go to Anglesey again.

In the bitter cold morning they tackled the notorious
Mousetrap on the South Stack cliff. The Irish sea flung icy
venom at the extraordinary cliff: like a pile of roughly-folded
bedding heaved vertically so that its fat crumpled folds and
edges sagged and wrinkled, it did not look like a cliff for
climbing on. Ant-like they crawled over the folds on disgust-
ingly loose and dirty rock, following a blanket-edge of hard
rock upwards. It was extremely cold and exposed, the wind
surging in gusts so that every loose hold seemed looser.
Although it was not particularly hard it was spectacular,
surreal: Bob was satisfied but Luke had none of his usual
elation. He sat in a fold watching the sea and talked to Bob
about the Alps.

That night in the pub, face still stinging from the salt spray,
he stood alone and listened to the voices.

". . . laybacking up the side of this really sharp flake. . ."
". . . and then I 'it 'im. . ."

". . . a really horrendous epic. . ."

". . . straight up for 3,500ft., clean granite, and the weather's amazing. Routes a week long on a vertical face. . ."

Luke whirled round. "Where?"

"Yosemite. California." A small man whom he did not know blinked clear blue eyes in a boot-leather face. "Climbers' paradise." He swilled the bottom of his empty beer mug reflectively. Luke grabbed it from him. "Stay there." He pushed the two glasses into Kate's hand. "Get us a couple of pints, Kate."

"Get 'em yourself." She shrugged and turned away.

"Bitch," he muttered, but someone else took them and went to the bar. He returned to the brown man. He had heard of California climbing before, but only in terms of the ludicrous equipment they used: ladders of drilled bolts to get up blank walls, carts to haul equipment up vertical faces, pitons made of old stove legs, angle iron and model T Ford axles.

"Tell me about it."

The man said, "3,000ft. of granite, sheer, smooth, clean as concrete, with these vertical flaring cracks. . . over 3,000, man." His eyes lost focus, seeing again the immense majesty of it.

"It sounds ridiculously artificial, from what I've heard. Ladders and all that: that's not climbing."

"Remember Whymper," said the man easily. "It was only on the early ascents. If you've got the guts to pioneer a route up one of those things you're entitled to use just about anything, I reckon, except too many bolts. It can get silly; but so can all the arguments about ethics. Half of these pundits'd piss themselves just looking at El Cap. It's awful big."

"Did you climb there?"

"Only some of the little ones: 600, 1,000ft. jobs." He drank deeply, lost in memories again.

"Why not the big ones?"

"Just go and take a look," said the man softly.

He told Bob about it, words bursting out in a torrent of

excitement. "Tell me more," Bob said, with that look of cautious determination Luke knew so well. And he made love to those thousands of feet of sun-kissed golden granite, and Kate thought: no, it's all right, it's only that he drinks so much. . .

Luke hitched to London and found Jack still hard at work in the magazine office.

"Take a look at that," Jack said, thrusting a photo of Idwal's Suicide Wall at him as he walked in through the door, and Luke was forced to discuss plans for the magazine for half an hour before he could get a word in.

"Got anything on Yosemite?"

"Why, are you thinking of going there? I'd like to do an issue on that; it's high time British climbers woke up to it. It looks incredibly impressive. There's a pile of old Ascents there, and the AAJ: you should find things in those. Look, would you hold the fort for a few hours? I've got to go out and there's a few phone calls coming in. . ."

Luke buried himself in the American Alpine Journal and started learning. . . The photographs were unbelievable, the tales of 27-day ascents even more so. He made a pile of the relevant magazines, stuffed them in his sac and made a couple of phone calls. He did not want to be subjected to one of Jack's all-too-penetrating inquisitions all evening, and there was no shortage of climbers willing to put him up. He chose a flat likely to have food, and left.

In a fit of melancholy Kate walked up Snowdon. The last tatters of snow still clung to the summits, and despite the spring sunshine there was a bitter wind. Sheep, heavy in lamb, trudged away from her on the lower slopes or turned to stamp and whistle; but higher up there was no life, nothing but the vast bleak expanse of the mountain and its dry dead grass. Cloggy looked huge and foreboding, streaks of ice glistening like frozen tears in its gullies, and she felt sad and heavy plodding by. But on the summit, bare of tourists and trains, the icy loneliness lifted her depression, shrinking problems to trivia in the face of such immensity. She thought: everyone should be forced to sit here alone at least once a year, and then there'd be fewer wars and fewer fanatics. Blinking against the wind, she could see the irregularity of the Wicklow hills humping in the limpid light, and thought: I've got a fraction of a millisecond in terms of this; I'm not going to waste it worrying. Anyway there's no point: if I did come to some decision either or both of them might die the next day, or might be dead now. She went down to have a look.

Luke walked all the way through north London to the University, prowled around the Geography Department until he saw a name on an open door, went to the library and photocopied his articles.

"One pound seventeen and six," said the librarian.

"It's for Dr. Tomlinson. I'm one of his Ph.D. students."

"You should have written authorisation."

"Sorry, I'm new here. Do you want to phone him?"

While she was fighting her way past the chaos of the University switchboard Luke quietly slipped out to return the originals to Jack.

The city pulsated around him: he had no need for sleep but walked for hours through streets of sharp shadows, past the great grey-green greasy Thames, through high deserted districts and bustling noisy ones, past late-night tarts and fumbling junkies waiting for next day's prescription a minute after midnight, through after-theatre diners and hot oriental smells that made his mouth water. He started accosting people: "'Scuse me, I've just had my wallet pinched: could you give me a bob for the bus fare home?" and collected enough for a plate of rice and vegetable curry. The party on the next table left half their rice and he wolfed that too, left his last penny on the table and started walking again. Two hours later he was on the motorway, hitching to Sheffield. A lorry driver treated him to breakfast and he went climbing.

For days he stalked the high bleak tors with their dark gritstone outcrops, soloing route after route on the small savage cliffs until his hands were torn and bleeding from vicious hand-jamming. The burnt-brown rock with its sharkskin curves teased him and he flung himself at it, as if by mortification of the flesh, and dwelling in high places, he could purify himself like some ancient eremite. But the blood-red skies hanging above the city called too; he swept down like an eagle to find climbers in the pubs where he knew they would be. He was welcome among Black Jack's crowd now, and where they were there were always floors to sleep on, food and drink to be had, money to be borrowed. His sleight of hand in stealing bottles of whisky from behind a barmaid's turned back won eternal favour and even sleep; but he looked at them disdainfully with blank haggard eyes that unnerved them as much as his total disregard for caution. With a Crow on his shoulder, caution was pointless: to the others he seemed to lead a charmed life devoid of the normal restrictions, and though they laughed and jibed with him it was a relief when he went away and stopped haunting them.

He walked clear across the Pennines in a wet mist, with a vision of a great wall of granite in front of him, and knew that it would be all right; but even in his absence his dank spectre hung round Cae Ganol too, seeping in with the spring monsoon. Bob would have preferred Luke not to exist, which shocked him; both Kate and he knew that with Luke she was touchy and hurt, and with Bob she was mellow and merry, and yet that when the choice came she would always go to Luke, and it made them both wretched.

Luke made his way to his parents' house, arriving in the afternoon to find his mother, immaculately dressed, reading a magazine about house plants.

"Jonathan! What a lovely surprise! Have you come from Manchester?"

"Mm. How are you?"

"Oh, we're jogging along, you know. Here, put your bag down and we can have a nice cup of tea before Philip gets home. Dear, you do look tired. Have you been working hard?"

"Yes, very." He looked around the lovely house that he hated so much.

"Oh, before I forget: there's a letter for you, it says it's from the Manchester Magistrate's court. I put it in the safe.

Wait a moment — seven two three five seven, isn't it?''

"Seven two three five seven. I think so, yeah.''

Together they attacked the small squat safe in his father's room. There was a long brown envelope. The missive inside demanded his appearance in court for a list of offences that covered half a page. He thrust it into a pocket.

"Nothing bad, I hope?''

"Driving offence.''

"I didn't know you had a driving licence," she said, closing the safe. "Will they fine you? Will you have enough to pay the fine?''

"I don't know," he said, and after a minute went on: "To tell you the truth, it was all a silly mistake. I haven't got a licence, no, but I drove a friend's car for him, just round the corner, to help him out, and of course they got me before I'd gone about 20 yards. There was no insurance for me, of course, so they'll give me a whacking great fine. Stupid, isn't it? I was only trying to do him a favour.''

"Won't he pay?'' She led the way to the kitchen.

"He hasn't got any money: what student has, by the end of term? Anyway, it was me that did it.''

· "How much will it be?'' She produced bread, biscuits, a shop cake, and he forced himself to eat slowly.

"Fifty, a hundred quid, maybe.''

"Oh dear. Have you got any money?''

He had never spoken to her even half-honestly, nor she to him, and it unnerved him. "No, I'll have to get a job.''

She put the teapot on the table, laid out cups and saucers. "That's not very good, with your exams. coming up, is it? My, you are hungry! Don't you eat enough?''

"I'm all right.''

She regarded him with something resembling concern, which made him uneasy. He bolted the last of the cake and fled to his bedroom. It was exactly as he had left it, the relics of sixth-formerdom adorning the walls: his massive star chart, laboriously copied from *Norton's*, a collage of climbing photographs, a Rolling Stones poster and the Periodic Table of elements. He felt old, removed from that boy by alcohol, sex and cynicism, and began to search through the foreign possessions. There was nothing worth selling except his brother's train set; he repacked it into a suitcase, fingering the beautifully made engines with awe and making an inventory of each item. In the drawers he found his Bowie knife and, at the back, a secret store of illicit articles: an air pistol, a packet of Woodbines containing two and a half desiccated cigarettes, an open but unused packet of contraceptives, a letter protesting his passion for a girl he could not remember. He heard the slam of the door as his father came in, and their voices.

"Jonathan," his mother called presently, "your father's home."

"Coming." He made a pile of the things he wanted, hid them under the bed and went downstairs.

"Ah," said his father, "to what do we owe the pleasure of your company?"

It was the same as ever. His father preferred the older brother, Richard, and made no secret of it. Richard was doing well for himself with a firm of chartered accountants; Richard had bought a new house; Richard's wife Veronica had produced a second child, a girl this time (the implications alarmed Luke); Richard and Richard's wife and Richard's son and Richard's daughter visited almost every weekend in Richard's new car. The man looked at his second effort with disgust. This wastrel, who swilled Martinis like water, intended to continue to live on the taxpayers' money for three more years, apparently, appearing in court at regular intervals between climbing cliffs in the company of plumbers. His hair covered his collar, his hands looked like a common navvy's, and his shoes were filthy. He never had been any good; plump fair Philip had always had his doubts that the dark boy was in fact his. . . He developed indigestion and had an early night.

Luke could hear them talking in the bedroom, lying on their twin pink-eiderdowned beds, as he stealthily removed the Hoover and brushes from the wine cupboard. His father's taste was conservative and well-advised; Luke took a bottle of excellent Chateau neuf du Pape, opened it and set it upstairs by his radiator while he had a bath.

Clean, warm, shaved, and with a glass of good wine, he reread his favourite bits: "If there ever existed an Eden, surely it was here. . ." "El Capitan rock. . . 3,300ft. high, a plain, severely simple, glacier-sculptured face of granite. . . unrivalled in height and breadth and flawless strength." "While strenuous and a bit scary — nailing around the right side of the 180 degree overhang with 2,000ft. of space below — it proved to be not nearly as difficult as we had thought. The following seven days blurred into a monotonous grind — if living and working 2,500ft. above the ground on a vertical granite face can be considered monotonous." He studied the photographs again: the vast sweeps of rock, the neat lines of pitons soaring up overhanging cracks, men prusiking up ropes that hung far out in space, so overhanging was the wall; and he read of the heat, of the psychological stress, the enormous stamina and strength required, and fell asleep sighing.

He was reading next morning when his mother came in with tea and biscuits.

"Are you staying tonight?"

"No, I've got to go back."

"Oh. It's very nice to see you dear, we don't see very much of you."

"Thanks for the tea."

"I spoke to Philip last night. I — wanted him to give you some money, but he refused. But I've got a little in my own bank account so I'd like you to have this." She handed him a folded cheque. He said:

"It's all right, Mum, I —"

"No, I'd like you to have it. After all, we're not exactly hard up; it seems wrong that we should have everything we want when you go short of food. It's only enough to pay your fine. Richard had a car and £250 for his twenty-first."

She glanced out of the window, seeming nervous at this voicing of opinion and Luke, who had had a watch for his twenty-first, thought: she hates him. Behind that dutiful wife bit, and with a brain stultified by honour and obedience, she hates him. He leaped out of bed, grasped her shoulders and kissed her. "Thanks, Mum, that's really nice, I'll pay it back.''

She touched his arm with a shaky laugh. "My, aren't you strong? You're like an athlete.'' He flexed his biceps with a grin. She sat down. "Oh dear. I remember you doing that when you were six, when you wanted to be Tarzan. My little boy.'' Luke leaped into bed again: that was far too much: "Jonty, I'm going out all morning. Do take some food with you if you go before I get back.''

When he went downstairs he found she had left a selection of tins and biscuits for him. Eating toast, he wandered into his father's room and sat, as he had so often done as a child, at the desk. That desk, with the safe and the filing cabinet, epitomised his father; at the time when he still wished for his father's approval he had sat there opening and shutting the cabinet drawers, pretending to add accounts. Later he had planned fiendish anti-personnel bombs, and acid-saturated cushions to burn that pompous posterior. Slowly he dialled the combination on the safe and withdrew his father's personal cheque book and American Express card. He closed the safe and went to retrieve the second slice of toast.

He sat drinking tea and practising. His father's handwriting was neat and definite: P. Fry, no frills or flourishes. When he was satisfied he rinsed the cup, collected the train set and set out.

He sold the train set to the same old dealer, who gave him a good price, and with a satisfying roll of fivers in his pocket attacked a travel agent's. After suitable deliberation about price, he bought three return tickets to San Francisco, departing in five weeks. On advice he also paid for three insurances and collected three US visa forms. It was like taking candy from a baby.

Back at home he replaced the cheque book and card in the safe, packed and left for Wales.

He bought wine, stole brandy and burst in to Cae Ganol like a tornado, seizing Kate from where she lay sprawled against Bob and throwing her up in the air like a child, then pouncing on Bob and wrestling with him.

"What have you been doing with my woman? H'm?'' he

demanded between grunts. "Own up. You've been fancying her again."

Bob silently heaved and manouevred until he had Luke's head wedged under one arm, where Luke howled until Kate stuffed a ball of paper in his mouth.

"You seem to be on form," Bob said, while Luke tried to extricate paper from his back teeth. "Won the pools?"

"Don't be facetious, my lad," Luke warned. "Many a true word spoken in jest. Out of the mouths of babes and sucklings. . ." He rooted in his rucksack.

"He found a tanner in the gutter," Bob told Kate. Luke waved brandy and wine at him.

"Ever heard of Premium Bonds?"

They both stopped moving, the same look of incredulous hope flitting across their faces, and as Luke whooped they broke out with shrieks and yells.

"Not one of those massive ones," Luke panted finally. "Only a seven-fifty job, but —"

"Seven hundred and fifty quid?" Kate gasped. "Only?"

"Hell, I nearly forgot. Look, would you save this for me? Hide it somewhere, anywhere you like, but don't let me spend it." He brought out the train set fivers, peeled off one and gave her the rest. She felt it dubiously.

"That's not seven hundred and fifty quid."

"I've spent a bit." He opened the brandy, took a swig. "We're going to California."

"Pull the other one, Cool," she said. "I mean, California? Us?"

He rummaged in the sack again. "Yosemite," he said, holding out the tickets. Bob looked at them in disbelief. "You never dreamed of anything so good, Bob. Those beautiful great walls just going straight up. No objective dangers, no stonefall, no storms, no avalanches, no broken crampons. Sun. Peaches. Wine. A valleyfull of big-wall nutters. Big stuff." He waved the brandy bottle. "Five weeks tomorrow."

"Five weeks?" They looked at him aghast.

"Yeah, check the date, Bob. It's no use after that until the autumn: it gets too hot. We've got to go then. Anyway, all

you need's a bit to spend there, we could last out three or
four weeks.''

Bob sat down, shell-shocked. Kate said: "It's crazy, I've
just landed a job. . . Hey, what about your exams?''

"Oh," he said, "well, they, er, advised me to take a year
off. . . I can do them next year. . . I was, well, the medics
said I was sort of beginning to crack up and I wasn't going to
make it. To tell you the truth, I was really creased up about it
but this came up the next day and it seemed like a sort of
booby prize. I thought, well, let's go for it.''

Bob was still examining the tickets. "I can't. I haven't got
the akkers. If you got these changed to the autumn we could
save all summer.''

"He wouldn't save, he'd spend," Kate said. "All that lot
burning a hole in his pocket.''

"Right," Luke said loudly. "Spot on. I don't want to
wait, anyway. You can pay me back later, if it bothers your
conscience. Hey, look at the pictures, look, here. . .''

There was no resisting that amount of enthusiasm and
brandy. Later in the evening, still buzzing like a top, Luke
said: "Pub's still open: let's go and get a carry out.''

"Na," said Bob.

"Bob!" Kate remonstrated.

"Take the van if you want. But Kate —" he had to shout
after them "you drive, not him." He returned to the articles.

Luke threw beer all over Kate in the pub, and got them
thrown out. He was in a wild mood, effervescent, full of
energy. "Let's go and do Crackstone Rib," he yelled, "come
on, Kate, there's a huge moon. . .''

They roared up the Pass to assault the cliff with a
minimum of gear. In the moonlight the large holds were
deceptive and the rock glistened as if wet. They climbed
barefoot, cold-toed above the dark drop, while the lights rose
and fell from the cars winding along the road below; Luke
went singing off to the moon, and Kate had a hard time
finding her way. When they came down, panting, triumphant,
she said: "Oh, God, look at the time: Bob'll be furious.''

"I'll drive: I'll be quicker.''

Within half a mile he had hit a sheep that lay warming on

the road.

"Made an awful mess of its head. . ."

"Made an awful mess of the van: look at the wing."

"Awful lot of lamb chops. . ."

Despite the sheep, Bob was furious, doubly so since he felt in no position to complain, and refused to have the sheep until they had found its owner and offered recompense.

It was one of those parties that are talked about for years, becoming positively boring to anyone who was not there. Kate took the day off and spent it solemnly basting the sheep as it hung above a slow fire while Luke dashed about the villages and cliffs inviting people. Even before the pubs had closed the pace was strong: limitless quantities of alcohol appeared, followed by a sack of potatoes and the quiet ones, the non-party-goers; the lane became clogged with cars and vans; Ed's sound system began to rock the whole mountain with Stones; and then they really started arriving, gabbling, shouting, laughing, with tales of driving epics on the way up. Sweat glistened on bare-chested dancers stomping to the insistent beat, while outside round the bonfire the hungry attacked the sheep and juggled hot potatoes. Stuffing was eaten by the handful and rubbed into hair; gnawed bones crunched underfoot with the broken glass; leaping flames glimmered on faces dripping with grease.

"Oh, 'ello, haven't seen you for a bit," they yelled.

"No, I've been in Seattle for two years."

"Christ, everybody's here tonight: they've just come back from Patagonia. . ."

Contests broke out, involving tall stories, drink, brute strength and vehicles. A detachment of drivers spent an hour timing each other up and down the narrow twisting lane leading to the main road, listening joyfully to the sounds of metal on stone wall and examining the damage with delight. Shorn wings, mirrors, number plates and two complete wheels littered the course as the night wore on. Ethics were discussed and epics recounted, and while the dancers danced and the talkers talked and the competitors competed, the hedonists crept upstairs with a girl and a bottle of brandy and united the two in a monster licking orgy. Kate, who had been used as a towel by sticky-handed eaters, went up to change her T-shirt and found a helplessly giggling group on their knees round the girl, who was wearing brandy and nothing else. The man attending to her left breast was Luke. When he saw Kate he gave her a V sign and carried on.

Kate seized a pillow and hit him over the head with it. Cheering, the others grabbed it, ripped it apart, and disappeared under a cloud of feathers. She kicked several people, not caring who, and left. Dirty Dick followed her downstairs and started stomping with her and she flirted outrageously with him but there was no point because Luke was not there. After a diligent search she found Bob sitting halfway up a big ash tree, sucking the remains of a shoulderblade and arguing fiercely with Jack about the magazine's editorial policies. She climbed up.

"How's it going? Sheep was good."

"Luke's being a pig."

"Luke *is* a pig."

"Well I've had enough. Honestly. *Enough*." He kissed her and gave her a bottle of wine and went back to the argument, which alcohol had deprived of all semblance of logic. Later they evicted several people from Bob's bedroom, barricaded the door and went to bed.

"Get up, you lazy bugger, get up!"

It was Luke, full of life, who had climbed in through the window with two mugs of tea. "Come on, get out of there, get up." Sun streamed in through the open window, catching on the hills rolling away to the sea. In the room next door music started up again. Bob moaned and snuggled closer. Luke reached across Kate and shook him, slopping tea all over Kate.

"Stop it, get out of here," she cursed, but he got into bed beside her instead and started running his hands up and down her. "Get out, Luke, get out."

"What's the matter, don't you like it? When I do this? And this?"

"Get out, get out, get out," she screamed, kicking and biting. He got out.

"Bitch," he said. "Tell that two-faced bastard we're supposed to be climbing, will you? Here's your tea." He threw it over her and left.

The cliff looked grimly forbidding, emerging from six months of winter with a fearsome air of brooding endurance. Bob shivered. It seemed foolish to seek out this sunless face when there were others ready to maximise what little warmth there was. Nobody else had thought it worthwhile to visit the gaunt greasy walls, and they were alone in the dark cul-de-sac. He glanced at Luke, who was gazing at it with the enraptured look of a man who has sighted the Holy Grail.

Woubits, right at the top of the cliff, looks as if it should drain well, but as they stood on the high terrace below it the rock glistened evilly.

"You go?" Bob offered him the rope.

"No, you do the first pitch. I want to do the Left Hand." He waved his left hand and danced a little, impatient to get on to the hard variation finish.

"You'll be lucky. In fact we'll be lucky to get up anything in these conditions."

"What's the matter with you all of a sudden? Washed out after a hard night?"

There was no humour, none of the usual fooling: he was as savagely serious as the cliff itself. Bob did not like it. Although the terrace protected them from the exposure they were already 300ft. up, and the atmosphere was unpleasant.

"Come ON!" Luke screeched. Bob made his preparations and set off, pulling powerfully up over an overhanging wall to swing out over the long drop. The next few moves were hard and greasy; he did them slowly, deliberately deaf to Luke's barrage of questions and complaints, pulling into a steep groove. This, he knew, had to be climbed on nothing more than fingerjams. He managed the first few moves but higher up it was even wetter, soap-slick, and he thought: well, O.K., I know I could do it in the dry, and I might even do it as it is, but there's really no point. It was like Russian roulette, and he was no gambler.

"Coming down!" he yelled, and retreated back to Luke. It

was hard. "It's a mug's game," he told Luke. "Toss a coin stuff. Let's come back later. It's too early to be climbing on Clog."

"What, you just want to back out now?" Luke looked in disgust from Bob to the rock and down the cwm. "Ah, hell, Bob, don't be such a wanker. A little bit of water and you chicken out? Where's your balls, man?"

They managed to avoid the next few seconds.

"Bloody hell, man, we've been waiting to do this for yonks. I mean, we could've been climbing somewhere else — or I could have been climbing with someone else." Bob ignored him and coiled the rope, thinking of the time when, flushed with their first success, they had aspired to this route. It had all been much simpler then. . . "Well, I'll lead it. If you get gripped seconding you can have a tight rope."

"There's no —"

"Climbing."

Luke climbed it very fast indeed, barely pausing in his upward flight. Bob, following, was horrified to see how little protection he had used. He's in a real tantrum, like a child, he thought. The great black cliff was no playground, though, and despite his apparent oblivion to danger Luke was scared. Climbing the crack he had been icily afraid, so frightened that the fear had, as it were, overflowed and dissipated, and he had defiantly climbed on. The fact that he had managed it was a triumph to irrationality, but even he had to admit he could not lead the Left Hand in those conditions.

Bob smoked silently, gazing at the dark lake below, until Luke nudged him. "Well, shall we go?" Bob assumed the second's position. "Aren't you going to lead? Since when did we stop leading through?"

"O.K., fine," Bob said, "but it'll be the ordinary finish. I'll not lead the Left Hand now. It can wait."

Luke sighed.

It was an impressive lead. A big steep groove led up to a roof, which Bob turned by moving on to the left wall of the groove and, after climbing a big flake, making a mantelshelf. He did it so perfectly, easily, despite the horrific exposure, that even Luke was compelled to admire. By the time he had joined Bob he felt all right again.

Bob, however, felt it was one of the most unpleasant, and therefore pointless, routes he had ever done. He wondered at Luke's apparent joy in the fact that they had done it, and mentioned it to Kate later.

"Maybe I am gutless, but I climb for pleasure, not masochism. It was just a senseless risk."

"I think the University thing's screwed him up more than he cares to admit. I know he says it's what he wanted, but I think he feels an awful failure. He always climbs like a nut when he's upset."

Bob wanted to say: you're not helping either, but that made him feel even worse because he knew it was his fault, not hers. He was too passive; but he dared not make the bold move for fear of losing her. She said:

"I'm sure it'll be better in America. It'll be a triumph getting there, and all due to him. He'll be his old self again, honest."

"He'd better, because sure as hell I wouldn't go on El Cap with him in the mood he's in at the moment."

In April the monsoon dribbled to a close and the hurricanes blasted in. The new lambs were swept off their feet in the gales, blown bewildered far from their mothers in the blustery drafts. Luke dashed hither and thither, obsessed by Yosemite, collecting and collating every scrap of information he could glean and hitching hundreds of miles to talk to the few British climbers who had been there. All had been overawed by the big walls, and none had climbed them.

"Oh, boy," they would say, shaking their heads, "they are *big*." He learned about 'psyching up' and 'psyching out', the mental preparation for the climb and the succumbing to psychological pressures that had become too great; the impossibility of retreat or rescue beyond certain points on certain climbs; the character of the climbing and the stamina required; about fixing pitches and cutting loose; and the more he learned the more certain he was that Bob and he could do it. In near-perfect conditions mere technical difficulty would not 'psych' Bob out; he had the steadiness, and Luke had the nerve, and they both had the ability. They were ready to be tested to the ultimate. Luke wanted to go to that ultimate and have a baptism of fire, a cleansing, an unknown and unknowable experience from which he would emerge, like tempered steel, the stronger.

Bob battened down his shaky roof and did his homework. He did not want a voyage into the unknown or any other romantic quest; he wanted to get it right, to make a flawless ascent of that flawless cliff, and that, he had learned, came from being able to handle whatever problems might arise. Luke's interest in the problems was anticipatory enjoyment; Bob's was training, and he pored over the books and photos to try to gain a feel for that alien, sun-baked precipice.

Kate found herself whisked away like thistledown by the onslaught of the great cliff. She had landed a second job, so that she cooked and skivvied in a hotel all day and barmaided all night; Bob or Luke would find her swathed in blankets on the sofa in the morning, when she would swear and dash off late to work. She was almost too busy to notice her eclipse, and too tired to care, though she looked forward to her re-emergence.

The mounting tension made them hyperexcitable, like nervous players before a match, and as the piles of gear grew steadily and their plans began to fall into place all that keen energy became directed to one end. Private doubts were privately quashed. Like a mountain torrent they sped towards their end, flowing over obstructions, and it seemed that they were attracted to it by a force as strong as gravity. Luke hitched to Manchester for his court case, appearing tidy and nervous before a magistrate who decided to ban him severely and fine him lightly. Licences were dispensable in Wales, but not fines. He fell into the student bar to celebrate.

"I wondered where you'd got to," said the barman. "Lost anything?"

"Lost anything? Only my licence."

"I thought you was pissed. You gave me near on fifty quid a month or so back, and I'm that simple I've kept it for you." He produced an envelope from the back of the till.

"I gave you fifty quid? I must have been out of my mind.

Where did it come from?"

"Your bike, remember. What you just lost your licence for."

Count Dracula, so named after his abseil down Cemetery Gates anchored only by a bootlace, flapped into Cae Ganol one night.

"Heard you were going to Yosemite. D'you want some nuts?" He produced a handful of shiny metal hexagons from capacious pockets. "I've just started making 'em. See what the Yanks think, would you?"

"Sure," said Bob. "I might even use them."

But the flow did not include Kate. For her there was only work, which exhausted her, and a curious feeling of nausea.

"Got to go home to see the old man," Bob said. "If you want a lift I could do it on Wednesday, Kate."

"Oh God, I'll have to, or I won't get that visa."

He drove her to the school which, deserted of boys, lay in mellow holiday sunshine. Kate's father was standing outside, hands in pockets, sniffing the air and bouncing on his heels in a way that the boys mocked.

"Kate!" he cried warmly. Hospitality outweighed her past sins. "I was beginning to find solitude oppressive. Would you care to swim? We have just completed the swimming pool, the boys and I. Won't you introduce us?"

"Sorry, this is Bob. Yes, I'd love a swim, wouldn't you, Bob?"

"No, I'm all right."

"So refreshing after a journey. We can lend you a costume, here, come this way."

"I can't swim," Bob whispered as they filed past the vegetable garden but the old ears, used to tuning in on little boys' secrets, overheard.

"Can't swim? Good Lord, why not? Not afraid of water, surely, at your age?"

"No, just lack of opportunity. I've always wanted to," he said, abandoning self-consciousness and remembering the opportunities at Orkney.

"Then let us provide, let us provide."

They bounced about dutifully in the cold pool. Kate taught Bob to float on his back and splash himself along.

"What a nice young man," said her father over lunch, after Bob had gone. Kate was surprised. "Opportunity, opportunity, I strive to give these boys opportunity and they will not make the most of their privileges. No sense of responsibility. Thornton Major — remember him? — visit from his father. The boy's 17 and taking drugs. Drugs! Health, education, money, poured into that boy. Willoughby, expelled from Rugby. Scarisbrooke, one of our brightest, ran away from Ampleforth to play in a 'pop' group. Conjugated Latin verbs like a Roman, to sing *la la la honey*. I don't know. Finish this ham."

Poor old you, Kate thought, seeing a tired, frustrated elderly man. Six months apart has done us both good.

"I'm glad I've been away so long," she said. "It looks different."

"Fly the nest." He flapped his hand. "Can't be tied to Matron's apron strings. What are you doing with yourself?"

"Seizing opportunities." She told him about her job, and Yosemite.

"America! What a wonderful thought." He laid his knife and fork together, clasped his hands as if in prayer, and said: "Ah, Catherine, such a continent! Such richness! Such diversity! Hope! Opportunity! Are you going with that young man?"

"Him and another."

"Ah."

"They're going climbing. I'm just going for fun."

"Oh, a climber, is he? Did you know I was at University with Mallory? Extraordinary chap. Because it's there. What an extraordinary chap."

"America, is it?" Bob's father asked. "Just to climb a rock? You're off your rocker, lad. When are you going to settle down? You haven't even got yourself a girl friend yet, have you?" Bob produced a photograph of Kate that she had given him. It was taken on the beach at Hoy. She looked particularly good. "Eh, she's pretty, isn't she? Nice-looking young wench, I could fancy a bit of that myself. . . No, I'm only teasing you, lad, you know I'm not like that. She does look nice, though. Where d'you say she comes from? Not Welsh, is she?" Bob explained what he knew of her background. His old man poked the fire and said: "I don't know. Isn't she a bit out of your class? Public schools and the like. . . Fancy stuff, that."

Bob wanted to say: she's still pig-ignorant about politics, the structure of society, history, economics, and a host of other things, and she's only just learning how to be a woman; instead he said: "No, she's not like that, Dad. You'd like her. She's no snob. D'you want a pint?"

When he returned to pick Kate up her father insisted he stay to lunch. They talked of Mallory and Irvine, of climbing, of motivation. Kate was at first ready to be embarrassed but ended up impressed by his analysis, his ability to explain his own deep pleasure in climbing, his resume of climbing history in social terms. Her father was totally absorbed in the conversation; she sat silent, relegated to waitressing.

"Nice old fellow," Bob said as they drove away.

"You bowled him over," she said. "I'm amazed — not by that, but by his whole attitude. I thought he was a narrow-minded old fart, but he's not at all. It's as if I'm not merely his child any more; he treated me like a proper person."

"You are a proper person," Bob said, squeezing her thigh. "Roll us a cigarette."

CHAPTER 8

If You Need Me

The bus swung out of the tunnel and into the blazing sunlight
and the Valley was before them, a great corridor gouged
through the high rolling Sierra, guarded by massive portals of
vertical granite: El Capitan soaring implacably severe on the
left, with the softer mass of Cathedral Rock on the right, and
Half Dome like a hunched eagle towering beyond amongst
rioting waves of bare granite. But for them there was only the
Captain, that smooth clean ocean of golden rock frowning
over the dwarf forest below, and the jutting line of its fierce
nose, and then they were down amongst the huge trees in the
Valley proper, straining to peer out of the windows for
truncated glimpses of waterfalls and the never ending
precipices. When a hungry shark cruises into a tight-packed
shoal of fish he is momentarily overwhelmed, not knowing
which way to turn, killer instincts briefly confused; so they,
too, were stunned, openmouthed, five weeks' plans lost in
wonder as the huge vertical walls and spires slid by one after
another, rising sheer and fluted out of the dark pine forest.

"Camp Four!" announced the driver at last, and plump
tourists craned for a glance at the crazies while Luke, Bob
and Kate scrambled for their rucksacks. "Have a good day,"
he added, watching them fall off the bus in an unco-
ordinated jetlagged heap. "Take care."

The heat and the smell of pines hit them like the waft from
an oven; they lay bewildered, unable to move. Despite so
much anticipation, so much preparation, the reality was still
incomprehensible.

Behind the gas station they found Camp 4. A Ranger with
a surly face and matronly hips stopped them at the entrance
to demand fees and told them the number of a site. Notices

informed them of restrictions which Luke found difficult to believe. The camp was noisy and chaotic: dogs barked and fat ladies in Bermuda shorts bawled conversations above the blare of radios; children shrieked and flung little flying saucers at each other; a longhaired girl fed a naked baby from a slack brown breast, chatting to a trio of Jesuses in headbands; hippies with hubble-bubbles grinned dreamily. But in the dappled light filtering through pine trees there was evidence of climbers too: tents, open-air beds of pine needles, beer cans and bottles, sacks cunningly strung between trees, sacks bulging with the angular outlines of pitons, more gear laid out on a table with a clean and serious-looking climber arranging it. They had arrived.

Luke dropped his sack. "I've got to go and see that cliff," he said, and strode purposefully down the valley.

They lay out in the riverside meadow amid shrilling crickets and gazed, and the more they gazed the more they realised the limitations of their understanding. It was like discovering another dimension, for there was nothing in the familiar three to admit the possibility of so many acres of clean, lovely rock. El Capitan's south-west face, bounded from its south-east face by the haughty prow of the Nose, sprawled gold in the evening sun, streaked with the tears of a million rainstorms. It was too big: the eye could not take it in; there was no way to grasp its enormity. Tiny 200ft. pine trees bristled on its summit like a night's unshaven stubble, but even with these as a reference there was no comprehending whether the shadowed cracks could hide sparrows or elephants, whether the roofs could be stretched over in one move or needed a morning's pegging. It was like trying to understand a light-year. They looked away; they looked back; it was still there, sheer, pure, ineffably beautiful.

Bob made an effort to clear his throat. "Boot Flake," he murmured, pointing.

"Texas Flake," went Luke.

"The Great Roof." They enumerated the features one by one, as if reciting the litany of known irregularities might bring comfort from the implacable unknown wastes of smooth rock. After the last of the sun crept away they were left shivering, amazed at their own presumption: *Are we really going to climb that?*

Kate slept outside in a borrowed hammock, listening to the night pulsating with the bombardment of the crickets, with ominous snuffles from the bears and occasional giggles from the insomniacs huddled around a last fire. She watched the moonlight creeping down the great grey walls behind the camp, the line of shadow dropping lower and lower like the level of water draining from a sink, and thought: when it reaches me then this awful feeling of fear and oppression will go. But it did not, for the knowledge of those terrible cliffs rising majestically in the moonlight made her hair stand on end.

During the next few days they watched and learned. They learned to recognise the cliffs and to hide food from bears, to find the bar across the road and avoid raccoons and rangers; about nickels and dimes, Californian champagne and Wild Turkey; about the unapproachably aloof big-wall climbers and the friendly punters, the kitchen-sink campers and the hippies whose desire for freedom and clean, wide-open spaces had led them to the crowded Ranger-infested squalor of Camp Four. They tried the boulder problems behind the camp and got burned off, to Luke's fury and Bob's amusement; they listened to fierce discussions on climbing equipment and the ethics of big-wall routes as well as Vietnam, love not war, self-discovery and Martin Luther King; they found, to Luke's disappointment, that the climbers' extramural activities were mellow in comparison to their Welsh counterparts, and that for the majority having a fireside gallon of wine too late in the campsite made a good night. Anarchy, so beloved of British climbers, was stamped upon in this well-ruled wilderness and the few forthright rebels found their outlets in drugs too strange for Bob, Luke and Kate to understand or want to sample at first. And so they bathed in the river and ate ice-cream, and made a daily pilgrimage to El Cap until they could look at it without wincing, gazing boldly at its bland blank face and feeling the conviction building up inside them again.

Meanwhile they started climbing.

"We haven't done anything yet," Bob said to one of their new-found acquaintances, after he and Luke had been quizzed about British climbing and the old-world Mecca of Wales. "What's good free climbing, for a start?" An hour-long discussion replete with promises followed, and they were woken at a trying hour next morning and led to a mere 700ft. step called Manure Pile. They flashed quickly up an open-book corner, reached a broken section of cliff and rapelled back without bothering to finish the climb. With all that perfect, clean rock there seemed no sense in choosing the substandard.

"You didn't seem to find that too hard," their mentor commented. "Try Nutcracker: that's pretty new, about 5.8 or so, and there's a really wild mantel up there."

Luke did not want a break, despite the heat: he was aching for a real climb. He got it. Nutcracker was long, not too hard, and had a magnificently exposed wall at the top, affording a splendid view over the valley. He was triumphant at the top.

"We can do it, Bob: I know we can do it."

"Hold your horses, Luke me lad. The Nose is, um, more than seven times as long as this."

"Yeah, but if they think this is wild then their standards are a bit different from ours. They're all so serious. Have you seen how they tape up their hands so they don't scar their lily-white skins? Can you imagine us getting away with that at Stanage? Oh, we'll do it O.K., Bob, let's go for it soon."

"Tiger tiger."

They climbed all the daylight hours, more obsessed than ever, and at night gleaned what information they could without divulging their plans, for they did not want to seem presumptuous. One evening they spent with three dazed characters back from a six-day ascent of Half Dome with a mystical look in their eyes: they were like men from another planet. They talked about equipment and about mistakes; they listened to the epics; Bob spent hours admiring and absorbing the cold, calculating attitude necessary for a big climb, while Luke learned that of every ten parties that aspired to the big walls nine came down again with no sense of shame. They knew that the climbing itself was as safe as you cared to make it, that Harding's bolts were renowned for their safety, and that the weakest element was the human one. Mistakes springing from exhaustion, carelessness and plain fear after thirst-racked days and sleepless nights spent swinging in a spider's web of pins and ropes 2,000ft. up were the killers. The Nose haunted them at every turn: Luke was impatient for it, howling for that ultimate proof; Bob looked and learned, his slow-growing confidence based on preparation. The Nose, the Nose. . .

Where the heat and the dust and the climbers enveloped them, so that they began slowly to merge into Valley life, Kate found herself outside. The flat mile-wide chasm with its soaring walls oppressed her; she felt as if they were trapped in a hot grave together, and the Elysian meadows along the river, the huge peaceful ponderosa pines, the gentle deer, seemed to mock her fear of the awful walls that enclosed them. It seemed to her that all the fear that Bob and Luke should have felt had accumulated somehow in her and that she was bearing the load for them, liberating them to work on their suicidal mission; and she resented it fiercely. She feared the cliff; it was too powerful, a god of war. It took Bob and Luke from her, calling them to search for something that was beyond her; when she was away from them, she could feel as close to them as ever, but when she was with them they were mere shells, they were dull old Bob and sarcastic, hurtful Luke, both ignoring her. She hated that cliff.

She dragged herself up the twisting path to the top of Glacier Point, and hung exhausted overlooking the Valley. The air was clear, the massive block of the Sierra rolling away to the west, mile upon mile of bare granite and peeling-onion domes. She felt wasted, washed out, and sat chatting to a group of San Francisco flowers; they offered her a lift down and drove back via the tunnel, stopping at the point where they had first seen the valley from the bus.

It looked different: the valley seemed darker, an ominous cleft, and in a moment of mysticism she saw it as a well of darkness presided over by those three strange sentinels of wisdom, the fierce Captain, the gentle Cathedral, the aquiline

Half Dome, routes to the light above: Mars, Venus, omni-
potent Jupiter; the Yin, the Yang, the ultimate Tao; and she
saw why she hated the Captain and thought, giggling, I've
been talking to too many hippies.

She made herself walk by it and saw to her delight that
there was someone on the bottom of the Nose.

"Hey, bad news," she said, coming into camp, "listen,
bad news: there's a party on the Nose."

They sat silent, frozen. Jeff, one of their Nutcracker
friends, said: "Were you guys aiming for the Nose? Ah hell,
that's too bad. There's been a party up at the top and these
guys have been waiting for 'em to finish. It's their first day:
they'll be fixing the bottom pitches and coming down
tonight, and you know what it's like, anybody's guess when
they'll go up again, whatever they say. You could always wait
a while, but. . . Hell, that's bad if you came all the way from
Britain for it."

Bob shrugged. "There's others. It's just the most obvious,
that's all."

"There's one hell of a lot of bolts up there. I thought you
Brits were all purists: well I'd have guessed you'd have gone
for the Salathé anyway. There's no forcing on that: it seems
to wander about a lot, but it follows the lines of weakness
more logically. It's generally rated the finest on El Cap. . ."

"Sold to the lady in the brass hat," said Bob.

"What?"

Back to the meadow: they sat and studied the Captain's
face. Its massive south-west wall, to the left of the Nose, is
not quite vertical but slightly concave, sweeping gently
outwards both below and above its centre. If a book some
half a mile wide and nearly twice as high, with thin granite
pages, were stood upright and gouged out slightly across the
centre by the rumbling force of a glacier, it would produce
the same smooth walls, overlapping corners and vertical
cracks. Huge flat-topped splinters of rock press against the
lower face, mirrored above by roofs, and the exfoliated pages
of granite spring away in expanding flakes. The Salathé Wall
route ascends the face from right to left via a series of

irregularities that time has honoured with evocative names —
Half-Dollar, the massive indented Heart, the protruding
Ear, El Cap Spire, the Headwall — and ledges so few that
they too are christened: Mammoth Terraces, Lung Ledge,
Sous le Toit, Thank God. Thirty four pitches of a full 150ft.
each makes a mile of climbing: four, five, even six days in
blazing heat.

When they looked at it they knew, with a conviction that
they had not felt about the Nose, that this was their route.
Bob counted belay stations and Luke prepared himself like a
young savage for his initiation. During the next few days they
collected plastic water-bottles (six pints per man per day, but
how many days?), racked up equipment and advice, and
found people quietly watching. But the fierce competition
that bristled among Valley climbers, and between the East
coast and West coast contingents, did not, it seemed, include
British climbers. The old world was protected by diplomatic
immunity; Bob and Luke were treated with friendly interest
that bordered on compassion: "Do you want us to give you a
shout each day?" "John's just topped out from the Nose;
he'll lend you more bottles. I'll ask;" or, before the neatly-
arrayed variety of pitons: "You won't need all those rurps,
man, but you could do with more two-inch bongs, and more
nuts if you can get 'em. Those ones of yours look interesting:
what's the breaking strain of that wire?"

They chose a practice route to accustom themselves to all
the gear and the type of aid-climbing: the day-long Steck-
Salathé route on Sentinel Rock. The towering pinnacle was
huge when they woke below it, yet it was smaller in
comparison to El Cap than the Old Man of Hoy was to the
dominating mass of St. John's Head. It was long and varied,
and though they had encouragingly little difficulty with the
climbing they were dreadfully slow.

The roar of the bar was around them.

". . . some really wild stemming up that dihedral. . ."

". . . blank wall up there; they had to put a bolt in and do
a pendulum across an outside corner. . ."

". . . crack system you're following peters out six, seven

pitches up. . .''

"Hi!" A couple of college-student types turned to Luke. "Saw you on the Steck-Salathé. How d'you find it?"

"Good. There was less aid than we'd thought. I liked the headwall."

"What about the Narrows? Not so hot, huh?"

"'orrible thrutchy claustrophobic load of choss," grinned Bob.

"Oh yeah? You know, the way you guys talk is really neat. We heard you were going on the Captain."

"We thought we might take a look at the Salathé."

"Uh-huh. Well, if you need any help. . . First British party on it: we'll all be watching."

"That's what I was afraid of," said Bob.

She counted the days, again and again, but it still came out the same. And then there were the swollen breasts, the feeling of oppression, of self-protection. . . She waited until she caught Luke alone.

"Luke," she said. "I'm pregnant."

"Oh shit," he said, "that's just what we need. You are sure, are you? Well, it's not necessarily mine, anyway: I guess it'd be fairest if we split it three ways. Can you wait till we get back to have it done?" He noticed the look on her face. "Sorry about that, kid, mucks up your holiday a bit, doesn't it? Look, there's a bloke over there who I've got to speak to. . ."

"Bob," she said, "I'm pregnant."

He waited, almost too long, took a deep breath and said: "Would you marry me?"

"Oh yes," she said, incredulous. "Then —"

"When I get to the top of that cliff I'm going to be the happiest man alive."

After Bob went to bed she sat poking the fire and remembering the feel of Luke, knowing that it all had to be over and that she could not bear it to be, that she wanted him more than ever; and then Luke was beside her and she was running her hand up his leg, pulling him down over her, drawing him into the shadows with her. . .

Bob found them before dawn. She saw the disbelief, pain, fury, on his face and thought: he's going to say that they can't go now, that I've messed it up. But even as she braced herself against the guilt he had turned on his heel and picked up the sack, and Luke was pulling on his jeans and then they were gone to the cliff.

They stood under the great wall to the left of the Nose. The sun had not yet reached round the corner, and the bay in front of them was dark. The headwall hung over them, miles above.

"I bet that crack'd go free," Luke said, squinting up the first pitch. He was still nervous of Bob's silence.

"Don't piss about."

"O.K., pardner, here we go." And may the best man win, thought Bob bitterly, watching Luke clip the weighty rack of ironware round his waist and start climbing. On the Sentinel route they had learned how to rack the vast selection of pitons logically so that a practised hand could reach automatically for an unseen pin. The sequence of actions was methodical and repetitive: Luke banged in a pin, yanked on it, clipped in his etriers, stepped into them, moved the knotted sling attached to his harness from the pin below and clipped it into the pin he was now standing on, clipped the climbing rope trailing from his waist into the pin below, banged in another pin. . . It was soothing at first. The crack ran straight up for a pitch. Bob, watching, thought: so this is really it. He wondered if he were up to it now, or if his dull anger would interfere. He did not doubt Luke, for Luke could turn anything into drive, and would; but he himself was still reeling, and could not throw himself at it wholeheartedly. He feared his lack of commitment, and he was afraid that Luke might pressurise him, or irritate him, into some predicament he could not handle. He looked up: the wall was measureless in its immensity, so that he could only sense that it was bigger by far than anything he had ever known. He could not know whether he would be capable or not.

"Well all *right*!" Luke sang out, "yeah, all right!" and continued in an off-key rendering of Buddy Holly. He had forgotten everything except the clean rock and was enjoying himself. When he reached the belay and tried to set up the Jumar clamps to work the pulley for the haul bag, his merriment turned to howls of frustration. Time and obscenity finally made the pulley work, but even then it was exhausting. He pumped with his foot, sweating heavily now that the sun had reached across the wall. The bag seemed full of lead instead of water, and since the rock was far from vertical it dragged horribly. Bob, removing the pins as he jumared up the rope, wished he would shut up.

Bob's pitch was a long free jamcrack. Even stripped to his shorts he was hot as he grunted his way up, realising he would have to haul the ironware up as well as the bag. He had to belay in slings, for there was nowhere to stand, so that arranging the pulley became even more difficult. He could not see how he and Luke and both bags could possibly extricate themselves from the spider's web he had woven. He saw the river over 300ft. below and longed for a drink as he pumped the gear up. The thirst and heat grated like the sickness within him.

It seemed to take hours of rearrangement before Luke could leave the belay, and Bob found his closeness irksome. No sooner had one of them worked out which ropes to unclip than the other realised a different system. Each time they tried to move, the haul bag lay mulishly in the way, and in trying to keep their tempers they resorted to noncommunicative silence. But finally Luke freed himself and set off.

His head hurt, and he could not think. Slabs ran across each other and he found the placements and the route finding time consuming. Bob grew more depressed. It was late afternoon, and unless Luke speeded up there would not be enough time for the fourth pitch, the day's quota. He did not speed up. Even the haul bag conspired against them, for it scurried stubbornly from one hiding place in the cracks to another, and Bob had to struggle to free it. They were both exhausted and thoroughly fed up when they perched on the small belay ledge in the slanting evening light.

"That's it," Bob said. They were already a long way up but the Half Dollar, the huge semicircular flake slightly less than quarter of the way up the wall, looked no closer.

"Aren't you going to do that pitch?"

"It'd be dark. Let's go."

Luke started to remonstrate, but fortunately stopped. They left all the gear and rappelled down for a day's rest. They picked their way through the talus in silence. Bob thought: I'll have to sort it out with her. I wish I could turn it all to energy, as he would: maybe I really don't have the makings. . . Luke thought: the bastard, he's chicken after all. He said:

"Well, that was O.K., wasn't it? Nothing too desperate."

"Three pitches a day? It'd take over eleven days."

"It gets quicker further up, you know that, and we'll get better at the knitting. At least we've got the Jumar-hauling bit worked out. We'll be O.K. We're only a pitch behind."

"One in four: 25 percent error. Six and a half days, not five."

"Come on with you, Bob, it'll be O.K. when we're on it for real. A day's —"

"We need more water."

"More water's more weight, more hassle, more sweat loss hauling it."

"Not enough's dead."

"Christ, Bob, if you go at it with that attitude you'll never get up there." Damn him, damn him, Luke raged, I'll bloody tear him limb from limb if he chickens out now. He's got to go on, he's *got* to.

In the tent there was a note: Gone to camp above Bridalveil Falls. See you in five days!! Love, Kate.

"Thank God for that," Luke said. "Let's go and get drunk." And Bob felt the weight drop from his shoulders, and knew that for once Luke was right. Even the air felt cleaner as they shambled to the bar together, knowing that it would be all right.

All next day they did practically nothing. Luke could not face the questions and stalked through the woods wildeyed, jumpy as a cat, charging himself up; Bob lay in the long grass in the meadow, smoking cigarette after cigarette, gazing at the wall and letting its immensity seep into him. Their ropes reached as far as an I on a printed page. . .

They slept out beneath it, silent, wondering.

The sun struck the wall before they were at the top of their ropes, beading their foreheads with sweat. Bob was carrying the sack with the sleeping bags and two giant tins of fruit salad to allay his worries. He could feel the damp trickling down his bare back. He looked up, and Luke yelled at him to hurry. That was the beginning.

It was hard work. The heat pressed on them unmercifully, dizzying the senses until as they reeled from pitch to pitch there was nothing but the great molten gold sea of rock studded with flashing, burning pins. They were moving like snails, urgency nagging like the thirst. Bob hung on a belay watching Luke try to drive pins home into a shallow crack, but only the tips would go in. He tied tapes round them against the rock to reduce the leverage if he fell.

"Here we go, man. It's the infamous bottoming cracks. Have to be mine. Hey, here's a new one."

"The bashie?"

"It certainly looks bashed."

It was a tiny square of aluminium beaten into the rock where the crack ran out. Luke looked down at the jumbled cracks pouring down to the talus below, and wiped the sweat off his forehead. It looked incredible that such a device could hold his weight. He clipped into the antique weathered tapes dangling from it. Panting with fear and disbelief, he pulled at it. It did not fall off; but it was still a long way down.

"Just thank your bloody stars you're not in my shoes, Bob." He licked his dry lips and stepped up, barely daring to breathe. He could not look at it, but stretched gingerly over an overlap to the left. There were holds there and, far above, a bolt. It was desperately thin. He struggled up to it, ironware clanking, clipped into the bolt and howled.

"Screaming abjabs. Horrors. Christ, this is *hard*. That was nasty."

I wish you'd shut up, Bob thought.

Above was a safe ladder of three bolts. Luke blessed them

like a Holy Trinity and belayed in slings above. They were in an area of steep, crumpled slabs and the haul bag, which had revealed itself as a living thing hybridised from a donkey and a limpet, became even more obstinate as the temperature and altitude rose. It hid in corners and refused to move; the more fiercely it was pulled the more it dug its heels in; Luke kicked it every time he saw it, which only made it sullener, and he was still berating it when Bob sorted himself out and climbed on.

There was nowhere particular to go, no helpful cracks, no leading lines, just a hot wall rearing up. After a few moves he found an unsatisfactory placement for a peg. He wandered on. It was difficult. He was not sure what to do, and cursed his own indecision. He tried to climb it free, decided he must have gone wrong, retreated, tried again, meandered. . . Luke screeched at him to stop messing about and use skyhooks, but he felt doubtful: he had never used the little butcher-hooks made to hang on tiny projections.

"Got to be a first time," Luke bawled. All the first day Bob had dragged him down, and he was determined to put a bomb under the old slug. Bob wavered, balanced a skyhook on a knob and stepped up on it. It jiggled, teetering slowly towards the edge of the knob. Slowly, smoothly he stepped off it and it fell off behind him. Above he had to try another, and then another. The third rocked drunkenly, and then he was falling. He did not go far: his pin below held him, but he banged against the rock and felt sick with the heat, the stress, and Luke's unspoken condemnation.

"Damn those stupid hooks," he muttered. "I'll do it free." He took a long time, forgetting where he was, blocking out the exposure and Luke's barrages to concentrate on the sparse holds and the delicate shifts of balance. There was only him and the cliff, and he climbed it. It took an age. Then the holds ran out and another ladder of bolts led across the blank wall. More free climbing brought him to a little ledge. He was a very long way from anywhere. If the water holds out, he thought, we should make it. He looked up, and it went on for ever.

They were tired, and it was hot. Baked air swept the

crickets up from below, where tiny figures splashed in the river. Luke ran up the next pitch, mostly easy free climbing, and belayed in slings. It was late afternoon. They had to move faster.

Above them was the Half Dollar, a huge semi-circular flake hanging out from the wall to form a chimney that later narrowed to a crack. Bob found it awkward: he had to keep turning one way and the other, and the rock scraped his bare flesh. He wrestled his way up slowly, feeling Luke's impatience wafting up with the hot air, rounded the top of the curve and found a ledge big enough to take several paces on. Luke was directly below him; he called:

"Good ledge." His throat was so dry it was hard to shout. "I'll pull the haul rope up and chuck it down so it doesn't have to go out round the curve." Why not spell it out slowly, thought Luke, you must think me dim. The haul bag went straight up easily, but Luke had to jumar the long way round to retrieve the ironware. When he reached the ledge his face was as dry and seamed as the rock itself.

"We're not going to make Mammoth Terraces," Bob said. "It's another two pitches and there's not much daylight left."

"You took a hell of a long time," Luke said, hitting the rock with the side of his fist.

"I know. Still, if you fix the next pitch we'll only be one behind, and that's what we were at the beginning of the day." He sat watching the valley in the evening light, listening to Luke's hammering above and thinking: I mustn't let him get to me, it only makes me worse.

Luke rappelled down in the dark and they forced themselves to eat oranges and candy. Bodies heavy with exhaustion, they had no desire for food, only water and sleep; but there was little water left from the day's quota and sleep would not come. Luke itched where his harness had already begun to chafe; Bob could not stop an interminable newsreel of each move, each pitch, rolling through his mind, ending with the questions. Will we make it? Will the stress get too big for me? Will I be able to hold out, not only against the cliff and the heat and the thirst, but Luke too? He was afraid of fear itself, of what it might do to him after days of exhaustion and searing heat, rather than of the climbing. He remembered his father's stories of men suddenly cracking up, of shell-shocked submariners gibbering themselves into garbage heaps of men, unable to walk. Luke, open-eyed beside him, did not seem to have real fear at all, only an outward scaredness that he shrieked about and mutated into furious energy. Bob had no such process: he controlled his fear by referring to his strength and ability, but he was not sure he had enough for this. He felt his weakness undermining him.

Luke, rolling cigarette after cigarette, thought: he's so bloody slow, and speed is the essence. If there were two of me we'd be flashing up it. I've got to hurry him up, got to hurry him up, got to hurry him up. . . During the heat of the day Luke had reached screaming point with impatience, and tired as he was he could not sleep, for the scream was still there in the back of his mind and his aching muscles. Bob, like a placid old cow, was snoring gently.

They woke later than they had hoped. It was still cold; they were stiff with it, moving sluggishly. Luke slapped himself and went up his fixed ropes while Bob methodically repacked the sack. They ached and shivered; Luke whined. It was queer, jumbled rock, the first part of the gouged-out section; Bob found his route-finding hard, especially since neither his mind nor his body was properly awake. Then the sun came round the corner, warming his back, making blood flow into cramped muscles, and he climbed beautifully, rhythmically, and knew that he was doing so, and did not care about Luke. He swung leftwards on to Mammoth Terraces, a long series of ledges along the cut-off tops of the granite plates. "Many lying down" said their diagrammatic notes. There was room for a small army up there. He imagined a cavalry platoon, the patient horses munching their hay on the narrow ledges, and started to giggle. I must eat something, he thought, I'm getting light-headed. He felt as if he had drunk a bottle of champagne.

Luke joined him, and he was tense again. They walked leftwards along the terraces until they could see Heart

Ledge, the lowest tip of the Heart, 130ft. below them. They set up a rappel and Luke went over the edge. The first moment of an abseil, the first step over into the void, is always sickening. Stepping into 1,000ft. of air provoked a wave of sheer terror in Luke: for a moment he thought that his knees would give way, and that he would find he was pissing himself. The icy claw of nausea gripped him; then it was gone, and he was finding it fun.

Heart Ledge was lovely, five feet wide by twenty. He felt extremely happy. From one end of it you could rappel all the way to the ground, for the valley's Mad Bolter had passed by and left a line of bolts a full rope-length apart right down the blank walls to the green below. Luke belayed on the top bolt. He did not want to move when Bob joined him; suddenly he understood why people went down again. . .

The heat was appalling as he forced himself to go on. The rock danced in front of his eyes and he wondered if he was ill. When he belayed in slings the straps of his harness bit into his chafed flesh. The changeover seemed to take hours, and he noticed with fury that Bob had an easy pitch again.

Bob thought: well, that's almost it. We've left the last way down, and once we're past this next pendulum pitch we're totally committed. If he'd said let's go down from Heart Ledge I'd have gone: it's his determination that clinches it every time. He reached Lung Ledge and sat alone for a moment on the sun-baked platform before hauling the bag up.

"You jammy sod," panted Luke as he reached Bob. "You got all the easy ones. Isn't this the pendulum?"

Bob nodded. "That is, unless you fancy bivvying here too."

"What d'you mean?"

"Nothing."

"No, what do you mean?"

"Nothing, it was a lousy joke. I thought you wanted to stop down there, that's all."

Luke shot him a look of pure venom whose ferocity was startling, and Bob thought: I want to go down, I don't want to go on with him. But Janus Luke was smiling again: "To tell you the truth, I'd hate it if it were your lead. I don't want to do it but I do want to have done it, if you see what I mean." But his voice did not sound right.

He hammered off, up and leftwards, heading for a bolt some 50ft. away. It was straightforward pegging but he took a long time. The bolt was the point of no return: after it there was no possibility of retreat, and on the overhanging upper part of the cliff rescue would be practically impossible even if one of them were injured. I hope we're up to it, Bob thought, because I'm going. He'll be O.K., old Luke, he always is in the end. Luke still had not reached the bolt. Bob grinned. The lad's got the wind up: I'm glad he's not completely nerveless.

When Luke clipped in to the bolt he was over 1,500ft. up and he had to swing on an 11-millimetre rope, like a lunatic trapeze artist, right across the wall. A bitter taste of chocolate came to his mouth. He forced words out.

"O.K., Bob, lower me down."

Bob let out the rope slowly until Luke was hanging to his left and slightly below him. Further to the left the blank wall ended in a corner which they could not see round.

"I'll just kind of crawl over and take a butchers." He worked his way over to the corner and peered round it. For 20ft. the wall was smooth and featureless; then there was a vertical crack, the edge of Hollow Flake. He looked at the distance and walked back across the wall towards Bob.

"I can see the crack," he said. "I'll have a go now." He looked at his feet. There were people doing one of the short climbs at the bottom of the face, tiny dots moving like mites across the rock. He looked up. The headwall looked exactly as it had done three days ago, no nearer, rearing endlessly above him. He began to walk across the wall to the right, below Bob, and then to run. When the rope pulled at him he turned and ran to the left. He did not reach the corner before he had to turn and run back again. Back and forth he went, increasing the arc of his swing until when he ran leftwards he could jump across the corner and take a few paces across the blank wall beyond. He could not get anywhere near the crack. He gave up trying and hung, panting, from the bolt.

After a while he tried again, running with more determination, but the momentum he worked up was still not enough to carry him across to the crack. It was a bitter anticlimax.

"Got to be third time lucky," he told Bob. "I'll just have a fag. How much further can you lower me? I'd get a bigger arc if I were lower."

His head hurt with the pounding of the sun. Bob lowered him another 20ft. He felt quite alone. He lit a cigarette, tossing the empty packet away. It fluttered down into infinity, a tiny dot vanishing long before it reached the level of the mites below. He knew that he had not made his two tries with total conviction, and resolved to go crazy for the next one. He did. Bob saw the sudden freedom of his movements as he ran wildly to and fro, screaming shrilly like a pig going to slaughter. Then, with a leap, he was gone, and a second later a howl of victory echoed across the cliff.

Luke thrust his hands and feet into the crack and yelled again: "SLACK!" The rope eased, no longer pulling him out. Heart thumping, he glanced up the crack. He knew that he had to free climb it without any protection, for if he put a runner in there would not be enough rope for him to reach the ledge reputed to lie above. If he made a mistake he would fall vertically for some ten feet before being whisked off towards Bob again, battering himself against the wall. He swallowed with difficulty and started to jam up the crack. It was straightforward at first, but then it reached a niche and widened so that it was too wide to jam yet too narrow to get into properly. Sweating heavily, he forced himself up it in an ungainly series of shuffling moves, using any part of himself that kept him in it. Nothing mattered except getting up it. After 100ft. of climbing he reached the ledge and lay on it, panting and shaking.

When the call came Bob let go of the haul bag and watched it career round the corner, banging against the wall; then he jumared up to the bolt. They had spent hours working out the best way to manoeuvre the next part. The climbing rope stretched slightly upwards, to the left; a moment later the haul rope, weighted with a bunch of pins, came whizzing down it. Bob collected the rope, doubled it, clipped it into the sling on the bolt and, unclipping the climbing rope, let himself down on the haul rope as far as he could. Clinging to the wall, he retrieved the haul rope and then, heart in mouth, half swung and half scurried across the wall until he was hanging below Luke.

They were now totally committed to finishing the climb. There was no way out except up. As they looked at each other it seemed that the world had, as it were, changed gear, entering that dimension whose fringes they had glimpsed from below. Hitherto their climbing, on this route even, had been a game, albeit a dangerous one; but at that moment it ceased to be a game: it was life itself.

CHAPTER 9

High And Dry

It was late. They forced themselves to eat and organise themselves for the night, before lying cramped and openeyed in the dark silence, lost in wonder at the extraordinary predicament in which they had placed themselves.

Things came at Luke all night: jaws, rats, trains, ants. . . He did not know whether he was awake or asleep: the cliff was full of them, rustling in the cracks behind him, alive in the night, and he was bound and helpless on the belay while they heaved and writhed behind him or came at him from in front. He knew that unless he held on tight the cliff would burst open, spewing them out from the bulging cracks, and so he held on while Bob, unaware of the danger, slept on. But later he was waking, with Bob shaking him and holding out the water, so he knew he must have slept a little too. He felt exhausted with the night-long battle.

"It's early," Bob said, "but I'll start on this pitch as soon as I can. The next decent ledge is seven pitches up: El Cap Spire." Luke looked up. The night had not left him; it crowded him still. Bob went on: "We'd make that tonight if we pushed it. We could do the changeovers miles quicker." He crawled out of his bag and relieved himself. They watched in childlike fascination as the products fell for ever downwards; then, stuffing food in Luke's day bag with some water, Bob started climbing.

He was cold and stiff, and so was the rock. He climbed badly, longing for the sun yet realising how he would curse it half an hour later. Luke let out the rope and finished the packing. Suddenly out of the corner of his eye he saw a movement and whipped round to see the dark tendrils flit back into the crack behind the ledge. He was right, then: they were there, oozing out. He remembered how Warren Harding's bag had been chewed by rats on the first ascent of the Nose, and shuddered. A jerk on the rope and a furious cry of "Slack!" from above woke him from his nightmare: he had not let out enough rope, and had been about to pull Bob off.

They had entered a featureless area, some 500ft. of vertical desert where the wall was sheer and smooth except for the crack system they were following. Peg followed peg in aching, sunbaked monotony; the rock throbbed in the heat. Hoarse with thirst, they sat for hours immersed in their thoughts. Bob allowed himself cautious pleasure at their progress, happy with the view and the security so paradoxical in such a vertiginous place; he was not aware, though, that as he sat paying the rope out he was examining every inch of it, like a man unconsciously telling his rosary. Luke's thoughts shot like a flock of grasshoppers all over a field. He was all right when he was climbing but the moment he stopped it was terrible, and he yelled impatiently at Bob. He found to his irritation that Bob was watching him, checking his every movement.

"Stop peering at me, dammit," he snapped as they reached the bottom of the Ear halfway through the day. "What's the matter, is it getting to you or something?" He clipped and unclipped karabiners at a speed which would have been impressive if he had made all the transfers right; as it was he had just unclipped the day-bag completely. Bob grabbed it in time.

"Think it must be," he grinned, thinking: maybe an admission will calm him down. "I keep finding I've put three times as many pegs on a belay as I usually would. Still, it's an error in the right direction." He looked up at the Ear directly above. A huge flake, it hung out from the wall like the lobe of an ear, creating a bottomless chimney up which Luke had to struggle. "Well, there's your bomb-bay chimney."

Luke thought: he wouldn't be so cheerful if he had to climb it. He started up the crack towards it. In fact it was not difficult climbing, but there was nowhere to put a runner and since it flared out beneath him he felt it was trying to drop him down to explode on the talus a third of a mile below. He hugged its curving lip, hiding in its shadow so that it boomed around him like a big shell held to the ear. He climbed silently, watching the dark shapes flitting in the shadows further in, and he was afraid. When he finally emerged at the top and could place a runner he had gone 80ft. without protection. He swung round the top, made a belay.

Bob's jumar was horrific: that solitary runner was far to his right and the rock was sheer, so that when he unclipped from his belay he shot sickeningly off to the right, unable to contain a yelp of terror. He swung to and fro before coming to rest facing blank rock. As he jumared up it seemed to pulsate with heat.

Dazed by the sun and thirst, they pegged on up the sheer wall. As their strength lost its edge the hauling grew easier, for the rock was steeper and featureless. Bob plugged on like a steam-engine; Luke waited on the belay gazing at the huge mass of Middle Cathedral opposite, the fluid bulges of rock hanging suspended in time. He remembered the falling candles of water of Bridalveil Falls hanging motionless for seconds on end in minor parody of the frozen rock and he thought: we too are trapped in it, in this time that does not move, as if we were approaching the speed of light. It's non-Euclidean, non-Newtonian, that's the difference. *Day after day, day after day, with neither breath nor motion,*

As idle as a painted ship upon a painted ocean. . . Shouts bothered him; he jumared up a rope. Bob was there, asking: "You're not getting sunstroke, are you?"

"For Christ's sake leave off, will you? Gimme some water." He shivered violently, throwing a glance over his shoulder to the moth-eaten mat of forest far below. When he was climbing it was all right, it was all mechanics and go for it, like being drunk; belays came too soon, and lasted for eternities.

The crack ran straight up, widening, until it became a chimney behind the free-standing El Cap Spire, a vast splinter of rock prised away from the wall at its top. Bob's lead ran up the right-hand edge where the chimney was perfect, running straight and true, exactly the right width for back-

and-footing. He shuffled up happily as the sun dipped behind the hills to the west, humming to himself. He could not place a runner but he could hardly fall either. He peered down, and saw that if he did drop he would plop into the ever-narrowing chimney and stick as fast as a cork in a bottle. It amused him, since he could not have been safer sitting in an armchair: he called down to Luke, but got no reply.

Luke, rigid, trembling, was thinking: but what if it unfreezes, this ocean of rock, what if this dam cracks? All that fluidness behind it, all those black things, pouring out. . . it's just a vertical facade, a sheet of ice, bulging at those cracks. I must not let it, I have to hold it, hang on, God it's hard. . .

Bob reached the level summit of the Spire, as flat as the floor of his cottage and as large, glowing with the last of the light. It was a miracle in that vertical desert; the whole Valley and the peaks beyond were flung out in the slanting golden rays, and there was room to stretch, to stroll about and enjoy it.

Luke went berserk when he reached it. "Yippeeee! Yaaaaa-hoooo!" While the echoes were still rolling down the Valley he tore off his harness, delighted to be free of the chafing straps, and did a war-dance. When he started doing hand-stands Bob began to worry.

"Hey, slow down, Luke, you'll get dizzy."

"You make me dizzy Miz Lizzie!" Luke sang, leaping about like a drunken teenybopper, and suddenly he nearly went over the edge. He threw himself back and crawled back to the centre, shaking his head. Trembling, he lit a cigarette and sat down. "You can do it if you try," he said, as if pronouncing a world-shaking theorem. "It's all — Bob — it's all, all, all in the mind, this business. It's a cinch, it's a doddle, it's a piece of overblown *bullshit*." He walked deliberately to the very edge and stood posing with his arms straight ahead as if about to dive; then he walked back. "I'm thirsty: give us some of that fruit salad, Bob, I'm *starving*."

It seemed to Bob that he was revving like a car with a slipping clutch. He sat down, ate a mouthful of fruit salad, leaped up, peered over the edge, threw himself down, showed

Bob the scarlet stripes across his back where the webbing had chafed, complained about monotony, scratched and repeated the whole process.

"Peace, man, peace," Bob said.

"Peace! For God's sake, you're in the most incredible position you've ever been in and you sit there as if you were watching the telly. Where's your imagination? Where's that famous appreciation? You've got a mind like a fucking armadillo sometimes."

"I'm knackered."

"Go to sleep then, if you can't take the pace, just go to sleep."

Luke did not stop for hours. He walked up and down, smoking, talking in nonsensical snatches until Bob swore at him and, pulling his harness on, crawled into his sleeping bag. He could not sleep as long as Luke was sitting on the edge, legs dangling into the blackness.

"Tie yourself to something, there's a good chap."

"What's the matter now? I'm not going to fall off."

"Makes me nervous."

"You don't get nervous when I sleep on the sofa."

"Please."

"Ah, just to please me, come on, just this once. You're beginning to sound like Kate. Piss off."

Bob sighed and dozed. Later Luke had curled up too.

The jaws came at him, spinning out of the dark at him, snapping their white teeth, dozens of them. They had eyes, little shining eyes peering at him while he shrieked and squirmed out of their way. In the moment when Bob, clutching at him, shook him awake he knew what they were: his father's dentures, grinning horridly in their hygienic cleanser, deliberately distracting him, tormenting him. He fought Bob's grasp.

"That was some nightmare," Bob said.

The sweat was pouring off him, icy cold. The cliff was bulging, shifting, the pillar they were on slipping down inexorably; he could not hold it. In the fluid rush the call of a hoot-owl drifted up from below, creating a nucleus; stillness crystallised around it. "It's O.K.," he said. "It'll be all right

now," and Bob relaxed his grip, helping him with the
harness. "God, I wish I had a drink." He longed for alcohol
as never before. They lay side by side, smoking, until Bob
drifted off to sleep again and he was left alone in the infinity
of the night.

Luke woke brisk, invulnerable, impatient. His first pitch
was a good crack leading rightwards in an ocean of rock
whose waves ran vertically across the wall. It was wide: he
had to use nuts and bongs, those onomatopaeic wide pins
whose placement set long echoes rolling down the wall. He
felt exhausted but the steep rock warmed him. He reached a
corner where the narrowing crack could be climbed free, and
looked down the trough to the vast sweep below him. But the
headwall above, hanging like the crest of a wave, was still so
far away that the sight of it drained him, and in the shimmering heat the rock between pulsated, in and out, in and out.

As the sun took its toll they climbed in silence. Heat seared
their throats. Hour after hour they plugged doggedly
upwards. The wall was no longer long and rolling but
choppy, requiring thought and decision that strained their
fatigued minds. One of Luke's leads brought him to a section
which he stared at uncomprehendingly; the series of hard
moves that followed led him to a crack which was too
shallow, so that the pins bottomed and had to be tied off. He
made the moves mechanically, barely bothering about the
precariousness of the position because the whole thing was
unreal, a mental exercise anyway. Then the crack ran out.
There were holes in the rock; he stuck a pin in, aware it was
too small for the hole but belief was enough. They always
held even if they were no good. He was falling. . . The one
below held him but he scraped against the rock and swore
bitterly.

"Haven't got the right pegs: the hole's too big."

"Put two in back to back."

The fall had shocked him to his senses: he banged the
paired pins in and made the next few awkward moves with his
customary fury. Then came the chatter.

"Hey, Bob, it's just like Wales up here. There's this big
chimney thing, all black and wet. It's smashing, just like the

Black Cleft on Clog.'' Thank God, thought Bob, dry lips
cracking in a grin, Thank God, old Luke back again; maybe
it is getting to me and I'm worrying too much. The burbling
continued, as welcome as a mountain stream. ''It's great up
here. None of this salamander stuff, it's all green and oozy.
Must be a drainage channel.''

It was another sling belay. Bob led the chimney above,
bridging to avoid the vegetation at the back, and suddenly
found himself looking into the gold eyes of a small green
frog. Its soft, moist throat vibrated surprise, and then it was
gone. He was delighted that such delicacy, such tiny fragile
hands, could exist on this cliff: his own stubby fingers were
raw and bleeding; ironware clanked around his waist; yet he
found it almost impossible to exist here for four days, let
alone a lifetime. He climbed on carefully despite the steepness, fearful lest he should harm one of them. At the top he
stepped leftwards out of the cool oasis and back on to the
desert wall. The sudden exposure was heart-stopping.

Luke joined him, looked down, and did not want to go on.
A big clean crack reared out above them and there was
nothing below but the vast scoop of the wall and the talus
way, way down. The wall was so overhanging that a line
would not have touched rock for over 2,000ft. The damn
thing was moving again; it was heaving and swaying and he
could not keep it still and he could not climb on a heaving
ocean splitting at the seams. The dark things were there in the
cracks; he could not. . . And then he cried out, for they shot
out of the crack alongside and whirled and shot back in
again, and he could feel the blackness on his shoulder and he
was holding on. . .

''Swifts,'' Bob said. ''Jesus, look at 'em go! They're still
doing about 30 going back in again. Look, look! They must
be nesting. Precision!''

''Fucking birds,'' said Luke, and suddenly it was a piece of
cake: he was banging his way up a clean straight crack as safe
as houses, driving on with the sun glinting off pitons hot to
the touch. It was like flying. He reached the ledge at the top
of the block drained, parched; his lips cracked when he
passed his tongue, dry as a lizard's, over them. He stared out

over the top of Middle Cathedral at a helicopter trekking by, and when he leaned down to call to Bob he nearly fell off, for he had forgotten he was not belayed.

Bob led on, dizzy with heat, the heavy gear chafing at his neck. The rock, eroded by water, was un-American: no clean straight lines and open spaces, but tricky pockets and varied problems. Immersing himself in technicality he forgot the position and bent his throbbing mind to deviousness. Reaching a good pin festooned in old tape slings, he lowered himself off it and made a short pendulum leftwards round a corner. Suddenly he was in the middle of nowhere. A monstrous drop yawned below him. He had swung on to the bottom of a flake 80 or 90ft. high, cut off both above and below; then the wall plunged abruptly into space. The crack above looked horrific. The flake was an exfoliating plate: if he pegged it the pegs would prise it away from the wall, so that each one loosened the one below. Nuts would be better, but he did not have enough. He had to climb it free. It was an 80ft. overhanging layback 2,000ft. off the deck, with the certainty of damage, and probably death, if he fell, for he would plunge straight down before being yanked 50ft. horizontally to below his pendulum peg, where he would smash helplessly against the crumpled wall. There would be no rescue.

He stared at it quietly. He climbed a little way up, placed a nut, and retreated. He waited until there was nothing in his head but the edge, the shape of the flake, and then he climbed, shoulders cracking with the strain, unable to stop on the glaring orange rock, just moving up and up in the most single-minded effort he had ever made, grasping the edge with bloody hands that had set like claws.

At the top he reached Sous le Toit ledge, exhausted, glowing.

Luke could not believe his eyes when, after swinging sickeningly across the wall, he saw the crack. He can't have done that, he thought, he can't have done.

It was a small ledge, as big as a sofa. Below, there was nothing. Above, the wall reared out and out, seeming to push them out over the void, millions of tons of it thrusting them down.

Bob said: "Good day. Christ, I'm knackered." He arranged the gear in the last of the light, ate, drank, and sat in his sleeping bag, legs dangling. "One more, and one more night." He feel asleep.

The great wall hung raven-black over Luke's shoulders. He knew that the next part, the great roof leading to the headwall, was the worst, and it was his. He tried to sleep but could not: *Macbeth shall sleep no more*: and when he did the night was full of horror. Sheep with eyes like headlights, steaming entrails dragging bloodily on the floor behind them, advanced on him until he found he was backing over the edge of a bottomless abyss. It was not sheep but his father, dentures flying from his mouth. . . It was not night, but the blackness of a great bird above him. Kate screamed as he drove a line of pitons through her, slashing her open so that the little lights and bits of black came shooting out at him and he had nowhere to go. He woke and shook. Torrents of terror poured over him. His sweating, shaking fingers could not roll a cigarette. He lay back, defeated, and felt the headwall sitting softly on his shoulder, a dull black weight upon him, heaving and rolling, cracking open like a foetid corpse, and he had to let go because he did not have the strength any longer. And then the birds came, surging out of it in a flood of panic, and he could not stop them but crouched down, hands over his head, as they poured endlessly over him, their wings beating and roaring in his ears, overwhelming him, smothering him in their blind fear, their soft stinking feathers and their insidious filth.

His long, awful moans woke Bob, who saw the sinews standing out on the backs of his hands, string-white in the moonlight, as he crouched down.

"Hey! Wake up!" Bob grabbed an arm and shook, rocking the ball that was Luke until it uncurled and the face came out. But it was not a face: it was a skull, a death's head, the skin stretched tight over the bones like wet parchment, the eyes dead as a fish's, staring emptily into the dark. The moans went on, issuing from a mouth that was a pool of horror.

"Luke!" Bob shook again. He was frightened. "Luke, wake up!" But Luke was awake. He swung round with his other arm, plucking Bob's hand off and thrusting it angrily aside.

"Get your hands off me. Leave me alone, why can't you? You never stop it, peering and prying and poking and spying, on and on and on, peer, poke, peek, spry, cry why don't you leave me ALONE, I warn you, leave me alone alone alone." He writhed away, jerkily defensive. Then came a tiny voice: "Help me, for God's sake help me, Bob." A few seconds later he was brisk: "Sorry, a bit of a nightmare. I suppose that's how it catches up on me: I'm not at all scared really. Got a roll-up?"

They sat and smoked, staring out into the dark. The headwall hung over them. Luke said quietly: "If I were you I'd jump now."

"What?"

"I'll get you. You know I will. *Each man kills the thing he loves.* God I'm tired. You're my old mate, Bob." Bob felt as if he had been marked. He was afraid again. He waited a while, and gestured out into the dark: "Funny how the stars aren't quite in the right place, isn't it? I'd have expected Orion over there but I've no idea what that is."

"More like Virgo, this time of year. Orion's really a winter constellation. That's not Spica, though. You're right, they do seem to be in odd places. The Milky Way's too overhead, isn't it? Maybe that's Arcturus. . ."

"I don't know. I only know the Plough and —"

"Doesn't it look orange to you? I'm sure that's Arcturus. Then that must be Coma Berenices there; it's packed with galaxies, that one, and. . ."

Bob was asleep again before the stellar identification had finished. Luke went on for hours, for the contemplation of such known immensity soothed him; earth felt small and safe. Later he dreamed again. This time it was about a house, a tall Victorian monstrosity with castellations and a tower. He tried to get in but it was locked; he climbed up the outside and on to the roof, where there was a broken skylight. The house was empty, and shabbier inside than out. He was alarmed to find it so abandoned, but even as he walked downstairs it was disintegrating. He found a cellar door and hesitated; but he already knew that there was nothing any-where else. He tried the cellar. There was a dead horse in a far corner, its bloated body writhing with maggots which hatched into clouds of flies as he watched. He recognised the flies as ones that carried a particular disease, and realised that the house had been shut up to prevent a plague spreading over the whole earth. They came at him in a swarm, escaping past him up the cellar steps. He woke up. The first of the light was creeping over the east, and Bob was watching him.

"Find something else to stare at, can't you? Give me the water."

There was less than a gallon left. It would take them a day and a half — 18 pints of water, not eight — to finish, and the hardest bit was his. He was furious at Bob, who must have been swilling the water secretly, for fixing it so that Luke had all the hard pitches. He knew now that Bob was playing a canny game, driving him to the point where he gave up; that was why Bob was watching so carefully. He hated Bob's two-faced treachery.

Abruptly Luke stopped his muttering, got up and started to climb almost before Bob had time to realise what he was doing. It was a short, straightforward pitch leading up to a couple of bolts, with the roof still another short pitch above. But Luke seemed to be uncertain what to do, and as he fumbled about doing things in the wrong order Bob became increasingly alarmed. About 30ft. up, two-thirds of the way to the bolts, Luke stopped altogether. Bob waited. Nothing happened. Luke had simply stopped.

"You O.K.?" Bob called, not knowing what to do. "Luke."

After an endless pause Luke said: "Coming down." Bob lowered him slowly to the ledge. Luke looked crumpled, empty. He turned round and Bob saw, with a wave of fear, that his eyes were gone again. There was nothing behind them. Bob shook him. He said:

"I can't. I tell you honestly, Bob, honestly now, I — you — if you go up there you'll die." He looked up; he looked down. Two and a half thousand feet below the forest waited.

"Come on," said Bob, taking his arm, but Luke snatched away.

"Don't bloody patronise me, you bastard, you don't know what you're playing with. I'll kill you, I tell you, I'll kill you." He sat down. "Give me water, I know you've got it."

Bob said: "There isn't enough."

"I killed Carver, you know."

There was a long pause. "I said, I killed Carver."

They looked at each other, full of wonder.

"I didn't mean to. I killed him like I nearly killed Kate, like I'll kill my father, like I'll kill you. It's not me really, it's the crow; but he's got his eyes on you, and he'll get you. I don't want him to get you, Bob, help me. . ." He felt the weight of it on his shoulder, pressing down like the roof.

Bob thought: what the hell do I do? It was like being asked to climb on soap: there was no precedent, no way of knowing how to handle it. He realised that Luke was unclipping himself; he grabbed a sling and tried to clip it into Luke's harness, but he was too slow.

"You've got to do it, Bob. It doesn't matter for me, but if you jump he won't get you." He was trying to unclip Bob's harness too. Bob wrestled with him; together they slithered on the narrow ledge, legs hanging over that immense drop, until Bob held him with one hand and smashed his fist into his face. Luke's head hit the wall; he slumped. Trembling like a leaf, Bob belayed him.

Luke took a long time to come round, and when he did there was blood on his mouth and on the back of his head. He did not look like a person but a collection of features strung together at random, twitching and chattering by means of some galvanic force that was not human either. A rag-bag of tatters, he talked in tatters: there was not one Luke but several. There was a child that cried for help, throwing a tantrum when Bob could not give it; there was a sardonic, superior intellectual who quoted formulae at Bob to prove his ignorance; there was a terrified creature that gibbered about moving cliffs and the evil within; there was the old daredevil, the fearless Luke. . . *My name is Legion.*

"I loved her, Bob, and I killed her, killed that in her, don't you see? Fuck, of course you don't see. See? You? You're just a programmed automaton, eat, work, shit. . . And I'll kill her baby too, more death, one up for the old crow. *Help me, Bob, help me.*" He leaned close, his rank breath stinking, and looked down. "Oh, sweet Jesus. . ." He lay back, panting. Then: "You think I'm cracking up, don't you? Think I'm scared, don't you. I know your sort, you. . . I don't give a damn, I'm not chicken like you. . ." He had the belay sling off before Bob could stop him, stood up, perched on one leg on the narrow ledge. "Hey, look, they're all watching us down there, watching. . . He laughed suddenly, then started to sing: "My my my, said the spider to the fly: jump right ahead and you're dead."

Bob could do nothing. He did not know where to start, what the answer was, and he was frightened. He was facing death, not in the way he knew, a peg pulling out, a handhold going, a rope breaking, but in some unthought of manner from the grinning death's-head beside him. Luke was death, anti-life. . . As the sun beat down for hour after hour, hurting their heads, baking them dry, he felt worse and worse. Each time he tried to answer Luke he found it was a different Luke who was answering back, and he began to feel that the point of it was mainly to humiliate him. He longed for water, shade, then he might be able to think.

"I used to think," Luke said, "that that moment of complete annihilation that you reach on the good times, when you're climbing or screwing, that moment when you don't exist any more because you are the thing you're doing, that moment of death, actually, was what gave root to life. I thought that it was only by putting yourself into the position where that might happen that you could liberate all that energy from within, like splitting the atom. Destruction for creation. Out of death, life. All those mini-deaths releasing that potential energy into light, heat, radiating out. . . It did seem to add up, that those who were afraid to put themselves into the firing line never would be able to release it. That's how people are, isn't it? And so it seemed right to go on.

"But now I see that it isn't really like that: it's that each time you get there you lay yourself open to the Devil, and he infects you, bit by bit. I've been fertile grounds. I always was, but now it's really bearing fruit. Evil. Carver, Kate, my Dad, you. . ."

"That's wrong," Bob said, "you know that's wrong. Devils. You're off your rocker."

"You'd have said Christopher Columbus was off his rocker, or Einstein. Space is curved? Matter is energy? Anything that you can't comprehend with your little pea-sized brain is crazy, isn't it? You believe in the good, in God —"

"I don't believe in God," Bob said. There seemed to be no point in this discussion, dying of thirst on a precipice, and yet Luke had not been so rational before. Bob thought that maybe he could hold him there, fix him in that state. . .

"Oh yes you do. Maybe not the old man with the white beard, but good, right things, solidarity with your mates and the honest working man and all that. You don't believe in the Devil, in evil; you believe in mistakes, selfishnesses, petty things. And so you let him work too."

"Yes, I did see evil once," Bob said, remembering. "When you hit Kate. I thought that was evil. Not just because she's a woman, but that it wasn't really anything to do with her — at least, I'd bet on that — it was your piddling little problems and you weren't man enough to keep them to yourself."

Luke burst out laughing. "Not man enough, not man enough! Hell that's a good one." He laughed and laughed, peal after peal of it echoing down the wall. "God, you're funny sometimes. Not man enough. How big's yours, big boy?"

Kate reached the Meadow to find a knot of people clustered there, pointing, looking through binoculars. She recognised Jeff.

"Are they all right? What's happened?"

He gestured ignorance. "They were doing fine until last night, but they haven't moved all day. They're on Sous le Toit."

It was only what she had known, and had fled from. She had thought it would be over by now. He said, misunderstanding: "They're not waving or anything, and they're moving about, so they must be O.K."

She could not see them. An elderly tourist nudged her. "Here, take a look, there's two of 'em up there." He passed huge binoculars, but she still could not see them. Acres of blank rock smiled mercilessly, deserted. The man's comfortable paunch pressed against her as he helped her. "That dark triangle, now down a ways, move left. . ." Two tiny dots, impossibly small. Without the binoculars they vanished. "Those boys must be in trouble."

"Can't get to 'em," said a climber, "not till they're over the headwall: it overhangs too much. They've got to get to Thank God before you can reach 'em."

"I'm pretty sure they're O.K.," Jeff said. "We'll walk up and meet them at the top. Chris, you can signal us tomorrow. . . You coming, Kate?"

She was sitting on her heels in the long grass, small, alone, defiant, her eyes on the cliff, hands round her belly.

Bob did not realise he had slept until he woke. The heat made everything advance and recede, and he felt like a desiccated stick insect. Luke crouched on the haul bag like a mummy, gibbering softly, insane upon the monstrous cliff. Bob knew suddenly that they were both dying. We've got to get out of it, he thought, or we will die; but he knew that it was not finished yet, and until it was finished he would not be able to move Luke. He said:

"How did you kill Carver?"

Luke told him; then he told him about Kate's pregnancy, about the money, the fact that it was the only real way to hurt his father, about the University. . . It took hours. Voice dried to a whisper, he said:

"It's almost over. Just you. And Kate's baby. She'll end up another one of us, agents for the other side."

"No, you've lost that one," Bob said. "I'm going to marry her. You'll not kill that baby."

For a split second Luke's face pulled together, and Bob felt huge relief. But it was anger that was uniting the legions. Luke sprang at him, howling. They were both belayed, but they fell off the ledge, crawled back on again, fought, wrestled, beat at each other. Bob was the stronger, the better street-fighter, and though Luke was wilder Bob ended up on top.

"Have you finished now?" he demanded.

"Oh God, I didn't mean it, I didn't mean to hurt you, it's. . ."

"Shut up." Bob was completely disgusted. He looked down at the thing that had been his friend and thought: maybe I do believe in evil after all. He's destroyed something in me, or *it* has: I don't care whether he lives or dies any more; it's my own skin I care about now, and there was a time when I cared about his just as much.

Luke, staring straight ahead like a man who sees a vision, whispered: "Do you remember Orkney, Bob? The fishes? The lobsters? Ginger and the whisky? It was all right then, wasn't it?" And Bob looked down at the wasted face, the black, battered hands and despite himself felt a surge of compassion: it was as if they were both transported from the vertical desert, that parody of paradise, to those distant sea-lashed stacks, hearing again the boom of the Atlantic surf, the seagulls' cries, tasting the salt on their lips, the triumph of those turf summits amid the breakers, and it seemed to them both that they had been as innocent as children then.

"We never even knew Kate then," Luke said. "It was simple, wasn't it?"

Bob said: "You can't have that one either. It wasn't her fault. Nor the Devil. Just you, Luke. Jonathan. Whoever you are. And you've lost. You've lost everything. You've lost this game too. Hold this rope, I'm going to shin up these pins of yours and fix my pitch before it gets dark."

"Don't go, don't go, Bob you don't know. I tell you, he's looking at you."

Luke clutched at Bob's leg, and for a moment Bob was almost seduced again. But he bent down, took Luke's hand off his leg gently. "I told you," he said. "You lost."

He was still afraid, in a quiet cold way, and he did not want to do it because he did not trust Luke; nevertheless any other way meant certain death. He reached the top of Luke's pegs, finished the pitch for him, and clipped into the bolts. He was so dry he could barely move. He looked up at the overhanging crack above him.

It was desperate, the most difficult on the whole climb, and he was barely in condition to walk 100 yards. It was too wide to drive pins in: he had to cudgel his exhausted brain into thinking of ways to wedge the pins across hollows, indulging in jiggery-pokery he would have thought ludicrous in any situation. But he did not allow himself to think of the situation as he crawled from one wedged pin to another, barely daring to breathe: he fought the knowledge of that crumpled thing on the ledge below as stubbornly as he fought the crack. It was the hardest thing he had ever done and he took forever, the roof pressing down ever harder above as if determined to repel him.

"You O.K.?" Luke called.

"Yeah. It's hard." Two more steps and he would make it; two more placements, something, somewhere, no, careful now, Bob me lad, don't go and prove him right. . . And then he was under the roof in the dusk, hands wet with moisture he no longer thought he had in him, heart straining, limbs shaking.

"That's it." He came down.

For the first time in months Luke slept all night, a long dreamless rest, and it was Bob who sat awake, wondering what it was all about. Luke slumped against him, breathing evenly like a tired child. Follow my leader, that's what it was, Bob thought: it's all up to me now but I'll do it, I'll do it all right. He fell asleep.

Luke was calm in the morning but they were terribly dry. Even their bones seemed dry as they jumared up to the roof. It jutted out in tiers for 20ft. and there was no looking down, for it was like crawling across the sky. There was no line of weakness across it: Luke had to traverse rightwards, then back left on pins driven straight up so that there seemed to be nothing to hold them in. Like a spider on a ceiling he inched across. Once, only once, he stopped, jammed up because he knew what was below him; Bob said:

"It's like Kilnsey, isn't it? Have you done that?"

"Soloed the bugger, couple of months back," said Luke, and went on, while Bob's lips bled where he grinned. For a moment Luke hung right on the lip, the Sierra foothills rolling away behind him and the river, thousands of feet below, glinting in the sun; and then he was over it and it had not been too hard, hairy as hell but not too bad really, and there was a crack like a climber's dream running straight and true, the right width, perfect, up that wonderful headwall.

"Oh Bob, you'll never believe it, it's mind-blowing, it's the ultimate. . ." His voice gave out but Bob could still feel the joy of it and thought: by God that lad's got some powers of resistance; I thought he was finished. But when he too pulled over the lip he could see why, for there was no exhaustion, no thirst, no agony, just the perfection of it, the wall smooth as concrete and slightly overhanging, with the pins sparkling in the sun and a faint breeze fanning him as he swung and jumared. On the stance, in slings, he felt Luke's hand on his arm and saw his face, crumpled again, gasping, done in, and he patted him back: "Not much further. What a wall, eh?"

"Miraculous. We've done it." But there was anxiety, a question there.

"Yeah, we've done it. Nearly. Champers for breakfast." Then he was driving on up steadily, mindlessly, the clean hard rock warm and true, the whole world beneath his feeth and he rejoicing in it because he had earned it, that ultimate of all ultimate walls. One hundred and fifty feet of the Holy Grail, he thought, pulling over a small overhang and stopping for a rest. He was so tired that when he paused he thought he might never start again, feeling the weight of Luke on him too. He knew that it all depended on him now, on his decision and strength, and he felt that he had none left; but when he did move the wall took over again, feeding him with momentum and rhythm. It was a long haul. He belayed under a second small roof, wedging his bottom snugly into a niche and watching the swifts shoot out into the sunshine.

Grey with fatigue and desiccation, they were making slow progress. There was half a pint of warm water left and they could not top out that evening. It had to be another night, but Thank God ledge was above. Luke's pitch. Bob made the changeover knowing that Luke was hanging on to the last shreds of determination for the long pitch; he wanted to exude his support as Luke had done for him once, long ago.

"Remember the Ben?"

Luke managed a smile. "Imagine snow." He pulled over the overlap and it changed. The crack narrowed as he climbed, thinning down to almost nothing until he was hanging on tiny nuts wedged into it. He tried to swallow, but could not. When the crack ran out he was standing on a thin thin wire above nearly 3,000ft. of air, and there was nothing more. Above to the right was a chickenhead, a fist-sized lump of darker rock poking its head out of the smooth wall. He reached up carefully, curled his hand over it and found a good hold. There was another one further to the right. It took him minutes to make up his mind and even then he felt like screaming as he swung from the first to the second, feet flat against the wall in the airiest hand traverse of all time, pulling up and right again, and then again, and suddenly the wall was full of jugs and footholds too as he climbed alone over a bottomless abyss, pulling up and still right until there was Thank God ledge and he could collapse on it.

It was scooped out into a bucket seat, safe as a child's chair with the lip curving up under his knees so that he could slump in total safety and even dare to look. The sun was falling low over the mountains, slanting long shadows up the valley, and clouds were beginning to bank up to the west. He called to Bob, and started hauling.

Bob had to climb the last part to save himself from a swing off the last nut, and came up croaking: "Jesus, Luke, how did you do that, you necky old bastard?" They rested, and he thought of that wonderful headwall slanting below them, the prize for agony, that blazing glory. They were safe now; they had almost done it. He forced himself not to relax. There was still a little daylight left, and he still had some strength. There were only three pitches left, but after a waterless night he knew he would take a long time to warm up. He said: "I'll fix this next pitch. Give me a teaspoon of water."

It did nothing, and there was almost none left. He dragged himself to his feet and started climbing. It was an overhanging wall, hard at first; he made little progress, too tired almost to think but forcing himself to go on because he understood that it was only a question of decisiveness, of not considering defeat. The rock above was more complex, slabby and cracked, and in the growing dusk he was not sure which way to go. By the time he had explored one way and decided on another it was darkening fast, the clouds pulling over to blot out the last of the light, and he climbed on and on in the cool. He was sure there should have been a ledge and had just decided that he should have gone left and not right when Luke shouted that there was no more rope. None of his last pins was good enough to lower himself off. He was so tired he was fumbling. He called: 'I'll tie the haul rope on.'' He pulled it up and tied it on to the climbing rope. It was really dark. We'll have rain, he thought, rain. He could hardly bear to think of it.

A little higher up he nested three pins, hauled both ropes up, ran them through the pins and made to abseil off them. He knew that the ropes, doubled, would not reach the ledge but when he had sorted them out Luke called that they were only eight feet short and he knew they would stretch that much. He was pleased that Luke was managing to hold together. He started to abseil. This pitch, then his, then —

Then he was falling, the ropes tangling round him. The pins had pulled out.

He saw Luke, and he tried to cry out but he did not know what, and there was the cool and then merciful blackness as he fell, in a bundle, over half a mile clear to the talus.

Luke saw him go, heard the strangled croak. He sat motionless for a long while in his bucket seat, unthinking, breathing lightly. The black night settled around him, the darkness rustling softly like feathers as it folded itself round his ledge, and the rock beat warm behind him. His neck turned and he found himself looking along the ledge to the dying glimmer in the west. As he watched, the dark shape silhouetted against the clouds gave a croak like an echo of Bob's, and hopped a little closer. When it turned towards him he could see its eyes gleaming softly, like dull headlights seen through a mist.

GLOSSARY

Abseil   A method of descent using a doubled rope supported by an anchor sling or a piton. The climber fits the rope through a friction device (e.g. karabiner-brake or descendeur) which he attaches to his harness. He is then able to make a controlled slide down the doubled rope to gain the bottom of the cliff or a suitable ledge. The rope is retrieved by pulling one end. Another abseil can then be set up and the descent continued. Great care is needed to ensure that the ropes are positioned to run smoothly during retrieval — a jammed abseil rope is a serious problem on a big climb.

Aid   The use of slings or pitons to assist progress on a difficult section of climbing. Climbers always seek to minimise or eliminate the use of aid — free (or non-aided) climbing being the ideal.

Arête   A knifed-edged ridge or rock feature.

Artificial Climbing   Gaining height on a cliff by the repeated use of aid techniques involving pitons, nuts, slings, etc. In Yosemite, artificial climbing has reached very high levels of skill with climbers utilizing very faint crack lines, slots and rugosities to assist progress.

Belay   A secure anchorage to rock or ice using pitons, the rope, slings, nuts, etc. The term has several forms: *belaying* describes the action of the belayed climber paying out, or taking in, the rope to the climber who is moving; *running belays* are placed by the lead climber as he progresses. These work on a pulley principle. The rope is clipped to them with karabiners and they effectively shorten the length of any fall. In the event of a fall, providing rope and belay hold firm, the party is always secured to the cliff.

Bolt   A nail-like fitting used as a piton but requiring a hole to be drilled into the rock in which it is inserted on a rawlplug principle. The bolt has an eye which will accept a karabiner. The use of bolts is controversial and considered by many to be unethical.

Chimney   A wide crack, big enough to allow the climber to fit inside.

Cornice   An overhanging mass of snow or ice along the crest of a ridge, shaped like the crest of a wave and formed by wind action.

Crampons   Metal frames with spikes that are fitted to the soles of the boots for climbing on hard snow or ice.

Daisy Chain (Mare's Tail)   A knotted sling or tape used in artificial climbing. It is attached to the climber's waist harness and can be clipped into the support piton at a short or long length according to need.

Dollies   The Dolomites.

Ets, Etriers   A rope or tape stirrups, usually with three steps, that are used in artificial climbing.

Headwall   A dominant rock wall at the top of a cliff or route.

Jam, Jamming   Using wedged fingers, hands, fists or arms to climb cracks.

Jumars   A pair of mechanical devices that fit onto a fixed rope, slide easily up it, but lock solid when downward force is applied. Footslings and waistloops are added to enable the climber to use jumars for steep prusiking (climbing fixed ropes) without undue exertion. Jumaring is an important technique for climbing the big Yosemite aid routes: the second man invariably jumars, retrieving the pitons, etc. as he gains height. Meanwhile jumars are also used in a different manner by the leader (belayed on the stance above) to assist the arduous process of sack hauling. A big-wall team can clean a pitch and haul the sacks with methodical efficiency if good jumar technique has been perfected.

Karabiner   A strong metal snaplink that is used to link the climber to the rope, belays or running belays.

Mantelshelf   A method of climbing onto a ledge by first pulling up on the arms and then pressing down on them, until a foot can be placed on the ledge and a stand-up achieved in precarious balance — a similar technique to getting out of a swimming pool.

Nuts   Small metal chockstones fitted with wires, tapes or rope loops. Nuts are manufactured with a wide variety of designs and sizes and they can be jammed into cracks to provide secure anchors for belays or running belays.

PA's   Lightweight rock climbing shoes. The original PA's were marketed by the famous French climber, Pierre Allain. The manufacturer, E. Bourdonneau, later decided to market the shoes himself and they were thereafter retitled EB's. Pierre Allain subsequently introduced his own shoe (the new PA), but the original design (the EB) retained great popularity and, despite many challenges, is still the most favoured rock climbing shoe on both sides of the Atlantic. Older climbers often refer to the shoes as PA's, their original title.

Pegs, Pins, Pitons   Metal nails of various shapes and sizes that can be hammered into cracks for secure belays or running belays. Ice pitons are sometimes designed on a screw principle enabling the climber to place them with one hand. All pitons have an eye that will accept a karabiner.

Pitch   A convenient section of climbing between belays.

Protection   The quality and number of running belays (runners) placed by the leader as he progresses up a pitch. 'Good protection' means secure and frequent running belays that can be relied on to hold a fall. 'Poor protection' means there is an element of unreliability about the runners which prompts greater care and circumspection by the leader, sometimes even retreat.

Prusik   Climbing a fixed rope using prusik knots or jumars (q.v.).

Rappel   (see abseil).

Roof   A large ceiling-like rock overhang.

Skyhook   A small metal hook with an attached sling that can be used as an aid on blank rock where the only weaknesses are slight rugosities and friable flakes. The skyhook provides a subtle, albeit insecure, method of gaining height.

Stance   A ledge that provides a good base for a belay.

Talus   An accumulation of scree (rock debris), usually below a cliff.

Tension Traverse   A method of traversing with aid from the rope. The leader places a runner and leans off the rope which is held in tension by the second man. In this manner he can traverse across a blank section of rock with few holds, where progress by normal free climbing would be very difficult.

Tyrolean   Using the rope to cross a gap. The technique is often used in sea-level cliff traverses (to cross difficult caves or zawns), or to climb sea stacks. It is sometimes possible to lasso an anchor-spike on the far side and pass across the tightened rope using a karabiner and a sit-sling. Another method is when one person swims across and fixes the rope and the others follow by the tyrolean traverse. In the mountains the technique can be employed to quit a spectacular pinnacle adjacent to a cliff. Having climbed the pinnacle the rope is thrown back and anchored on the main cliff. The climbers then traverse the doubled rope with the sit-sling, etc. and retrieved the rope from the pinnacle by pulling one end, a sling having been left on the pinnacle (q.v. abseil technique).